NIGHTSCAPE

NIGHTSCAPE

David Morrell

headline

The stories in *NightScape* originally appeared
in this order in the following places:
'Habitat', *Monsters*, Laurel Entertainment, broadcast in October 1989
'Remains To Be Seen', *Psycho-Paths*, Tor Books, ed. Robert Bloch, 1991
'Nothing Will Hurt You', *MetaHorror*, Tor Books,
ed. Dennis Etchison, 1992
'Elvis 45', *The King Is Dead: Tales of Elvis Postmortem*, Delta,
ed. Paul M. Sammon, 1994
'If I Should Die Before I Wake', *Revelations*, Harper Prism,
ed. Douglas E. Winter, 1997
'Front Man', *Murder for Revenge*, Delacorte, ed. Otto Penzler, 1997
'Rio Grande Gothic', *999: New Stories of Horror and Suspense*, Avon,
ed. Al Sarrantonio, 1999
'Resurrection', *Redshift: Extreme Visions of Speculative Fiction*, ROC Books,
ed. Al Sarrantonio, 2001

First published in Great Britain in 2004
by HEADLINE BOOK PUBLISHING

10 9 8 7 6 5 4 3 2 1

British Library Cataloguing in Publication Data
is available from the British Library

ISBN 0 7553 2172 3 (hardback)
ISBN 0 7553 2173 1 (trade paperback)

Typeset in Times New Roman by Letterpart Limited, Reigate, Surrey
Printed and bound in Great Britain by Mackays of Chatham plc, Chatham, Kent

Headline's policy is to use papers that are natural, renewable and
recyclable products and made from wood grown in sustainable forests.
The logging and manufacturing processes are expected to conform
to the environmental regulations of the country of origin.

HEADLINE BOOK PUBLISHING
A division of Hodder Headline
338 Euston Road
LONDON NW1 3BH
www.headline.co.uk
www.hodderheadline.com

To Henry James, who showed new ways in which tales of terror could be written – and the human secrets they could hide.

– we make guilty of our disasters the sun, the moon, and the stars;
as if we were villains by necessity, fools by heavenly compulsion

William Shakespeare
King Lear (Act I, scene ii)

CONTENTS

Introduction

My mother didn't like bedroom doors. Hated them, in fact. As I grew up, whenever we moved from apartment to apartment (sometimes above bars), almost the first thing she did was remove the bedroom doors. One reason for this, I suspect, is that she wanted to convert a normally private space into an area so public that my stepfather would feel uncomfortable making sexual overtures, knowing that I would hear everything where I lay close by in a doorless bedroom.

As it was, I heard plenty, for my mother suffered from nightmares, and I was often kept awake by her frightened murmurs, fidgets, and groans as she fought horrors in her sleep. She never talked about these persistent nightly onslaughts (and it wasn't a household where I felt comfortable asking), but from what she blurted while asleep, I gather it often had something to do with fire. That's the major reason she took the doors off the bedrooms, I believe: fear. For most people, closing a bedroom door before they go to sleep creates a feeling of security, of safe boundaries. But for my mother, that closed door made her feel imprisoned. Smothered. Trapped. As far as she was concerned, whatever haunted her in her sleep might in fact have been creeping along the hallway out there, crouching, about to pounce. Better to leave the door open so that she might hear the threat coming and be ready for it.

Although I never knew the content of her nightmares, I did learn the actual horrors she'd survived, for without prompting, she often told me about them (this was usually after my stepfather had picked a dinner-hour family fight so that he could storm away and play poker with his brothers). My mother's name was Beatrice, and whenever I think about her dismal life, I'm reminded of a contrasting Beatrice, Dante's representation of beauty and truth. My mother lied about her age, so it's difficult to reconstruct when the waking nightmare began, sometime around 1910 on a farm in southern Ontario, Canada, when the area had as many horses as automobiles. Her mother died giving birth to her. Her father married his dead wife's sitster (to some, this is a form of incest). The new wife blamed my mother for her sister's death. My mother had an older sibling, Estelle, who could do no wrong in the eyes of the stepmother. In contrast, the stepmother decided that my mother could do no right. The consequences were frequent, severe beatings. My mother described one occasion on which she hid all day under a porch while her stepmother waited with a club. She described another occasion on which she and Estelle put on their best clothes to go to a party. As they stepped from the farmhouse, their stepmother stalked toward them with a dead maggoty groundhog she'd found and threw it at my mother, splattering her dress. Meanwhile, Estelle was permitted to get into a buggy and ride off to the party (my mother loved her sister and never stopped mourning that Estelle died young from breast cancer). Somewhere in these accounts, never explained, only furtively alluded to, was a reference to being terrorized in the night; something about a fire.

The upshot of this hell was that when my mother was sixteen, she fled to a convent, where she somehow managed to remain until she was of legal age. She then moved to a city a hundred miles away, supporting herself by working in factories and also using her considerable skills as a dressmaker (to see her use a sewing machine was a joy). Eventually, she met my father, George, who was an RAF bombardier assigned to train Canadian airmen for the Second World War. In 1943, soon after I was born, he was reassigned to active status in Britain and was shot down during a bombing raid over France. Or so I was told as a child. The truth was inadvertently revealed to me when I was twenty-seven and my mother made a casual stunning comment. In actuality, my father had survived. Wounded, but having parachuted safely into a field, he was discovered by the French Resistance and smuggled across the English Channel to an RAF hospital, where he wrote letters to my mother and died from pneumonia. To try to repress her painful memories, my mother got rid of everything he left behind, his clothes, their marriage license, his letters, everything except a cigarette lighter and a very few photographs.

Then came more tough times. Trying to support the two of us in the final years of the war, my mother took in as many dressmaking jobs as she could manage. In our two-room ground-floor apartment, she fell sick on the Thanksgiving of my second year. I still remember how fiery her face looked and how impossible amounts of sweat kept streaming from it. I sat next to her on the bed, using an entire box of Kleenex to mop her cheeks. When hunger finally insisted, I climbed onto the kitchen table to the turkey my mother had taken from the oven just before she'd collapsed on the bed. A physician who lived down the street happened to walk past our window and look in at me on the table, clawing meat from the turkey. A half-hour later, my mother was in an ambulance on the way to the hospital. The disease that had felled her, an acute strep skin infection known as erysipelas, was potentially fatal and extremely contagious, but even though I had practically bathed myself in her sweat while I blotted her cheeks with tissue after tissue of Kleenex, I never got sick.

She spent weeks in the hospital, and subsequently, unable to support the two of us while remaining home and taking care of me, she made a difficult choice. I was around four, and I still remember the family friend who had a car and who took us for a ride in the country. We came to a remote, gothic-looking building, where children played on swings and slides. Invited to join them, I eagerly accepted, only to interrupt my laughter to look behind me and see my mother getting into the car and driving away. You may have guessed that the building was an orphanage. My mother claims I was there only a couple of months, but I seem to recall the passage of seasons and feel as if I was there a year, during which I twice attempted to escape. Eventually, my mother remarried and reclaimed me, but I never got over the sense that I might have been adopted, and I never got along with my stepfather, who disliked children and who on one occasion struck my face with his fingers curved like claws, ripping my mouth open. In *Lessons from a Lifetime of Writing*, I described how the fights between him and my mother were so frightening that at night I put a pillow under my covers, hoping to make it look as if I was there while I slept under the bed. The bedroom door had, of course, been removed.

That brings me to this collection, whose title, *NightScape*, is appropriate to what I've just told you. By and large, the kind of tales an author writes are metaphors for the scars in the nooks and crannies of his/her psyche. In my youth, thrillers and horror stories (both in print and on the screen) provided an escape from my nightmarish reality. Is it any wonder that, as an adult obsessed with being a writer, I would compulsively turn to the types of stories that provided an escape when I was a child? Perhaps I'm eager to provide an escape for others. Or perhaps I'm still trying to escape from my past.

In any case, when I was rereading and arranging these tales, I was struck by a common theme. I was startled, in fact, to recognize it. When I wrote each story, I didn't realize how important a factor this theme was throughout my work: the obsession and determination I just alluded to. In most of these tales, a character gets an idea in his head, a hook in his emotions, a need that has to be fulfilled, and he does everything possible to carry through, no matter how difficult. Truly, this emphasis on determination was a revelation to me, although probably not to my family and friends. It got me wondering *why*, and it led me to poignant memories about my mother, who died when she was eighty (maybe she was a little younger or older – as I said, she lied about her age) and whose genes should have allowed her to live to the functioning ninety-eight years that her father and stepmother did if not for the lung cancer that finished her (she never smoked, but my stepfather did, compulsively).

If I had to select a solitary memory about my mother, it would be this. My stepfather seldom failed to destroy a holiday. On Thanksgiving, Christmas, New Year's Day, and Easter, just as my mother (who hated to cook) was about to set a big meal on the table, he would pick a fight and leave. My mother and I would sit across from one another, trying to enjoy dinner. Usually, she was sobbing. And this is what she would say to me: 'David, you can be anything you want to be as long as you work hard enough.' Again and again, at every ruined family occasion. 'David, you can be anything you want to be as long as you work hard enough.'

Experience shows that isn't true. A person can work brutally hard every long day until death and still not achieve anything. I'm reminded of when I was a professor of American literature and taught the theme of naturalism in the works of Stephen Crane and Theodore Dreiser. Basically, naturalism can be defined as 'pessimistic determinism,' a compact way of saying that we're environmentally and biologically doomed for the worst. Although naturalism insists there is no God, the American version of it can be traced back to the Calvinistic sense of being damned that came to America with its early New England settlers. Calvinists believe that human beings are too unworthy and despicable to earn salvation. Only God's mercy can save us. Call it luck. And Lord knows, luck has a lot to do with getting along comfortably in life. We all know people who worked hard all their days and never got their just deserts. But even the colonial Calvinists believed that, against the logic of their fatalistic religion, we still couldn't give up working and trying.

That was my mother's attitude. Life had dealt her shock after shock. I think she hated every aspect of her existence. I think she hated being a woman (I'll explain in a few paragraphs). A week before my mother died, my wife asked her what she would have done differently if she could go through her life again.

'I wouldn't have gotten married,' my mother said.

'But then you wouldn't have had David.'

'What you don't have and don't know you'd have had,' she said, 'you don't miss.'

In my mother's experience, sex meant emotional pain. She was taught that, by being born, she had caused her own mother's death. Marrying my father, who was an Anglican while my mother was a Catholic, she caused life-long tension with her stepmother, a Catholic who believed that marrying out of the faith was a sin. I've always had a sense of a deeper source of tension between her and her stepmother, and I wonder if that wasn't caused by pregnancy before marriage, conception out of wedlock, a grievous social taboo back then. Then shortly after my birth, the already considerable emotional pain was followed by an even greater one – my father's death.

All related to sex and its consequences. I think my mother

wished she'd been a man. I also suspect that if she'd lived during our less judgmental age, she'd have been far more content inasmuch as she was probably, without knowing it, gay.

'David, you can be anything you want to be as long as you work hard enough.'

Yes and no. Determination was the mainspring of my mother's existence. The obsession to make something of herself, to survive her past and achieve something in her future, was what kept her going. Sometimes, she had as many as three jobs: upholstering furniture in a factory, then mowing lawns, then making buttons in the basement until midnight. So that she could buy a house and stop living over bars. So that she could have a degree of comfort and possibly a relief from fear. In many ways, she achieved her goals. But she was never really happy, and as her persistent nightmares indicated, she never really got over her fears.

You can be anything you want to be as long as you work hard enough.

She instilled that into me. Work? Hell, if it's only a matter of work, let's roll up our sleeves. No big deal. All it takes is obsession, discipline, and determination. Which might be a good description of what it takes to be a writer. In the obsession of the characters in *NightScape*, I recognize myself. I recognize my youth. I recognize my *mother's* youth.

And the absence of bedroom doors.

With slight exaggeration, the events in this story actually happened. In the late 1980s, I flew from Iowa City to Ottawa, Canada, to attend that year's World Fantasy Convention (a wonderful opportunity for writers and fans to mingle). I remember it as an interminable journey. During a long layover in Toronto's airport, I dug into a book I'd brought along, a history of the Vatican, that I needed to do research for a thriller I was writing, The League of Night and Fog. *Fighting fatigue and weary eyelids, I resolutely turned the pages and suddenly straightened when I came across the fascinating real events, only tangentially about the Vatican, that form the basis for what you're about to read. If you're tempted to say I've got a sick imagination, remember that history is much sicker. A few years later, Robert Bloch asked me to write a story for an anthology he was putting together,* Psycho-Paths. *Wondering what kind of weird tale the legendary creator of* Psycho *might find amusing, I remembered Toronto's airport and what I'd read about Argentina's dictator Juan Peron.*

Remains To Be Seen

'On my honor, Your Excellency!' Carlos clicked his heels together and jerked his right arm upward, outward, clenching his fist in a salute.

'More than your honor! Your life, Carlos! Swear it on your life!'

'My life, Your Excellency! I swear it!'

The Great Man nodded, his dark eyes burning. His once robust face had shrunk around his cheekbones, giving him a grimace of perpetual sorrow. His pencil-thin mustache, formerly as dark as his eyes, was now gray, his once swarthy skin now sallow. Even if a miracle occurred and His Excellency's forces were able to crush the rebellion, Carlos knew that the strain of the past month's worsening crisis would leave the marks of its ravages upon his leader.

But of course the miracle would not occur. Already the rattle of machine-guns from the outskirts of the city intensified. The echo of explosions rumbled over rooftops. The shimmer of fires reflected off dense black smoke in the night.

A frantic bodyguard approached, his bandoleer slapping against his chest, his rifle clutched so rigidly his knuckles were white. 'Your Excellency, you have to leave now! The rebels have broken through!'

But the Great Man hesitated. 'On your life, Carlos. Remember, you swore it.'

'I'll never disappoint you.'

'I know.' The Great Man clasped his shoulders. 'You never have. You never will.'

Carlos swelled with pride, but sadness squeezed his heart. The gunfire and explosions reminded him of the massive fireworks that had celebrated the Great Man's inauguration. Now the golden years were over. Despondent, he followed his leader toward a truck, its rear compartment capped by a tarpaulin.

A crate lay on the cobblestoned courtyard. It was wooden, eight feet long, four feet wide. The Great Man squinted at it. His gaunt cheeks rippling, he clenched his teeth and nodded in command. Six soldiers stepped forward, three on each side, and hastily lifted the crate. It tilted. Something inside thumped.

'Gently!' His Excellency ordered.

Straining with its bulk, glancing fearfully toward the shots that approached the heart of the city, the soldiers slid the crate inside the truck. One yanked down a section of the tarpaulin. Another raised the creaky back hatch. The Great Man himself snapped the lockpins into place.

'Your Excellency, please! We have to go!' the bodyguard implored.

An explosion shook windows.

The Great Man seemed not to have heard. He continued to stare at the truck.

'Your Excellency!'

The Great Man blinked and turned toward the bodyguard. 'Of course.' He scanned the flame-haloed outskirts of the city. 'We must leave. But one day . . . one day we'll return.' He pivoted toward Carlos. 'Do your duty. You have the itinerary. When I'm able, I'll contact you.' Flanked by bodyguards, he rushed toward his armored limousine.

'But Your Excellency, aren't you coming with me?' Carlos asked.

Racing, the Great Man shouted back, 'No! Separately, we have a greater chance of confusing the rebels! We have to mislead them! Remember, Carlos! On your life!'

With a final look at the truck, the Great Man surged into his limousine, guards charging after him. As the car roared out of the palace courtyard, speeding southward from the direction of the attack, Carlos felt suddenly empty. But at once he remembered his vow. 'You heard His Excellency! We must go!'

Men snapped to attention. Carlos scrambled into the truck. A sergeant slid behind the steering wheel. The truck raced eastward, a jeep before and behind it, each filled with soldiers clutching automatic weapons.

They'd gone five blocks when a rebel patrol attacked. The front jeep blew apart, fragments of metal and flaming bodies twisting through the air. The truck's driver jerked the steering wheel, skidding around the wreckage. Gunfire shattered the windshield. Glass showered. The driver gasped, his brains erupting from the back of his skull. While the truck kept moving, Carlos lunged past the shuddering corpse, shoved open the driver's door, and thrust the dead sergeant onto the street. The body bounced and hit a wall. Stomping the accelerator, Carlos rammed through a wooden barricade, gripping the steering wheel with his right hand while using his left hand to fire his pistol through the shattered windshield.

He and the remaining jeep swerved around a gloomy warehouse, raced along the murky waterfront, and screeched to a stop beside the only ship still in port. Its frightened crew flinched from nearby gunfire and scurried down the gangplank toward the truck. They yanked the crate from the back. Again something thumped.

'Gently!' Carlos ordered.

Heeding the nearby gunshots more than his order, they dropped the crate on a sling and shouted commands to someone on deck. A motor whined. A derrick raised the crate. A rope broke. Carlos felt his heart lurch as the crate dangled halfway out of the sling. But it kept rising. He held his breath while it swung toward the freighter and slammed onto the deck.

An explosion followed a moment afterward as, a block from the freighter, a building erupted in a thunderous blaze. The freighter's crew raced up the gangplank, Carlos and his men rushing after them, the gangplank beginning to rise.

Already the freighter was moving. Scraping from the dock, it mustered speed. Ghostly reflections from the fires in the city guided it toward the harbor's exit.

Carlos barked orders to his men – to remove the tarpaulins from the fifty-caliber machine guns at the bow and stern. As they armed the weapons, he tensely watched the freighter's crew repair the sling and lower the crate through an open hatch. Sweating, he waited for the shout from below that would signal the crate's safe arrival in the hold.

Only then did he feel the ache of tension drain from his shoulders. He wiped sweat from his brow. The first stage of his mission had been completed. For now, he had nothing to do except wait until he reached his next destination and then wait again for further orders from His Excellency.

Behind him, a woman whispered his name.

'Maria?' He turned.

Beaming, she hurried toward him: short, with ebony hair and copper skin, handsome more than beautiful. Her pregnancy emphasized her stocky build. Her strong-boned features suggested faithfulness and endurance.

They embraced. During the previous hectic week, Carlos hadn't seen his wife at all. Despite his devotion to the Great Man, he'd felt the strain of being separated from her – a strain that must have shown, for the Great Man had finally told him to send Maria a message asking her to meet him on this freighter. Carlos had been overwhelmed by the Great Man's consideration.

'Is it over? Are we safe?' Maria asked.

'For now.' Carlos kissed her.

'But His Excellency didn't come with you?'

'No. He plans to meet us later.'

'And the crate?'

'What about it?'

'Why is it so important that you had to bring it here under guard?'

'His Excellency never said. I would never have been so bold as to ask. But it must have tremendous value.'

'For him to entrust it to you, to ask you to risk your life to protect it? By all the saints, yes, it must have tremendous value!'

Maria gazed worshipfully into his eyes.

At three a.m., in a cabin that the Great Man had arranged for them, Carlos made love to his wife. Hearing her moan beneath him, he felt a pang of concern for his benefactor. He prayed that the Great Man had escaped from the city and would contact him soon. His wife thrust a final time against him and went to sleep with a patient sigh as if proud that her marital duty had been accomplished.

Obedience, Carlos thought. Of all the virtues, obedience is the greatest.

At dawn, he was startled awake by a soldier pounding on the cabin's door. 'Rebel boats!'

'Maria, stay here!'

The two-hour battle was fierce, so much so that Carlos didn't realize he'd been wounded in his left arm as he manned the stern's cannon after the soldier at the trigger was sprayed by machine-gun fire.

The freighter, too, sustained damage. But the rebel boats were repelled. The crate was protected. The mission continued.

As one of his men bandaged his bleeding arm, Carlos ignored the throbbing pain, concentrating on a message that the radio operator had given him. His Excellency had escaped from the city and was fleeing through the mountains.

'May God be with him,' Carlos said.

But the radio operator looked troubled.

'What is it? What haven't you told me?' Carlos asked.

'The boats that attacked us. I monitored their radio transmissions. They knew His Excellency was in the mountains. They knew *before* they attacked us.'

Carlos frowned.

The radio operator continued. 'If they knew His Excellency wasn't on board, why were they so determined to attack us?'

'I have no idea,' Carlos said.

But he lied. He did have an idea.

The crate, he thought.

In the hold's fish-stinking darkness, Carlos aimed his flashlight toward the wooden planks that formed the crate. Pensive, he walked around it, examining every detail. A bottom corner had been splintered – not surprising, given the rough way the crew had brought it aboard. But fortunately no bullets had pierced the wooden planks. He leaned against a damp bulkhead and stared in puzzlement at the crate.

What's in it? he wondered.

Twenty minutes later, while he continued to stare at the crate, a crew member brought a radio message.

Carlos aimed his flashlight at the sheet of paper. *Escape from the mountains accomplished. Avoid first destination. Proceed to checkpoint two. Instructions will follow. Remember, on your life.*

Carlos nodded to the messenger. He folded the piece of paper and tucked it into a pocket. Pushing away from the bulkhead, he fully intended to follow the crew member from the hold.

But he couldn't resist the impulse to aim his flashlight at the crate once more.

'Your arm!' Maria said when Carlos at last emerged onto the deck. 'Does it hurt?'

Carlos shrugged and repressed a wince.

'You mustn't strain yourself. You need to rest.'

'I'll rest when His Excellency reclaims his property.'

'Whatever it is,' Maria said. 'Do you think it's gold or jewels? Rare coins? Priceless paintings?'

'Secret documents, most likely. It's none of my business. Tomorrow evening, thank God, my responsibility ends.'

But the Great Man wasn't waiting when the freighter docked at the neutral port that was checkpoint two. Instead a nervous messenger raced up the gangplank. Wiping his brow, he blurted that although His Excellency had reached a neighboring country, the rebels persisted in chasing him. 'He can't risk coming to the freighter. He asks you to proceed to checkpoint three.'

'Three days to the north?' Carlos subdued his disappointment. He'd looked forward to showing the Great Man how well he'd done his duty.

'His Excellency said to remind you – you vowed on your honor.'

'On my *life!*' Carlos straightened. 'I was with him from the beginning. When he and I were frightened peasants, determined to topple the tyrant. I swore allegiance. I'll never disappoint him.'

That night while the freighter was still in port, a rebel squad disguised as stevedores snuck on board and nearly succeeded in reaching the hold before a vigilant soldier sounded an alarm. In the furious gun battle, Carlos lost five members of his team. All eight invaders were killed. But not before a grenade was thrown into the hold.

The explosion filled Carlos with panic. He emptied his submachine-gun into the rebel who'd thrown the grenade. He rushed down to the hold, aimed his flashlight, and was shocked to discover that the grenade had detonated fifteen feet from the crate. Shrapnel had splintered its wooded slats. A jagged hole gaped in the side.

Carlos felt smothered. He drew trembling fingers along the damaged wood. If the contents entrusted to him had been destroyed, how could he explain his failure to His Excellency?

I swore to protect! Fear made Carlos stiffen. What if the shrapnel had stayed hot enough to smolder inside the crate? What if the contents were secret documents and they burst into flames?

Grabbing a crowbar, he jammed it beneath the lid. Nails screaked. Wood snapped. He jerked the lid up, desperate to peer inside, to make sure there wasn't a fire. What he saw made him gasp.

A footstep scraped behind him. Slamming the lid shut, he drew his pistol and spun.

Maria emerged from shadows. Caught by the beam of his flashlight, she frowned. 'Are you all right?'

Carlos exhaled. 'I almost . . .' Shaking, he holstered his pistol. 'Never creep up behind me.'

'But the shooting. I felt so worried.'

'Go back to our cabin. Try to sleep.'

'Come with me. You need to rest.'

'No.'

'What did you find when you opened the crate?'

'You're mistaken, Maria. I didn't open it.'

'But I saw you . . .'

'It's dark down here. My flashlight must have cast shadows and tricked your eyes.'

'But I heard you slam down the lid.'

'No, you heard me lose my balance and fall against the crate. I didn't open it! Go back to our cabin! Do what I tell you!'

With a plaintive look, Maria obeyed. As the echo of her footsteps dwindled, the flashlight revealed her pregnant silhouette. At the top of murky metal stairs, the hatch banged shut behind her.

Carlos forced himself to wait. Finally certain that she was gone, he turned again toward the crate and slowly lifted the lid. Before he'd been interrupted, he'd had a quick glimpse of the contents, enough to verify that there wasn't a fire, although he didn't dare

15

tell Maria what was in there for fear she'd reveal the secret. Because what he'd seen had been more startling than a fire.

The coffin was made of burnished copper, its gleaming surface marred by pockmarks from shrapnel.

His knees faltered. Fighting dizziness, he leaned down to inspect the desecration. With a sharp breath of satisfaction, he decided the damage was superficial. The coffin had not been penetrated.

But what about the body?

Yes, the body.

It was none of his business. The Great Man hadn't seen fit to let him know what he'd pledged his life to protect. No doubt, His Excellency had his reasons.

Carlos subdued his intense curiosity, lowered the lid, and resecured it. He'd exceeded his authority, granted. But for a just motive. To protect what had been entrusted to him. His duty had been honored. The coffin wasn't in danger for the moment. He could have its copper made smooth again. He could replace the crate with one that hadn't been damaged. His Excellency would never know that Carlos had almost failed.

But the mystery still wasn't solved. The ultimate questions remained. Why were the rebels so determined to destroy the crate? Who was in the coffin?

Burdened with responsibility, Carlos climbed from the hold and ordered a crewman, 'Bring down a mattress and blankets. A thermos of coffee. Food. A lantern.' He told Maria, 'I'll be staying in the hold tonight. *Every* night until His Excellency reclaims what's his.'

'No! It's damp down there! The air smells foul! You'll get sick!'

'I made a vow! I've tripled the guards on deck! No one but me is allowed down there! Not even you!'

Three awful days later, Carlos shuffled from the hold. Unshaven, gaunt, and feverish, he squinted through blurred vision toward the northern neutral port that was checkpoint three. But again His Excellency wasn't waiting. Another distraught messenger rushed on board. 'It's worse than we feared. The rebels are determined to hunt him to the ends of the earth. They've cut off his route here. He has to keep running. These are your new instructions.'

Shuddering, Carlos studied them. 'To *Europe*?'

'Marseilles. That's the only chance to complete the mission.'

Carlos wavered.

'His Excellency said to remind you. You swore on your life.'

Carlos trembled. 'My oath was solemn. Not just my life. My *soul*.'

In the hold, enduring turbulence, nausea, and delirium, Carlos felt more compelled. During the seemingly endless route across the Atlantic, the crate and its contents beckoned. The coffin – his only companion – drew him. As his lantern hissed and his wounded arm throbbed, he paced before his obligation. The crate. The coffin. The corpse. Whose?

At last, he couldn't resist. Again he grabbed the crowbar. Again he pried up the wooden lid. Leaning down, trembling, he fingered the catches on the coffin's seam, released them, and pushed upward, gradually revealing . . .

The secret.

This time, he gasped not from surprise but reverence. His knees wavered. He almost knelt.

Before Her Majesty.

The patroness of her people. The blessed mother of her country. How many days – and far into how many nights – had she made herself available to her people, allowing endless streams of petitioners to come to her, dispensing food, comfort, and hope? How many times had she interceded with His Excellency for the poor and homeless whom she'd described as her shirtless ones? The Church had called her a saint. The people had called her a God-send.

Her works of mercy had been equalled only by her beauty. Tall, trim, and statuesque, with graceful contours and stunning features, she embodied perfection. Her blond hair – rare among her people – emphasized her uniqueness, her locks so golden, so radiant they seemed a halo.

The cancer that ravaged her uterus had been both a real and symbolic abomination. How could someone so giving, so emotionally fertile, have been brought down by a disease that attacked her female essence? God had turned His back on His special creation.

The world would not see her like again.

The people mourned, His Excellency more so. He grieved so hard that he felt compelled to preserve her memory in the flesh, to capture her beauty for as long as science could make possible. No one knew for sure the process involved. Rumor had it that he'd sent for the world's greatest embalmer, the mortician who'd been entrusted with the corpse of the secular god of the Soviets, Lenin himself. It was said that the Great Man had instructed the embalmer to use all his skills to preserve Her Majesty forever as she had been in life. Her blood had been replaced with alcohol. Glycerine, at one hundred and forty degrees Fahrenheit, had been pumped through her tissues. Her corpse had been immersed in secret chemicals. Even more secret techniques had preserved her organs. Although her skin had tightened somewhat, it glistened with a radiance greater than she'd had in life. Her blond hair and red lips were resplendent.

Carlos froze with awe. The rumors were true. Her Majesty had been made eternal. He cringed with expectation that she would open her eyes and speak.

In turmoil, he remembered the rest of the tragedy. Her Majesty's death had begun the Great Man's downfall. He'd tried to maintain his power without her, but the people – always demanding, always ungrateful – had turned against him. It didn't matter that His Excellency had planned future social reforms while his wife had soothed social woes merely from day to day. From the people's point of view, the good of now was greater than that of soon. When a rabble-rouser had promised immediate paradise, a new revolution toppled the Great Man's government.

Now Carlos understood why the rebels were so determined to destroy the crate. To eradicate all vestiges of the Great Man's rule, they had to destroy not only His Excellency but the immortalized remains of the Great Man's love and source of his power, the goddess of her country.

Burdened with greater responsibility, Carlos bowed his head in worship. An hour having seemed like a minute, he lowered the coffin's lid and resecured the top of the crate. He trembled with reverence.

During the turbulent voyage across the Atlantic, he twice gave in to temptation, raised the lids from the crate and the coffin, and studied the treasure entrusted to him. The miracle continued. Her Majesty remained as lifelike as ever.

Soon the Great Man will have you back, Carlos thought.

But His Excellency wasn't waiting when the freighter docked at Marseilles. Yet another frantic messenger hurried aboard, reporting that their leader was still being chased, delivering new instructions. He frowned at Carlos's beard-stubbled cheeks, flushed skin, and hollow eyes. 'But are you well enough? Perhaps someone else should—'

'I vowed to His Excellency! I *must* complete his mission!'

When Maria privately objected that he *wasn't* well, he told her, 'You don't understand what's involved!'

Distressed, he arranged for the crate to be unloaded from the freighter and placed in a truck. Under guard, it was driven to a secret airstrip, from where it was flown to Italy and placed on a train bound for Rome. Three times, rebel teams attempted to intercept it, but Carlos was watchful. The teams were destroyed, although at the cost of several of his men.

He paced in front of the crate in an otherwise empty boxcar. How had the rebels anticipated the itinerary? As the train reached Rome, he was forced to conclude that there was a spy. One of His Excellency's advisers must be passing information to the rebels. The itinerary had to be modified.

As scheduled, the crate was rushed to a warehouse. But twelve hours later, Carlos had it moved to the basement of a church and two days later to a storage room in a mortuary. After an uneventful week, only then was it taken to its intended destination, an abandoned villa outside Rome. Carlos hoped that his variation of the schedule had confused the rebels into thinking that the entire itinerary had been altered. Further variations tempted him, but he had to ensure that His Excellency could get in touch with him and, more important, rejoin Her Majesty.

The villa was in disrepair, decrepit, depressing. The stained-glass windows were cracked. The lights didn't work. Cobwebs floated from the great hall's ceiling. In the middle of the immense dusty marble floor, the crate lay surrounded by candles, so Carlos could see to aim if any of the ruin's numerous rats dared to approach the crate and its sacred contents. His men patrolled the grounds, guarding the mansion's entrances, while Maria had orders to remain in an upper-floor bedroom.

Periodically Carlos opened the crate and the coffin to remind himself of the reason for his sacrifice, of his need for constant vigilance. His vision of the blessed mystery became increasingly profound. Her Majesty seemed ever more lifelike, beatific, radiant. The illusion was overwhelming – she wasn't dead but merely sleeping.

He couldn't remember the last time he'd bathed. His hair and beard were shaggy. His garments were wrinkled and filthy. As he slumped in a musty chair, unable to fight exhaustion, his chin on his chest, his gunhand drooping, he vaguely recalled a time when his dreams had been restful. But now he had only nightmares, assaulted by ghosts.

A scrape of metal jerked him awake. A footstep on marble made him spin. His skill defeated his sleep-clouded eyes. He shot repeatedly, roared in triumph, and rushed toward the enemy who'd brazenly violated Her Majesty's sanctum. Preparing to deliver a just-to-be-certain shot to the head, he gaped down at Maria, unmoving in a pool of blood, every bullet having pierced her pregnancy.

He shrieked until his throat seized shut.

Maria was buried behind the villa in one of its numerous untended gardens. He couldn't risk sending for a priest, who in spite of a bribe would no doubt inform the authorities of the killing. What was more, to leave the villa to take his wife to a church and then a graveyard was out of the question. At all extremes, his duty remained. Her Majesty had to be guarded. Weeping, he patted his shovel on the dirt that covered Maria's corpse. He knelt and planted a single flower, a yellow rose, her favorite.

His grief was mixed with anger. 'You were told to stay upstairs! You had your orders just as I have mine! Why didn't you listen? How many times did I tell you? Obedience is the greatest virtue!'

Holding back sobs, he returned to the villa's great hall, relieved the guards who had taken his place, and commanded them to remain outside. He locked the great hall's door and wearily approached the crate to open the coffin, wavering before Her Majesty. Her blond hair glowed. Her red lips glistened. Her sensuous cheeks were translucent.

'Now you understand how solemnly I swore. On my soul. I sacrificed my wife for you. I killed my unborn child. There is nothing I wouldn't do for you. Sleep in peace. Never fear. No matter the cost, I will always protect you.'

His tears dropped onto her forehead. Her eyelids seemed to flicker. He inhaled sharply. But he was only imagining, he told himself. The movement had simply been the shimmer of light through his misted eyes.

He wiped the tears from her forehead. 'I'm sorry, Your Majesty.' He tried to resist but couldn't. He kissed her brow where the tears had fallen.

A messenger at last arrived. After restless nights of sleeping beside the crate, Carlos sighed, anticipating that the Great Man had escaped and intended to reclaim his treasure. At the same time, he surprised himself by regretting that his mission had come to an end. It hadn't, however. With an odd relief, he learned that the Great Man was still being chased. Carlos studied his new instructions. To take the crate to Madrid.

'His Excellency is obliged to you for your loyalty,' the messenger said. 'He told me to tell you he won't forget.'

Carlos fought to still his trembling hands, tugged at his unkempt beard, and brushed back his shaggy hair. 'It's my privilege to be the Great Man's servant. No sacrifice is too burdensome.'

'You're an inspiration. His Excellency heard about the unfortunate loss of your wife. He sends his deep condolences.'

Carlos gestured in grief as well as devotion.

But devotion to whom? he wondered. 'As I said, any sacrifice.'

In Madrid, he noticed Her Majesty's lips move and knew he had to feed her.

Three months later, having been ordered to move the crate to Lisbon, he knew that Her Majesty would be cold en route and covered her with a blanket.

Six months later, having relocated in Brussels, he knew that Her

21

Majesty would have trouble breathing in the coffin and ordered his men to bring him an electric drill.

Finally the message arrived. *Escape accomplished. Faithful friend, your obligation is at an end. Directions enclosed. With heartfelt thanks and immense anticipation, I ask you to return what is mine.*
Yours?
Carlos turned to Her Majesty and sobbed.

The motorcade fishtailed up the snowy road that approached the chateau outside Geneva. The Great Man waited anxiously, breathing frost as he paced the driveway. Pressing his chilled hands under the crate, he helped his servants carry it through the opened double door. Impatient, he ordered it placed in the steeple-roofed living room and commanded everyone to leave, except for the genius mortician who had used his secret skills to preserve the Great Man's love and who now had been summoned to validate the results of his promise.

Each breathed quickly, ready with crowbars to raise the crate's lid but finding that it wasn't secure. Distressed, they reached to open the coffin but discovered that it wasn't locked.

Her Majesty looked astonishingly lifelike, even more than the genius had guaranteed.

But a hole had been drilled in the lid of her coffin.

There was a matching hole in her skull, the drill having gone too deep.

And rotten food bulged from her mouth.

And brains and blood covered her face.

Carlos lay on top of her, a bullet hole in his skull, a pistol in his hand, a beatific expression on his face.

In 1987, my fifteen-year-old son Matthew died from strep and staph infections, the consequence of complications in a bone-marrow transplant that was a desperate attempt to cure his rare form of bone cancer. Thereafter, my imagination dwelled on the theme of grief. Eventually, I wrote a novel, Desperate Measures, *and several stories on the subject, some of which appeared in my earlier collection* Black Evening. *In the following one I couldn't help thinking of the serial-killer Ted Bundy. Commissioned by writer/anthologist Dennis Etchison, it appeared in the 1992 anthology* MetaHorror *and was nominated for that year's Horror Writers of America best novella award.*

Nothing Will Hurt You

Later the song would have agonizing significance for him. 'I can't stop hearing it,' Chad would tell his psychiatrist and fight to control his rapid breathing. His eyes would ache. 'It doesn't matter what I'm doing, meeting a client, talking to a publisher, reading a manuscript, walking through Central Park, even going to the bathroom, I hear that song! I've tried my damnedest not to. I hardly sleep, but when I manage to, I wake up feeling I've been humming it all night.'

Chad vividly remembered the first time he'd heard it. He could date it exactly: Wednesday 20 April 1979. He could give the time precisely: 9.46 p.m., because although he'd found the song poignant and the singer's performance outstanding, he'd felt an odd compulsion to glance at his watch. It must have been a tougher day than I realized, he'd thought. So tired. Nine forty-six. Is that all?

Sweeny Todd. The Demon Barber of Fleet Street. Stephen Sondheim's musical had opened on Broadway in March, a critical success, tickets impossible to get, except that Chad had a playwright client with contacts in the production company. When Chad's wife, Linda, broke one of their marriage's rules and gave Chad a surprise birthday party, the playwright (pretending to be a magician) pulled two tickets from behind Chad's ear. 'Happy forty-second, old buddy.'

But Chad remembered the precise date he saw the musical not because it had anything to do with his birthday. Instead, he had a deeper reason. The demon barber of Fleet Street. Come in for a shave and a haircut, have your throat slit, get dumped down a chute, ground up into hamburger, and baked into Mrs Lovett's renowned,

25

ever-popular, scrumptious, how-do-you-get-that-distinctive-taste meat pies.

Can't eat enough of them. To startle the audience, a deafening whistle shrilled each time Sweeney slashed a throat. Blood spurted. And one of Mrs Lovett's waiters was an idiot kid who hadn't the faintest idea of what was going on, but he had misgivings that *something* was wrong. He confessed his fears to Mrs Lovett, who thought of him fondly as her son. She promised that she'd protect him. She sang that nothing would hurt him – a magnificent performance by Angela Lansbury of a tune that forever after would torture Chad, its title: 'Not While I'm Around.' A lilting, heart-breaking song in the midst of multiple murders and cannibalism.

After the show, Chad and Linda had trouble finding a taxi, and didn't get back to their Upper East Side apartment until almost midnight. They felt so disturbed by the plot yet elated by the music that they decided to have some brandy and discuss their reactions to the show, and that's when the phone rang. Scowling, Chad wondered who in hell would be calling at such an hour. Immediately he suspected one of his nervous, not to mention important, authors with whom he'd been having tense conversations all week because of a publisher's unfavorable reaction to the author's new manuscript. Chad tried to ignore the phone's persistent jangle. Let the answering machine take it, he thought. At once, he angrily picked up the phone.

A man's gravelly voice, made faint by the hiss of a long-distance line, sounded tense. 'This is Lieutenant Raymond MacKenzie. I'm with the New Haven police force. I know it's late. I apologize if I woke you, but . . . There's been an emergency, I'm afraid.'

What Chad heard next made him quiver. In response, he insisted, 'No. You're wrong. There's got to be some mistake.'

'Don't I wish.' The lieutenant's voice became more gravelly. 'You have my deepest sympathy. Times like this, I hate my job.' The lieutenant gave instructions.

Chad murmured compliance and set down the phone.

Linda, who'd been staring, demanded to know why Chad was so pale.

When Chad explained, Linda blurted, 'No! Dear God, it can't be!'

Urgency canceled numbness. They each threw clothes into a suitcase, hurried from their apartment to the rental garage three blocks away where they stored their two-year-old Ford (they'd bought the car at the same time they'd bought their cottage in Connecticut, so they could spend weekends near their daughter), and sped with absolutely no memory of the drive (except that they kept repeating, 'No, it's impossible!') to New Haven and Lieutenant MacKenzie, whose husky voice, it turned out, didn't match his short, thin frame.

Denial was reflexive, insistent, stubborn. Even when the lieutenant sympathetically repeated and re-repeated that there had *not* been a mistake, when he regretfully showed them Stephanie's purse, her wallet, her driver's license, when he showed them a statement from Stephanie's roommate that she hadn't come back to the dormitory last night . . . even when Chad and Linda went down to the morgue and identified the body, or what was left of the body, although it hadn't been Stephanie's *face* that was mutilated . . . they still kept insisting, no, this had to be someone who looked like Stephanie, someone who stole Stephanie's purse, someone who . . . some mistake!

Nothing would hurt him, Angela Lansbury had sung to the boy her character thought of as a son in *Sweeney Todd*, and the night before when Chad had listened to the lilting near-lullaby, he had been briefly reminded of his own and only child, dear sweet Stephanie, when she was a tot and he had read to her at bedtime, had sung nursery rhymes to her, and had taught her to pray.

'Now I lay me down to sleep,' his beloved daughter had obediently repeated, 'I pray the Lord my soul to keep. If I should die before I wake, I pray the Lord my soul to take . . . Daddy, is there a bogeyman?'

'No, dear. It's just your imagination. Go to sleep. Don't worry. Daddy's here. Nothing will hurt you.'

'Not While I'm Around,' the song had been called. But two years earlier Stephanie had gone to New Haven, for a BA in English at Yale, and last night there *had* been a bogeyman, and despite Chad's long-ago promise, he had *not* been around when the bogeyman very definitely hurt Stephanie.

'When did it . . .' Chad struggled to breathe as he stared at

Lieutenant MacKenzie. 'What time did she . . .'

'The body was discovered at just before eleven last night. Based on heat loss from the brain, the medical examiner estimates the time of death between nine thirty and ten p.m.'

'Nine forty-six.'

The lieutenant frowned. 'More or less. It's difficult to be precise.'

'Sure.' Chad bit his lip, tasting tears. 'Nine forty-six.'

He remembered the odd compulsion he'd felt to glance at his watch the previous night when Angela Lansbury had sung that nothing would hurt her friend.

While the bogeyman killed Stephanie.

Chad knew. He was absolutely certain. Nine forty-six. That was when Stephanie had died. He'd felt the tug of her death as if a little girl had jerked at the sleeve of his suit coat.

'Daddy, is there a bogeyman?'

'Not while I can help it.'

Chad must have said that out loud.

Because the lieutenant frowned, asking, 'What? I'm sorry, sir. I didn't quite hear what you just said.'

'Nothing.' Sobbing uncontrollably, holding Linda whose features were raw-red, dripping with tears, contorted with grief, Chad felt the terrible urge to ask the lieutenant to take him down to the morgue again – just so he could see Stephanie one more time, even if she looked like, even if her . . .

All he wanted was to *see* her again! Stephanie! No, it couldn't be! Jesus, not Stephanie!

Numbness. Denial. Confusion. Chad later tried to reconstruct the conversations, remembering them through a haze. No matter how often he was given details, he needed more and more clarification. 'I don't understand. What the hell happened? Have you any clues? Witnesses? Have you found the son of a bitch who did this?'

The lieutenant looked bleak as he explained. Stephanie had gone to the university library the previous afternoon. A friend had seen her leave the library at six. On her way back to the dormitory, someone must have offered her a ride or asked her to help him carry something into a building or somehow grabbed her without attracting attention. The usual method was to appeal to the

28

victim's sympathy by pretending to be disabled. However it was done, she had disappeared.

Afterward, the killer had stopped his car at the side of a road outside New Haven and dumped Stephanie's body into a ditch. The absence of blood at the scene indicated that the murder had occurred at another location. The road was far from a highway. At night, all the killer had to do was drive along the road until there weren't any headlights before or behind him, then stop and rush to open the trunk and get rid of the body. Twenty seconds later, he'd have been back on his way.

The lieutenant sighed. 'It's only coincidence that a car on that road last night happened to have a flat tire where the killer left your daughter. The driver's a farmer who lives in the area. He switched on his flashlight, walked around the car to check his tire, and his light picked up your daughter. Pure coincidence, but clues, yes, because of that coincidence, this time we've got some. Tire tracks at the side of the road. It rained yesterday afternoon. Any tracks in the dirt would have to be fresh. Forensics got a *very* clear set of impressions.'

'Tire tracks? But *they* won't identify the killer.'

'What can I say, Mr Dolan? At the moment, those tire tracks are all we've got – and believe me, they're more than any other police force involved in these killings has managed to get, except of course for the consistent marks on the victims.'

Plural. On that point, at least, Chad didn't need an explanation. One look at Stephanie's body, at what the bastard had *done* to her body, and Chad knew who the killer was. Not the bastard's name, of course. But *everybody* knew his nickname. One of those cheap tabloids at the supermarket checkout counter had given it to him. The Biter. And reputable newspapers had stooped to the tabloid's level by repeating it. Because in addition to raping and strangling his victims (eighteen so far, all Caucasian females, attractive, blonde, in their late teens, in college), the killer left bite marks on them, police reports revealed.

The published details were sketchy. Chad had grimly imagined teeth impressions on a neck, an arm, a shoulder. But nothing had prepared him for the horrors done to his daughter's corpse, for the killer didn't merely bite his victims. He *chewed* on them. He gnawed huge pieces from their arms and legs. He chomped holes in their stomachs, bit off their nipples, nipped off their labia. The son of a bitch was a cannibal! Multiple murders and . . .

Sweeney Todd.

Nothing will hurt you.

Imagining Stephanie's lonely panic, Chad moaned until he screamed.

In a stupor, he and Linda struggled through the nightmare of arranging for a funeral, waiting for the police to release the body, and collecting their daughter's things from her dormitory room. On her desk, they found a half-finished essay about Shakespeare's sonnets, a page still in the typewriter, a quotation never completed: 'Shall I compare thee to a summer's . . .' On a shelf beside her bed, they picked up textbooks, sections of them underlined in red, that Stephanie had been studying for final exams she would never take. Clothes, keepsakes, her radio, her Winnie-the-Pooh bear. Everything filled a suitcase and three boxes. So little. So easily removed. Now you're here, now you aren't, Chad bitterly thought. Oh, Jesus.

'I'm sorry, Mr and Mrs Dolan,' Stephanie's roommate said. She had freckles and wore glasses. Her long red hair hung in a ponytail. She looked devastated. 'I really am. Stephanie was kind and smart and funny. I liked her. I'm going to miss her. She was special. It just isn't fair. Gosh, I'm so confused. I wish I knew what to say. I've never known anyone close to me who died before.'

'I understand,' Chad said bleakly. His father had died from a heart attack at the age of seventy, but that death hadn't struck Chad with the overwhelming shock of *this* death. After all, his father had battled heart disease for several years, and the massive coronary had been inevitable. He'd passed away, succumbed, joined his Maker, whatever euphemism hid the fact best and gave the most comfort. But what had happened to Stephanie was cruelly, starkly, brutally that she'd been *murdered*.

Dear God, it couldn't be!

Chad and Linda carried Stephanie's things to the car, returned to the police station, and badgered Lieutenant MacKenzie until he finally gave them directions to the road and the ditch where Stephanie had been found.

'Don't torture yourselves,' the lieutenant tried to tell them, but

Chad and Linda were already out the door.

Chad didn't know what he expected to find or feel or achieve by seeing the spot where the killer had parked and dumped Stephanie's body like a sack of garbage. As it turned out, he and Linda weren't able to get close anyhow – a police officer was standing watch over a section of the side of the road and a portion of the ditch, both enclosed by a makeshift fence of stakes linking yellow tape labeled POLICE CRIME SCENE: DO NOT ENTER. On the grass at the bottom of the ditch, the outline of Stephanie's twisted body had been drawn with white spray paint.

Linda wept.

Chad felt sick and hollow. At the same time, his heart and profoundly his *soul* swelled with rage. The bastard. The . . . Whoever did this, when they find him . . . Chad imagined punching him, stabbing him, choking him until his tongue bulged, and at once remembered that *Stephanie* had been choked. He leaned against the car and couldn't stop sobbing.

Finally, after seemingly endless bureaucratic delays, they were given their daughter. Following a hearse, they made the solemn drive back to New York for the funeral. Although Stephanie's face had not been mutilated, Chad and Linda refused to allow a public viewing of her remains. Granted, mourning friends and relatives wouldn't be able to see the obscene marks on her body beneath her burial clothes, but Chad and Linda *would* see those marks – in their minds – as if the burial clothes were transparent. More, Chad and Linda couldn't tolerate inflicting upon Stephanie the indignity of being forced to lie in her grave for all eternity with that monster's filthy marks on her. She had to be cremated. Purified. Made innocent again. Ashes to ashes. Cleansed with fire.

Each day, Chad and Linda drove out to the cemetery to visit her. The trip became the event around which they scheduled their other activities. Not that they *had* many other activities. Chad had no interest in reading manuscripts, meeting authors, and dealing with publishers, although his friends said that the thing to do was get back on track, distract himself, immerse himself in his literary agency. But his work didn't matter, and he spent more and more of each day taking long walks through Central Park. He had dizzy spells. He drank too much. For her part, Linda quit teaching piano, sequestered herself in the apartment, studied photographs of Stephanie, stared into space, and slept a great deal. They sold the cottage in Connecticut, which they'd bought and gone to each weekend only so they could be close to Stephanie in New Haven if she had wanted to visit. They sold their Ford, which they'd needed only to get to the cottage.

Nothing will hurt you. The bittersweet song constantly, faintly, echoed in the darkest chambers of Chad's mind. He thought he'd go crazy as he trembled from stress and obeyed the compulsion to visit places he associated with Stephanie: the playground of the grade school she'd attended, her high school, the zoo at Central Park, the jogging track around the lake. He conjured images of her – different ages, different heights, different hair and clothes styles – ghostly mental photographs, eerie double exposures in which then and now coexisted. A little girl, she giggled on a swing in a neighborhood park that had long ago become an apartment building. I can't stand this! Chad thought in mental rage and imagined the blessed release that he would feel if he hurled himself in front of a speeding subway train.

What helped him was that Stephanie told him not to. Oh, he knew that her voice was only in his mind. But she sounded so real, and her tender voice made him feel less tormented. He heard her so clearly.

'Dad, think of Mother. If you kill yourself, you'll cause her twice the pain she has now. She needs you. For my sake, help her.'

Chad's legs felt unsteady. He slumped on a chair in the kitchen, where at three a.m. he'd been pacing.

Nothing will hurt you.

'Oh, baby, I'm sorry.'

'You couldn't have saved me, Dad. It's not your fault. You couldn't watch over me *all* the time. It could have happened differently. I could have been killed in a traffic accident a block from our apartment. There aren't any guarantees.'

'It's just that I miss you so damned much.'

'And I miss *you*, Dad. I love you. But I'm not really gone. I'm talking to you, aren't I?'

'Yes . . . At least I think so.'

'I'm far away, but I'm also inside you, and whenever you want to talk, we can. All you have to do is think of me, and I'll be there.'

'But it's not the same!'

'It's the best we can do, Dad. Where I am is . . . bright! I'm soaring! I'm ecstatic! You mustn't feel sorry for me. You've got to accept that I'm gone. You've got to accept that your life is different now. You've got to become involved once more. Stop drinking. Stop skipping meals. *Start* reading manuscripts again. Answer your clients' phone calls. Get in touch with publishers. Work.'

'But I don't care!'

'You've *got* to! Don't throw your life away because I lost mine! I'll never forgive you if . . .'

'No, please, sweetheart. Please don't get angry. I'll try. I promise. I will. I'll try.'

'For *my* sake.'

Sobbing, Chad nodded as the speck of light faded.

But Angela Lansbury's voice continued echoing faintly. Nothing will hurt you. No matter how hard he tried, Chad couldn't get the song from his mind. The more he heard it, the more a lurking implication in the lyrics began to trouble him, a half-sensed deeper meaning, dark and disturbing, felt but not understood, a further horror.

The Biter's next victim was found by a hiker on the bank of a stream near Princeton. That was three months later. Although the victim, a co-ed who worked for the university's library during the summer, had been missing for two weeks and exposed to scavenging animals and the blistering sun, her remains were sufficiently intact for the medical examiner to establish the cause of death as strangulation and to distinguish between animal and human bite marks. That information was all the police revealed to the press, but Chad now knew what 'bite marks' meant, and he shuddered, remembering the chunks that the killer had gnawed from Stephanie's body.

By then, Linda had started taking students again. Chad – true to his promise to Stephanie – had forced himself to pay attention to his authors and their publishers. But now the news of the Biter's latest victim threatened to tear away the fragile control that he and Linda had managed to impose on their lives. Compulsively, he wrote a letter to the murdered girl's parents.

We mourn for your daughter as we mourn for our own. We pray that they're at peace and beg God for justice. May this monster be caught before he kills again. May he be punished to the limits of hell.

In truth, Chad didn't need to pray that Stephanie was at peace. He knew she was. She told him so whenever he stumbled sleeplessly into the kitchen at two or three a.m. and found her speck of light hovering, waiting for him. Nonetheless Chad's rage intensified. Each morning he mustered a motive to get out of bed, hoping that today would be the day when the authorities caught the monster.

What they found instead, in September, soon after the start of the fall semester, was the Biter's next victim, maggot-ridden, in a storm drain near Vassar College. Chad urgently phoned Lieutenant MacKenzie, demanding to know if the Vassar police had found any clues.

'Yes.' MacKenzie's voice sounded even more gravelly. 'It rained again. The Vassar police found the same tire marks.' He exhaled wearily. 'Mr Dolan, I understand your despair. Your anger. Your need for revenge. But you have to let go. You have to get on with your life, while we do our job. Every police department involved in these killings has formed a network. I promise you, we're doing everything we can to compare information and—'

Chad slammed down the phone and scribbled a letter to the parents of the Biter's latest victim.

We share your loss. We weep as you do. If there's a God in heaven – as opposed to this Devil out of hell – our beautiful children will not have died unatoned. Their brilliantly speeding souls will be granted justice. The desecrations inflicted upon their innocent bodies will be avenged.

Chad never received responses from those other parents. It didn't matter. He didn't care. He'd done his best to console them, but if they were too overwhelmed by sorrow to muster the strength to comfort *him* as he strained to comfort *them*, well, that was all right. He understood. The main thing was, he'd assured them that he wouldn't rest until the monster was punished.

Each day, he made phone calls to all the police departments in the areas where the Biter had disposed of his victims. Canceling lunches with publishers, postponing meetings with authors, leaving manuscripts unread, Chad concentrated on questioning homicide detectives. He demanded to know why they weren't trying harder, why they hadn't achieved results, why they hadn't tracked down the bastard, allowing his victims to rest with the knowledge that their abuser would be punished, at the same time preventing other potential victims from suffering his brutality.

Just before Thanksgiving, the Biter's next target – the same profile: female, late teens, Caucasian, blonde – was discovered in a Dumpster bin behind a restaurant a mile from Wellesley College. Sure, Chad thought. A Dumpster bin. The monster treated her the same way he did Stephanie and all his other victims. Like garbage.

He wrote another letter, but again he didn't receive an answer. The parents must be too stunned to react, he concluded. Whatever, it doesn't matter. I did my duty. I shared my grief. I let them realize they're not alone. I'm their and my daughter's advocate.

New Year's Eve. Another victim. Dartmouth College. More phone calls to detectives. More letters to parents. More visions in Chad's kitchen at three a.m. A speck of brilliant light. A tender voice.

'You're out of control, Dad! Please! I'm begging you. Get on with your life. Shave! Take a bath! Change your clothes! Most of your authors have left you! *Mother*'s left you! I'm afraid for you.'

Chad shook his head. 'Your mother . . . What? She *left* me?'

With a shudder, Chad realized that Linda had packed several suitcases and . . . Dear God. He remembered now. Linda had shouted, 'It's been too long! It's bad enough to grieve for Stephanie! But to watch you do this to yourself? It's too damned much! Don't destroy *my* life while you destroy *yours*.'

Ah.

Of course.

So be it, Chad dismally thought. She needs a comfort I can't give her. God willing, she'll find it with someone else.

Vengeance. Retribution. With greater fury, Chad pursued his mission. More phone calls, more frantic letters.

And then a breakthrough. What the detectives hadn't told Chad – but what he now learned – was that the tire tracks left by his daughter's desecrator had been identified last year, back in April, as standard equipment on a particular model of American van. Not only Stephanie's corpse near Yale but the later victim near Vassar had been linked with the tire tracks on that year and model of van. Because the Biter's numerous targets had all been students at colleges and universities in New England, the authorities had concentrated their search in that area.

When a blonde, attractive female student narrowly escaped being dragged inside a van as she strolled toward her dormitory at Brown University, the local police – braced for the threat – ordered roadblocks around the area and stopped the type of van that they'd been seeking.

The handsome, ingratiating male driver complied too calmly. His responses were too respectful, not at all curious. On a hunch, an officer asked the driver to open the back of the van.

The driver's eyes narrowed.

Chilled by the intensity of his gaze, the policeman grasped his revolver and repeated his request. What he and his team discovered . . . after the driver hesitated, after they took his keys . . . were stacks of boxes in the rear of the van.

And behind the boxes, a bound, gagged, unconscious co-ed.

That night, the police announced the suspected Biter's arrest, and Chad shouted in triumph.

Finally! A textbook salesman. The bastard's district was New England colleges. He stalked each campus. He studied his variety of quarry, reduced his choices, selected his final target, and . . .

Chad imagined the Biter's enticement. 'These boxes of books. They're too heavy. I've sprained my left wrist. Would you mind? Could you help me? I'd really appreciate . . . Thank you. By the way, what's your major? No kidding? English? What a coincidence. That's *my* major. Here. In the back. Help me with this final box. You won't believe the first editions I've got in there.'

Rape, torture, cannibalism, and murder were what he had in there.

Step in farther. Nothing's going to hurt you.

But now the bastard had finally been caught. His name was Richard Putnam. The *alleged* Biter, the media carefully called him, although Chad had no doubt of Putnam's guilt as he studied the television images of the monster. The unafraid expression. The unemotional eyes. The handsome suspect should have been sweating with fear, blustering with indignation, but instead he gazed directly at the cameras, disturbingly confident. A sociopath.

Chad phoned policemen and district attorneys to warn them not to be fooled by Putnam's calm manner. He wrote letters to the parents of every victim, urging them to make similar calls. Each night at three a.m. as he wandered through his cluttered apartment, he always found Stephanie's brilliant light hovering in the kitchen.

'At last they found him,' she said. 'At last you can give up your anger. Sleep. Eat. Rest. Distract yourself. Work. It's over.'

'No, it won't be over until the son of a bitch is punished! I want him to suffer! To feel the terror *you* did!'

'But he *can't* feel terror. He can't feel *anything*. Except when he kills.'

'Believe me, sweetheart, when the court finds him guilty, when the judge pronounces his sentence, that sociopath will suddenly find he can definitely feel emotion!'

'That's what I'm afraid of!'

'I don't understand! Don't you want revenge?'

'I'm speeding so brilliantly. I don't have time to . . . I'm afraid.'

'Afraid about what?'

Stephanie's radiant light faded.

'What are you afraid of?'

Nothing will hurt you. The song kept echoing in Chad's mind. While he hadn't been able to protect his daughter as he had promised when she was a child, he could do his utmost to guarantee he was there to make sure that the monster suffered. Calls to police departments revealed that the various states in which the murders had occurred were each demanding to put the Biter on trial. The result was bureaucratic chaos, arguments about which city would have the first chance to prosecute.

As the authorities persisted in quarrelling, Chad's frustration compelled him to visit the parents of each victim, to convince them to form a group, to conduct news conferences, to insist that jurisdictional egos be ignored in favor of the strongest evidence in any one city, to plead for justice.

It gave Chad intense satisfaction to believe that his efforts produced results – and even greater satisfaction that New Haven was selected as the site of the trial, that Stephanie's murder would be the crime against which the Biter was initially prosecuted. By then, a year had passed. As part of his divorce settlement, Chad had sold his co-op apartment in Manhattan, splitting the proceeds with Linda. He moved to cheaper lodgings in New Haven, relying on the income he received from his ten percent of royalties that his former authors were required to pay him for contracts that he'd negotiated.

Successful.

Sure.

Before Stephanie was . . .

Nothing will hurt you?

Wrong! It hurts like hell!

Each day at the trial, Chad sat in the front row, far to the side so he could have a direct view of Putnam's unemotional, this-is-all-a-mistake, confident profile. Damn you, show fear, show remorse, show anything, Chad thought. But even when the district attorney presented photographs of the horrors done to Stephanie, the monster did not react. Chad wanted to leap across the courtroom's railing and claw Putnam's eyes out. It took all his self-control not to scream his litany of mental curses.

The jury deliberated for ten days.

Why did they need so long?

They finally declared him guilty.

And yet again the monster showed no reaction.

Nor did he react when the judge pronounced the maximum punishment Connecticut allowed: life in prison.

But *Chad* reacted. He shrieked, '*Life in prison*? Change the law! That son of a bitch deserves to be executed!'

Chad was removed from the courtroom. Outside, Putnam's lawyer made a speech about a miscarriage of justice, vowing to demand a new trial, to appeal to a higher court.

Thus began a different kind of horror, the complexities and loopholes in the legal system. Another year passed. The monster remained in prison, yes, but what if a judge decided that a further trial was necessary, that Putnam was obviously insane and should have pleaded accordingly? A year in prison for what he'd done to Stephanie? If he was released on a technicality or sent to a mental institution where he would pretend to respond to treatment and perhaps eventually be pronounced 'cured'...

He'd kill again!

At three a.m., in Chad's gloomy New Haven apartment, he raised his haggard face from where he'd been dozing at the kitchen table. He smiled toward Stephanie's speck of light.

'Hi, dear. It's wonderful to see you. Where have you been? How I've missed you.'

'You've got to stop doing this!'

'I'm getting even for you.'

'You're making me scared!'

'For me. Of course. I understand. But as soon as I know that he's punished, I'll put my life in order. I promise I'll clean up my act.'

'That's not what I mean! I don't have time to explain! I'm soaring so fast! So brilliantly! Stop what you're doing!'

'I *can't*. How can you rest in peace if he isn't—'

'I'm afraid!'

Putnam's appeal was denied. But that was another year later. In the meantime, Chad's former wife, Linda, had married someone else, and Chad's percentage of royalties from his past authors dwindled. He was forced to move to more shabby lodgings. He began to withdraw money – with tax penalties – from his pension. He now had a beard. Less trouble. No necessity to shave. So what if his unwashed hair drooped over his ears? There was no one to impress. No authors. No publishers. No one.

Except Stephanie.

Where in God's name *was* she?

She'd abandoned him. *Why?*

While Stephanie's murder had officially been solved, others attributed to the Biter had not. Putnam refused to admit that he'd killed anyone, and the authorities – furious about his stubbornness – decided to put pressure on him to close the books on those other crimes, to force him to confess. Before he'd been a book salesman in New England, he'd worked in Florida. A blonde, attractive co-ed had been murdered years before at Florida's state university.

The killer had used a knife instead of his teeth to mutilate the victim. There wasn't any obvious reason to link the Biter with that killing. But a search of that Florida city's records revealed that Putnam had received a parking ticket near where the victim had disappeared as she left the university's library. Further, Putnam's rare blood type matched the type derived from the semen that the killer had left within the victim, just as the semen that the monster had left within Stephanie contained Putnam's blood type. Years ago, that evidence could not have been used in court because of limitations in forensic technology. But now . . .

Putnam was arrested for the co-ed's murder. His lawyer had insisted on another trial. Well, the monster would get one. In Florida. Where the maximum penalty wasn't life in prison. It was death.

Chad moved to the outskirts of Florida State University. His pension and his portion of royalties from contracts he'd negotiated increasingly declined. His clothes became more shabby, his appearance more unkempt, his frame more gaunt. At some hazy point in the intervening years, his former wife, Linda, died from breast cancer. He mourned for her but not as he mourned for Stephanie.

The Florida trial seemed to take forever. Again Chad came to stare at the monster. Again he endured the complexities of the legal system. Again the evidence presented at the trial made him shudder.

But finally Putnam was found guilty, and *this* time the judge – Chad cheered and had to be evicted from the courtroom again – sentenced the monster to death in the electric chair. Anti-death-penalty groups raised a furor. They petitioned Florida's Supreme Court and the state's Governor to reduce the sentence. For his part, Chad barraged the media and the parents of the Biter's victims with phone calls and letters, urging them to use all their influence to insist that the judge's sentence be obeyed.

Richard Putnam finally showed a reaction. Apparently now convinced that his life was in danger, he tried to make a deal. He hinted about other homicides he'd committed, offering to reveal specifics and solve murders in other states in exchange for a reduced sentence.

Detectives from numerous states came to question Putnam

about unsolved disappearances of co-eds. In the end, after they listened in disgust to his explicit descriptions of torture and cannibalism, they refused to ask the judge to reduce the sentence. There were four stays of execution, but finally Putnam was shaved, placed in an electric chair, and exterminated with two thousand volts through his brain.

Chad was with the pro-death-sentence advocates in the darkness of a midnight rain outside the prison. Along with them, he held up a sign: BURN, PUTNAM, BURN. I HOPE OLD SPARKY MAKES YOU SUFFER AS MUCH AS STEPHANIE DID. The execution occurred on schedule. At last, after so many years, Chad felt triumphant. Vindicated. At peace.

But when he returned to his cockroach-infested one-room apartment, when at three a.m. he drank cheap red wine in victory, he blinked in further triumph. Because Stephanie's light again appeared to him.

Chad's heart thundered. He hadn't seen or spoken to her in so many years. Despite his efforts on her behalf, he had thought that she had abandoned him. He had never understood why. After all, she had promised that she would be there whenever he needed to talk to her. At the same time, she had also demanded that he stop his efforts to punish the monster. He had never understood that, either.

But now, in horror, he did.

'I warned you, Dad! I tried to stop you! *Why didn't you listen?* I'm so afraid!'

'I got even for you! You can finally rest in peace!'

'No! Now it starts again!'

'What do you mean?'

'He's free! He's coming for me! *Don't you remember?* I told you he doesn't feel emotion except when he kills! And now that he's been released, he can't wait to do it again! He's coming for me!'

'But you said you're soaring so brilliantly! *How can he catch up with you?*'

'Two thousand volts! He's like a rocket! He's grinning! He's reaching out his arms! Help me, Daddy! You promised!'

Based on the note Chad left, his psychiatrist concluded that Chad's final act made perfect, irrational sense. Chad bled profusely as he struggled over the barbed-wire fence. His hands were

41

mangled. That didn't matter. Nor did his fear of heights matter as he climbed the high tower while guards shouted for him to stop. All that mattered was that Stephanie was in danger. What choice did he have? Except to grasp the high-voltage lines. To be struck by twenty thousand volts. Ten times the power that had launched the Biter toward Stephanie. Chad's body burst into flames, but his agony meant nothing. The impetus of his soul meant *everything*.

Keep speeding, sweetheart! As fast as you can!

But I'll speed faster! The monster won't catch you! Nothing will hurt you!

Not while I can help it.

I admit that Elvis 45 *is the most cryptic title I've ever used, but I wouldn't change it for the world. You see, I never got over being on a high-school social committee that was empowered to select and buy the records for the weekend dances. As this story indicates, in those ancient days there were listening booths in record stores. My friends and I could spend all afternoon there if we wanted. Not playing CDs, of course. That format hadn't been invented. Vinyl, along with Elvis, was king. A lot of you are too young to have heard vinyl (I continue to believe it sounds better than CDs do), or if you have, the word probably suggests LPs (long-playing records the size of pizzas) that held a half-dozen songs on each side and turned at thirty-three and one third revolutions per minute. But there was another vinyl format, the small, one-song-on-each-side 45 (forty-five revolutions per minute) that gives this story its title, as do the .45 revolvers Elvis liked to play with. The title also refers to a number of a course at a university, as in English 101 or Presley 45. Hey, I told you it was cryptic. In any case, the story was written for a 1994 anthology called* The King is Dead *and gave me a chance to experiment with an unusual technique. There is no exposition. No description. I avoided speech tags in the dialogue. The story is presented solely in dialogue fragments or in dialogue-like substitutes.*

Elvis 45

'**Y**ou want to teach a course on . . .?'
        'Elvis Presley.'
'Elvis . . .?'
'Presley.'
'That's what I was afraid I heard you say.'
'Do you have a bias against Elvis Presley?'
'Not in his proper place. On golden-oldie radio when I'm stuck in traffic. Fred, are you really serious about this? This isn't the Music Department. Not that I can imagine *them* offering a course in Elvis, either. Musical appreciation of Elvis. What a joke. So how could I justify teaching Elvis in the *English* Department? The subtlety of the lyrics? The poetry of "Jailhouse Rock"? Give me a break. The dean would think I'd lost my mind. He'd ask me to resign as chair. Fred, you don't look as if I'm getting my point across.'
        'Not a literature course.'
'What?'
'A culture course.'
'I still don't—'
'We already offer Victorian Culture. And Nineteenth-Century American Culture. This would be *Twentieth*-Century American Culture.'
        'Fred, don't you think you're interpreting "culture" rather broadly? I mean, listen to what you're saying. Elvis Presley, for God's sake. The department would be a laughing stock. And for *you* in particular to want to teach such a course.'
        'I?'

'That's what I mean. You said "I" instead of "me". Perfect grammar. You're the only person in the department who speaks as if he's writing an essay for *Philological Quarterly*. Correctness of language. Wonderful. But Fred, you're hardly the type to . . . You'd sound ridiculous teaching Elvis Presley. You're a little – how would the students put it – uncool for the topic.'

'Maybe that's why I want to teach the course.'

'High school. When I was fifteen.'

'What are you talking about?'

'If you'll stop interrupting me, Edna, I'll explain. When I was fifteen, my high school had a student committee that selected the records for the Friday-night dances after the football and basketball games.'

'So it's going to be another stroll down memory lane. Every night at dinner. Well, if I'm going to have to hear one more story, you'd better pass me the wine.'

'I don't need to tell it, Edna.'

'In that case, I have a phone call to make.'

'I was the president of the social committee. I had three subordinates, and every Friday after school, we went to our favorite record store.'

'I thought you said you weren't going to tell the story.'

'I was wrong. I do need to tell it.'

'And I still need to make my phone call.'

'To Peter Robinson?'

'What makes you think I'd be calling . . .'

'The two of you seem awfully chummy.'

'Are you insinuating . . .'

'Just drink your wine. The record store had sound-proofed booths. Customers were allowed to choose records they were interested in buying and to play the records in the booths. Each Saturday, my committee and I—'

'Fred, did anyone ever tell you you talk as if you're lecturing?'

'—would spend hours playing records there. The committee was allowed to buy only two records each week. The small ones. Forty-fives. That format had recently been introduced.'

'Fred, I know. I remember what forty-fives looked like.'

'But we played as many as thirty before we bought our quota of two. Strange. The owner didn't seem to mind. To me, that booth in the record store felt like—'

'Fred, how can I drink my wine if you don't pass the bottle?'

'—home ought to be. And I never had closer friends than the students on that committee. We debated each record with absolute fervor, determined to supply the best music possible for the dances. I was underweight even then. And of course, I'm short. And—'

'Fred, is there a point to this story?'

'—I didn't have a chance to be popular, as the football players and basketball players were. Come to think of it, all the members of my committee were, I guess you would say, geeky. Like me. So we tried to be popular in a different way. By controlling the music at the dances. Other students would have to come up to us and make requests. They would have to be nice to us or else we wouldn't play the records they wanted.'

'Fred . . .'

'Of course, I never danced. I was far too shy. The dances were really only the excuse that allowed me to be able to go to the record store after school on Fridays. I don't think I ever experienced anything as exciting as hearing Elvis Presley sing "Don't Be Cruel" in that sound-proofed booth. I sensed that he was singing directly to me. I felt his emotion – the feeling of being picked upon, of being an outcast. What a revelation. What a sense of being privileged to listen to that record before the students at the dance could.'

'Fred, I asked you before. Does this story have a point?'

'Since then, I don't think I've ever been so happy.'

'Two hundred and twenty-five students enrolled in the course. I must say I'm gratified. I never expected to attract so many Elvis Presley enthusiasts.'

('He's a funny-looking dude, isn't he? Check out the Coke-bottle glasses and the bow tie.')

'As I emphasized on the syllabus that I distributed among you, the subject . . . Elvis Aron Presley . . . may be misleading to some. You have concluded that this is what you call a fresh-air course, that you can expect high grades for very little work. Quite the contrary. I expect the same intense diligence that my students bring to my courses in semiotics and post-structuralism.'

('Talks funny.')

'Our subject is one of those rare individuals who through talent, character, and coincidence becomes the focus of the major trends in that person's culture. In this case, a young, Southern male, who adapted black musical themes and techniques, making them acceptable to a segregation-minded white audience. It can be argued that Presley's music, bridging the division between white and black, created a climate in which desegregation was possible. Similar arguments can be made about Presley's contribution to the counterculture of the fifties and the later sexual revolution.'

('That sexual revolution sounds interesting.')

'I must say, my initial instinct was not to let Fred teach the course. I'm pleased that I listened to his idea, however, and needless to say, the dean's very happy with our increased enrollment. Would I like another martini? By all means. These receptions make me thirsty. Speaking of the dean, look at Fred over in that corner, talking to him. Lecturing to him is probably more accurate. These days all Fred can talk about is Elvis. The poor dean looks like he's afraid there's going to be an examination after the reception. Fred's got Elvis on the brain.'

'And I'm one of the few people I ever met who saw Elvis's first television appearance. No, I don't mean *The Ed Sullivan Show*. Everyone knows about that and Sullivan's insistence that Elvis not wiggle his hips when he sang, that the camera focus on Elvis only from the waist up. The incident is a perfect example of the cultural and sexual repression that Elvis overcame. What I'm talking about is an earlier television show. When Jackie Gleason went on summer hiatus, the Dorsey brothers filled in for him, and it was the Dorsey brothers who introduced Elvis, gyrating hips and all, to viewers, most of them unfamiliar with rock and roll and most of them burdened by conventions.'

'Wigglin' his ass. Why, I never saw anythin' like . . .'

'Ought to be a law. The man's no better than a pervert.'

'And look at that long hair. What is he? A man or a woman?

Every time he jerks his head back and forth, his hair falls into his eyes. Them side burns is butt ugly.'

'Now he's wigglin' his . . .'

'Pa, you know what they call him, don't you? Elvis the Pelvis.'

'Shut your pie hole, Fred. Go to your room and study. I don't want you watchin' this junk.'

'It's difficult to overstate the importance of Elvis's appearance with the Dorsey brothers. Those who hadn't seen his performance were told about it and enhanced it with their own imagination. A phenomenon was about to—'

'Professor?'

'Please wait until the end of my lecture.'

'But I just want to say, don't you think it's ironic that Elvis was introduced on television by musicians who seemed as outdated to Elvis's generation as Elvis seems to the Metallica generation?'

'Is that a question or a statement?'

'I was just thinking, maybe some day somebody'll offer a course on Metallica. (Har, har.)'

'Fred, enough is enough! It's three in the morning! I can't sleep with that noise you're making! How many times do I have to hear "All Shook Up"? The neighbors will start complaining! There! I told you! That's probably one of them phoning right now!'

'Look at the sideburns Fred's trying to grow. They remind me of caterpillars.'

'As bald as he is, that's the only place he *can* grow hair.'

'Those blue suede shoes don't do anything for him, either. The next thing you know, he'll be taking guitar lessons.'

'And boring us with concerts instead of lectures.'

'Or making us read that book he's writing.'

The Corruption of a Legend
Chapter Six

The crucial demarcation in Elvis's career occurred in 1958 when he was drafted by the United States military and sent to

Germany. To paraphrase a lyric from one of his best-known songs, that's when the downfall begins. The episode is rife with implications. Politically, the government has proven itself stronger than the rebel. Sexually, the shearing of Presley's magnificent ducktail-style hair symbolizes society's disapproval and conquest of his virility: a metaphorical emasculation. Two years of military indoctrination have their effect. Elvis's long-awaited return to society is shocking. The constant sneer with which he signaled to his young audience his disdain for authority has been replaced by an eager-to-please grin. His 'Yes, sir, no, sir' manner earlier had the hidden insolent tone of a black servant who is hypocritically polite to his white employers, but now Elvis seems genuinely determined to suck up to the Establishment. Even his newly grown hair appears flaccid. If we discount the regional Southern hits that Elvis had from 1954 to 1956, it is clear that his astonishing career remained pure for only two years, for fourteen rebellious, million-selling records from 1956 to 1958. After the military interruption, the hits continued, but the self-mocking 'My Way' is a far cry from the innocence of 'Hound Dog.'

'He did it his way, all right. He became a tool of the Establishment.'

'Fred.'

'The Jordinaires were shunted aside. Instead of a small rhythm-and-blues section, he now had the equivalent of the Mormon Tabernacle Choir.'

'Fred.'

'The songs lost all pretense of substance. That wretched remake of "O, Solo Mio," for example, which was called "It's Now Or Never," sounded so Muzak-sweet it's a wonder his audience didn't die from sugar shock.'

'Fred, you haven't shut up since we started dinner. It's been forty minutes. I'm sick of hearing you talk about Elvis. In fact, I'm sick of hearing you, period. I'm certain the Robinsons would like a chance to get a word in.'

'Oh, I'm terribly sorry. I must have gotten carried away. Good gracious. What was I thinking? By the way, Mrs Robinson, did you know that your husband Peter here is fucking my wife?'

'Thirty-three wretched movies.'
   ('Word is our prof is getting a divorce.')
   'Each more insipid than the previous ones. Increasingly, their only theme seems to be that its audience should take a vacation at Las Vegas, Fort Lauderdale, Acapulco, Hawaii, or wherever the film is set, as if Elvis has become a travel agent or a chamber of commerce booster.'
   ('Maybe his wife isn't an Elvis fan.')
   'Las Vegas. That symbol of excess becomes synonymous with the decay within Elvis. His anti-Establishment zoot-suit appearance in the mid-fifties changes to a parody of bikers' leather after his return from the military and finally to sequined suits with capes that rival Liberace for ostentation. When Elvis reappears on television in 1968, he looks like the Vegas act that he'll soon become.'
   ('I hear the *Today* show is coming to do a story about him.')
   'Nine years later, he'll die on the toilet.'

'Professor Hopkins, what made you think that Elvis would be a proper subject for a university course?'
   'If you look closely at him, he represents America.'
   'What, Professor? I'm afraid I don't follow you.'
   'Bryant, I . . . Can you hear me?'
   'Yes, the remote transmission is coming through clearly.'
   'Bryant, you take a boy who was raised to sing Gospel music at his Pentecostal church, a boy who worshipped his mother, a boy who from all accounts ought to have blended with the Establishment but who instead chose to fight the Establishment. He was only nineteen when he made his first recording for Sam Phillips in Memphis, and it's hard to imagine that someone so young could have been such a significant force in cultural change. By making black music popular, he promoted racial understanding and was easily as important in the Civil Rights movement as Martin Luther King Junior?'
   'Professor Hopkins.'
   'In terms of the sexual revolution, he—'

'Professor Hopkins, your remark about Elvis, the Civil Rights movement, and Martin Luther King Junior. Don't you think that's somewhat overstated?'

'*Nothing* about Elvis can be overstated. For a brief moment in the middle of this century, he *changed* this century.'

'Professor Hopkins.'

'But the messenger became the victim. Society fought back. Society defeated him. Just as Elvis symbolized the rebel, so he eventually symbolized the vindictiveness and viciousness of American society. When he died on the toilet, a drug addict, a glutton, bloated, wearing diapers, he delivered his final message by showing how destructive capitalism is.'

'Professor Hopkins.'

'In effect, he'd already been dead a long while, and Graceland, that garish monument to decadence, was the mausoleum for his walking corpse.'

'Professor Hopkins, I'm afraid we're almost out of time.'

'I wore this sequined suit and cape today because in Elvis's perverted image there must be retribution. You see this revolver?'

'For God's sake, Professor . . .'

'One of the most publicized events in Elvis's life is the incident in which he shot the picture tube of a television set. Form without substance. Even in his drug-demented stupor, he knew that television was his enemy, just as television *is* the enemy, the manipulator and destroyer of the American people and proper values. In Elvis's name—'

'—shot the lens on the television camera being used for the remote broadcast of the *Today* show, shot and killed the remote segment's producer, shot several students whom he'd brought to the interview as representative of the other students on his course, went to the English department office and shot his chairman, went to the university administration building and shot his dean, went to his former home and shot his estranged wife along with a friend, Peter Robinson, who was visiting her, and finally went to a downtown record store where he clutched an armful of Elvis CDs, put his pistol to his head, shouted, "Where's the booth? Never been so happy! Long live rock and roll!", and blew his brains out. A note in his sequined suit coat pocket said simply, "All shook up." Officials continue to investigate one of the worst mass murders to take place at an American university. This has been an NBC News update.'

Due to its live coverage of what have been called the Elvis murders, the *Today* show last week received its highest ratings in two years. A TV movie has been announced.

Later in this collection, you'll read about the negative side of the film and television industry. In contrast, the background to the script for 'Habitat' was my most positive 'Hollywood' experience. I put 'Hollywood' in quotes because the company that produced this script was in fact located in New York City, just down the street from the Flatiron Building. The company's name was Laurel Entertainment. Its two main executives were Richard Rubenstein and Mitchell Galin, and their two main products (apart from occasional films such as Stephen King's Creepshow) were the fantasy and horror TV programs, Tales from the Darkside and Monsters. During the late 1980s, fans of Twilight Zone-type stories made these half-hour series popular on late-night syndicated TV. Periodically, Richard and Mitchell asked me to write a script for Monsters, but I had trouble complying because I couldn't imagine a story that would fit the show's strictly controlled budgetary requirement of a few characters and sets.

Meanwhile, they'd hired me to do a screen adaptation of Michael Palmer's medical thriller, The Sisterhood. As so often happens in the film business, the project never got further than the development stage, but in the process, Richard and Mitchell showed me remarkable courtesy. I'd been on the road for several weeks, promoting a new novel. When I returned home, exhausted, I received a call from them, suggesting various dates when we could get together to discuss revisions on the script. The way this normally works, the writer (being low in the food chain) goes to the producers. Always. But when Richard and Mitchell realized how tired I was, they immediately proposed that they would fly to Iowa City (where I then lived) to *have the script discussions at my home. And they actually did. I can't tell you how floored I was and how impressed I was by these two gentlemen as we sat on my back porch, tweaking the script. Eventually, in 1989, I had an idea that I thought would work for the limited budget of* Monsters. *If a few characters were good, a solitary character would be better, I decided. To my surprise, the script was in production two months after I submitted it. The actress Lili Taylor* (Six Feet Under) *portrayed the main character.*

Habitat

FADE IN:

INT. CONTROL ROOM – DAY

We open with a large vivid image of a moonscape: barren weathered mountains, waterless river beds, forbidding crevasses and canyons, rocky, gray, and dismal. We might be fooled for a moment but quickly realize that this is not the real thing, instead a huge mural. We hear a persistent electronic BEEP. As we PAN DOWN from the image of the black terrain, we see a model of a lunar habitat, domed, with arched corridors that lead to other buildings. The model is on a metal table. Along with the mural, it gives us the impression we're in a complex on the moon.

Lingering on the model of the habitat, we hear a further sound. It's out of place, surprising, A GUITAR BEING TUNED, and abruptly the guitar begins STRUMMING. A WOMAN'S LILTING VOICE begins singing a folk song about oceans and forests and how the earth and the sky belong to you and me.

We PAN AWAY from the habitat and discover that we're in a control room with electronic consoles and glowing lights on monitors. The BEEP we first heard is like a metronome that supplies the beat for the guitar and the woman's song.

We TRACK PAST the consoles and STOP on the SINGER. A woman, late twenties, wearing jeans and a Lakers sweatshirt, her hair in a ponytail. She's lithe and lovely, leaning back on a metal chair with her bare feet on a counter next to a console. Her name is JAMIE NEAL. She reminds us of a cheerleader grown up to be a graduate student in a college dorm.

Her eyes are closed. In a world of her own, she continues strumming, singing, her voice muted, tinged with melancholy. 'Yes, the earth and the sky belong to us all.'

Mid-way through a poignant line about a fertile majestic land, she hesitates, her strum becoming irregular. Her voice drops. Relentless, the electronic BEEP persists.

Jamie sighs, lowers the guitar, opens her eyes, and scans the control room.

Perhaps she expected the song to transport her magically to the glorious landscapes she sang about. If so, the spell didn't work. Despondent, she sets the guitar next to a monitor, rises sadly from the chair, and approaches the mural of the moon. The barren mountains and canyons look even more forbidding. She studies the model of the habitat, then squints toward the electronic equipment around her, tense, as if she's in prison.

With a sigh she raises her head, musters her thoughts, and starts talking. But as we've seen, there's no one else in the room. The initial effect is puzzling, disorienting.

> JAMIE
> I don't know if I'm supposed to say this . . .
> I mean, for all I know, this *isn't* what you want to
> hear . . . if you're listening.

The electronic BEEP continues. She cocks her head, frowning.

> JAMIE
> I wish you'd turn that . . .
> (she gestures in frustration)

noise off. You can't imagine how . . .
    (she gestures again)
annoying it is.
    (she exhales)
If you're listening.

She pivots from the model and approaches a computer.

              JAMIE
But of course you're listening. You hear every
breath I take. My heartbeat. The alpha waves in
my brain. The sounds I make when I need to
relieve my . . .
    (she hugs her chest, embarrassed)
Do I snore?
    (her eyes become bitter)
I had a fiancé once. Good old what's-his name.
He wanted a corporate wife. Translation: He
wanted me to be obedient. To conform. Wear the
right clothes. Say the right things. Advance his
career. He said I was too independent. I always
suspected he broke the engagement
    (chuckles)
because I snored. Even asleep, I had to conform.
I couldn't *ever* let my guard down.
    (stares at the ceiling)
So *do* I? Snore?

All we hear is the BEEP.

              JAMIE
Come on!
    (she glares)
You can tell me!
    (she looks all around her)
You know me better than *he* ever did. You and I,
we're closer than Yin and Yang!... ice cream and
peanuts!... Laurel and Hardy!... closer than my

mother and father ever were! So tell me! *Do I snore?*

The BEEP continues.

But the room seems terribly silent.

She hugs her arms again.

                    JAMIE
        Just talk to me.

BEEP.

                    JAMIE
        Look, I know we agreed. But . . .

Unclasping her arms, she lowers a hand to her guitar and STRUMS it.

                    JAMIE
            (teasing)
        Just once? Just one word? Just 'hello'? Just to let
        me know you're out there?

She smiles her best smile. No answer. The BEEP persists.

She sags against a console.

                    JAMIE
        Okay, so we made a bargain. No contact. No . . .
            (a frustrated gesture)
        communication . . .
            (a fatalistic shrug)
        which reminds me of whatever his name was. I
        hope the ceramic doll he married divorces him
        because . . .
            (a grin)

the secret I never told him was that *he* snored.

BEEP. She stares at the floor.

> JAMIE
> Just one 'hello'?

She turns and frowns toward . . .

A section of wall that's recessed. There's a glowing box above it. And a door.

> JAMIE
> See, I'm . . .
> (trembles)
> a little . . .
> (clutches her arms)
> after all this time . . .
> (shuts her eyes)
> scared.

She frowns harder toward the door.

> JAMIE
> Does that mean I failed? Lord, I hope so. Please stop this. Please say 'hello' and . . . Please unseal the hatch. Please let me out.

BEEP.

> JAMIE
> 'The forests are *my* land. The rivers are . . .' No. they're not *anybody's*. Except . . . Whatever's in . . . Please don't make me do it again. Don't make me go in there. I *know* I agreed. I signed your damned contract. Nine months in here in exchange for . . .
> (flinches)

61

> But all the money you promised doesn't matter
> now. Keep it! Just say '*hello*'. Then tell me I don't
> have to go in there again! I'm not . . .
>> (trembling)
> alone. Can't you *talk* to me? Can't we *discuss* what's
> *happening* to me? Don't you *understand*? I don't *care*
> about the money anymore. I want out!

She spins toward the mural of the moon. Glaring, she grabs the
model of the habitat and throws it across the room. Its glass and
metal SHATTER.

JAMIE

> Home! I want to go home! I want to see *people*!
> Breathe fresh air again! Eat chocolate cake! Walk
> barefoot in grass! Smile at the stars! I want to be . . .

Her shoulders sag. In despair, she rubs her forehead.

JAMIE

> Free.

She gazes up, hoping.

No response.

BEEP.

JAMIE

>> (her voice drops)
> Free.

She stoops to pick up sections of the model she destroyed.

JAMIE

> I never understood what that meant before.

Suddenly animated, she crushes the remnants of the model and hurls them away. They CRASH against the consoles.

> JAMIE
> (angry)
> But you won't release me from our contract, will
> you? This is what you wanted, isn't it? To watch
> me fall apart!
> (paces)
> *You think you're so clever?* No way! What you
> don't realize is you made a mistake! You didn't
> tell me *it* would be here with me!
> (gestures in fury toward the door)
> Full disclosure. Ever heard of it? You didn't tell
> me *everything*. You held back crucial informa-
> tion! And one thing I learned from my fiancé,
> whatever his name was, is a contract demands
> good faith.
> (another furious gesture toward the door)
> And that *thing* in there is definitely not good
> faith. *What kind of monsters are you?* Let me out
> of here!

Jamie storms toward a bare wall, the only one in the room, and
pounds on it in desperation.

> JAMIE
> Null and void! You hear me! The contract's . . . I
> want to be free!

Abruptly a SIREN WAILS. Jamie flinches and covers her ears.
THE SIREN KEEPS SHRIEKING.

> JAMIE
> No! Please! I'm sorry! I didn't mean it!

THE SIREN PERSISTS. Beneath it, the BEEP continues.

Jamie sinks to her knees, still clutching her ears.

                    JAMIE
I'm sorry! Don't! Please, stop the . . .!
        (cringing from the SIREN'S WAIL)
I'll do it! Yes! Whatever you want! Whatever
I promised! If only . . .! Stop the . . .! Forget what
I said!
        (tears trickle)
I'll keep my word! I'll obey the contract!
Whatever you want . . .!
        (she shudders, in pain)
I'll do it!

THE SIREN BEGINS TO DIMINISH, ITS WAIL LESS TOR-
TURING.

Jamie eases her hands from her ears, testing the threat.

As THE WAIL BECOMES FAINTER, she shudders again and
slowly relaxes.

                    JAMIE
Thank you. I will. I'll do it.
        (presses her hands together, as if in prayer)
Thank you. Thank you.

Wiping tears from her eyes, she struggles to stand. Unsteady, she
again surveys the control room.

The siren has finally stopped, but the BEEP continues.

                    JAMIE
        (as if hypnotized, to the rhythm of the beep)
'The oceans and the forests, the earth and the sky
belong to . . .'
        (faltering)
God help me.

THE SIREN BLARES, A SHRILL ATTENTION-GETTER.

She stiffens and glares toward the ceiling.

                    JAMIE
        I told you I promised!

With a frightened glance toward the door, she shuffles toward a section of the control room that we haven't seen.

There, she reaches a treadmill, breathes deeply, and straps what looks like a blood-pressure cuff to each arm. Wires lead out of the cuff to a monitor.

Nervous, she glances toward the door.

                    JAMIE
        If you'd just been honest . . . If you'd only
        prepared me . . .

THE SIREN WARNS HER.

JAMIE cowers.

                    JAMIE
        I know! I know! I *hear* you! But why won't you
        talk to me?

With a frantic gaze, she studies the ceiling.

No answer.

Distraught, she steps on the treadmill and pushes a button. The treadmill begins to move beneath her. She starts to walk.

CLOSE-UP on the monitor to which her cuffs and wires are attached. Like an EKG, it shows FLASHING RED NUMBERS – blood pressure, pulse, and other numbers that we don't understand.

Jamie walks in place, the treadmill moving beneath her.

A WHISTLE BLOWS.

Jamie presses another number on the treadmill.

The treadmill moves faster.

The monitor's numbers increase.

Jamie paces increasingly faster and begins to recite.

> JAMIE
> My name is Jamie Neal. I'm an assistant
> professor of deep-space psychology.

THE WHISTLE BLOWS AGAIN.

Flinching, Jamie presses another number on the controls. The treadmill moves faster. She hastens her pace.

THE FLASHING RED NUMBERS go higher.

Despite the effort of her increased pace, Jamie continues reciting.

> JAMIE
> Specialty – adaption to confinement. Reactions to
> a limited environment. Potential aberrant
> behavior caused by the stress of . . .

When THE WHISTLE SHRILLS AGAIN, Jamie presses another number on the treadmill's console. She's forced to pace even faster.

> JAMIE
> Claustrophobia.

Sweat beads on her brow.

> JAMIE
> Five rooms. Two here in this central unit . . .

(a nervous glance toward the door)
three others, an entrance bay, a solar power
station, and sleeping quarters, linked to this
central unit by corridors.
(swallows, wipes sweat from her brow)
But I can't reach my sleeping quarters . . .
(an even more nervous glance toward the door)
unless I pass through *there*.

ANOTHER SHRILL WHISTLE. Jamie hurriedly presses
another button. As the treadmill increases speed, she's almost
forced to run.

                    JAMIE
And we all know what's in there.

She shudders.

                    JAMIE
You bet. For sure. We all know what I have to
face in *there*.
(out of breath)
After you've made me fulfill my bargain.

The FLASHING RED NUMBERS on the monitor go higher.

Jamie's running now.

                    JAMIE
After you've put me through my paces for
today.
(wipes sweat from her brow)
Or is this yesterday? I don't know anymore. Isn't
that what you want to find out? How much stress
can someone take?

On the monitor, THE RED NUMBERS FLASH as if out of
control.

Instead of the whistle, THE SIREN ONCE AGAIN BLARES.

Breathing rapidly, Jamie presses another number on the treadmill's console. Her pace decreases. Nervous but relieved, she presses more numbers, reducing her speed until the treadmill stops and she steps off.

At once, after raising her Lakers sweatshirt to wipe her face, she stares toward the ceiling, then the door, in apprehension.

> JAMIE
> My name is Jamie Neal. I'm twenty-eight. I've
> been here . . . I think . . . for sixty-four days. I
> *think*. Why didn't you give me *windows*? I want to
> see . . .
> (paws at a wall)
> the stars. The sun sets even here. Not on the sched-
> ule I'm used to. But I could get *used* to that schedule.
> And I'd *love* to see it. After sixty-four days.

She squints toward the ceiling.

> JAMIE
> Or nights. *How can I know?* If only I could see . . .
> I bet the sunset . . . no smog here . . . the colors
> must be . . .
> (her voice drops)
> I remember . . . crimson . . . like a flower . . . a
> rose . . . in blossom . . .
> (melancholy)
> beautiful.

In a sudden rage, she kicks the remnants of the habitat's model she earlier crushed.

> JAMIE
> Never mind windows! Why didn't you give
> me . . .?

She spins toward the numerous consoles.

JAMIE

Computers! Temperature gauges! Pressure
readouts! Oxygen monitors! Humidity! Gravity!
Even *dust*! I can measure everything! Except the
single most precious thing in my life!

She slumps against a table.

JAMIE

Time. Maybe it's only sixty-*three* days. Or maybe
sixty-*nine*. Or maybe I've been here only a couple
of weeks. But it feels like . . .
    (despairing)
Eternity.

BEEP.

JAMIE

Why didn't you at least allow me to wear a watch?

She gestures frantically toward the consoles.

JAMIE

Or let me have a clock? Nothing fancy! No digital
astro-time calculator. No computerized star-date
monitor, with comparative readouts for here and
home and the Gemini galaxy and . . . Just a plain
old-fashioned clock.
    (makes a twisting motion with one hand, pre
    tending to hold an object in the other)
The kind you wind up at night, and it ticks, and
the hands go around, and if you want to wake up
at a certain hour, you set the alarm. And when it
rings, you know it's tomorrow. And if you make a
mark
    (pretends she has a pencil)

on a page every time the alarm goes off . . . and if
you count the marks, you're sure how many days
you've been here. You don't feel as if you're . . .
    (slumps against the wall)
going crazy. Is that the point of the test? How
would I react – not if but *when* I broke down?
Because of . . .

She stares in horror toward the door.

                    JAMIE
    Time.

The SIREN WAILS.

                    JAMIE
    No.

A SECOND WAIL.

                    JAMIE
    Please! Don't make me go in there again!

A THIRD WAIL.

Tears stream down Jamie's face.

A FOURTH WAIL.

Jamie walks toward the door, as if hypnotized.

                    JAMIE
    Fulfill my contract. Obey my orders.

Jamie's POINT OF VIEW – approaching the door.

                    JAMIE
    Go through my paces.

70

She pauses. OFFSTAGE, we hear the hiss of the door sliding open. We ZOOM TOWARD A CLOSE-UP of JAMIE'S FACE: contorted, apprehensive, horrified.

> JAMIE
> Time. Yes, again. Time.

The door has slid open. Beyond it, we see a CORRIDOR. But as if this is *Alice in Wonderland*, the corridor narrows and becomes lower.

THE BEEP PERSISTS.

> JAMIE
> Time.

She feels her pulse.

> JAMIE
> The beat of my heart. The only time I know.

She takes a Walkman-sized object from a counter, straps it around her wrist, stares at a suction cup at the end of the object, and reaches beneath her Lakers sweatshirt, apparently attaching the suction cup to her chest.

At once the BEEP BECOMES A LITTLE FASTER, as if the object on her wrist monitors the speed of her heart.

> JAMIE
> The constant motion of time. Except that
> it's meaningless without something to compare
> it to . . . Without something to appreciate . . .
> Without a sunrise. I could imagine a sun-
> rise if . . . *Why didn't you give me a*
> *watch?*

THE SIREN WAILS.

Jamie flinches, clutches her fists in fury, and glares at the ceiling.

JAMIE

All right, I'm going!

The BEEP that measures her heartrate INCREASES.

She shifts through the doorway.

The roof is low enough that she's forced to stoop now. The walls narrow until they touch her shoulders.

THE BEEP GAINS A LITTLE MORE SPEED.

JAMIE

(walking stooped, glaring up)
What I want to know is, when my heart beats faster, *does that mean I'm getting older?*
(swallows, staring at the crawlspace)
Would *sixty-nine* days that feel like *sixty-three* days . . . or however long I've been here . . . actually be the equivalent of a *hundred and twenty* days? Six months? The *nine* months you're paying me to stay here? Because time drags . . .

The lowering ceiling compels her to kneel. The narrowing walls squeeze her shoulders.

There's a crawlspace directly ahead.

Jamie shudders.

THE BEEP INCREASES.

JAMIE

But my heart feels like it's on rocket fuel. Speed.
Does the speed of my heart affect time? Have I been here . . .

The ceiling is now so low that she's forced to drop to her hands and knees.

                    JAMIE
    Forever?

She places a hand toward the crawlspace, about to insert her head. Trembles. Hesitates.

AND THE SIREN WAILS.

                    JAMIE
    Give me a break! I told you I'm going! I just need
    a minute to . . .!

Abruptly the door HISSES shut behind her.

She whirls.

THE BEEP INCREASES SPEED.

And something SIZZLES, the HUM AND CRACKLE of electrical current.

She flinches, in agony, raising one hand, then the other, trying to push herself off the floor. But the ceiling's so low she can't raise her back. She jerks one knee, then the other off the floor, desperate to minimize contact with the CRACKLING electrical current.

                    JAMIE
    No! Please, stop! *I'm going! I promise!*

She scurries into the crawlspace.

At once, the CRACKLING current stops.

Her face is contorted with pain as she sprawls on her stomach. The crawlspace is so small it reminds us of an air-conditioning duct.

She breathes heavily, exhausted by the electrical current, slumping in relief.

JAMIE
No more! This can't go on forever!

A sigh of despair.

JAMIE
Or maybe this is hell.

She crawls awkwardly, wincing, bumping her head on the ceiling, scraping her shoulders against the tight walls.

JAMIE
Maybe you never meant to keep your word.
Maybe you're just playing with me? Are you
enjoying this, putting me through my paces,
watching the way I react. Am I just some kind
of . . . Just a cruel sadistic *game* to you?

With effort, Jamie reaches the end of the crawlspace and squirms toward another compartment. Her brow is moist. Her elbows and knees are dirty. The shoulders of her sweatshirt are frayed and grimy.

She musters strength and struggles to stand . . . wavers . . . leans against a wall.

Wiping sweat from her forehead, she stares ahead. What she sees makes her close her eyes in despair. She reopens them, squinting. Her voice cracks.

JAMIE
Why did you . . . No! You broke the bargain
again! You changed the rules! You . . .!

THE BEEP INCREASES.

With a sob, she struggles not to sink to the floor.

> JAMIE
> It's not the same! Why do you keep changing
> the . . .

Now we see the room Jamie has entered. It's completely bare. More important, the floor tilts upward – severely.

> JAMIE
> Not the same. *Not the same.*

A SIREN WAILS.

> JAMIE
> I hear it, you . . .!

She staggers forward, reaches the incline, attempts to climb it while standing, but falls to her stomach and claws her way toward the top.

> JAMIE
> My name is Jamie Neal.
> (claws upward)
> I think.
> (claws upward)
> I'm twenty-eight.
> (claws upward)
> I think.
> (claws upward)
> Going on a hundred.
> (claws upward)
> I'm an assistant professor of . . .

Jamie hesitates, nods in fierce resolve, and continues crawling higher.

> JAMIE
> Deep-space . . .

Jamie hesitates again, shakes her head in confusion.

> JAMIE
> Psychology? I think. My specialty is . . .

She reaches the crest and slumps across it, head on one side, legs on the other.

> JAMIE
> Adaptation to confinement? How long, dear
> God? How long?

THE SIREN BLARES.

Jamie raises her weary head. Her determined eyes glare toward the ceiling.

> JAMIE
> I need to rest!

Again we hear the SIZZLE AND CRACKLE of electrical current.

Jamie screams. THE BEEP INCREASES. She strains to raise her body off the painful, torturing peak of the slope. In a frenzy, she topples over the rim.

On the opposite side, she tumbles, groaning, down a slope. She lands hard on a level surface.

She struggles for breath, kneels, and manages to stand.

> JAMIE
> My name is Jamie Neal. I'm twenty-eight. I'm an
> assistant professor of . . . I'm a *human being*. And
> no matter how much you break your word, no
> matter how much you torture me . . . I'll fight
> back! I swear it! I'll fight back!

THE SIREN WAILS.

Jamie flinches. THE BEEP INCREASES. But she stays in place.

Abruptly the current CRACKLES AND SIZZLES, and as if thrust by a cattle prod, she lurches forward. THE BEEP becomes EVEN MORE RAPID.

> JAMIE
> You broke *your* word! I'll break *mine*!

MORE CRACKLING AND SIZZLING.

Her face contorted with agony, Jamie stumbles across an open space and reaches a metal ladder. Prodded by the SIZZLING electrical current, she scurries upward.

> JAMIE
> Jamie Neal. Jamie Neal. Jamie Neal.

She disappears through a circle in the ceiling above the ladder.

The SIZZLING stops as Jamie topples from the ladder and lands hard in another area. Groaning, she slowly raises her head.

Squints.

Shakes her head to clear her vision.

> JAMIE
> (seeking refuge in her song)
> 'The oceans and the forests, the earth and the sky belong to you and me.'

The room is filled with mirrors, like a 'fun house' in an amusement park.

JAMIE
You changed it again!

With enormous effort, she stands.

THE BEEP INCREASES.

JAMIE
It's all a lie! You never meant to . . .!

She struggles forward, glaring toward the mirrors.

Each reveals a different image. She's fat. She's thin. She's tall. She's short. She's twisted. Concave. Convex.

JAMIE
Now I'm the one who's a monster! You've turned me into . . .!
(recoils from the mirrors)
You! I'll get even! I swear I'll get even!

OFF STAGE, WE HEAR A HISS.

Jamie spins in terror, THE BEEP EVEN FASTER.

A door slides open. A shadow fills the entrance.

Jamie cringes.

The shadow becomes a . . . what to call it?. . . not human . . . misshapen, with ganglia, and boils, and several eyes.

MONSTER
(voice distorted, an electronic simulation)
You've done very well. Today you've been
especially adaptive . . . and *especially* amusing.
You've earned your reward.

78

The monster raises a flat box.

MONSTER
Your nourishment. Just the way you prefer it.
With double cheese and black olives.

JAMIE
I'm *allergic* to black olives.

The monster's grotesque arm sags.

MONSTER
I'm sorry. I'm new at this. I was told that your
species craves those foods.

Jamie straightens, braces her shoulders, inhales, and glowers.

THE BEEP BECOMES VERY RAPID.

JAMIE
And I told *you* I'd fight back. You broke your
bargain. Now I'll break mine.

MONSTER
There's nothing more you can do. This is the way
things are.
You have only one more task to perform before
you can eat.

Suddenly horizontal RAYS OF LIGHT fill the space between
them. The rays are like transparent, multicolored poles in a
grotesque climbing gym. They CRACKLE AND HISS with electrical current.

Jamie looks more angry.

JAMIE
I'm Jamie Neal!

> MONSTER
>
> We know.

Jamie crawls under one of the rays. A portion of it touches her back and shocks her.

Groaning, she stands. She squeezes between two other rays but comes too close and again gets shocked.

> JAMIE
>
> I'm a human being!

> MONSTER
>
> We know that, also.

> JAMIE
>
> Wrong! You don't have the faintest idea! *Watch me prove it!*

She braces herself and walks straight into the remaining rays, electricity jolting her. As the CRACKLE becomes un-bearable, she takes slow, agonized, determined steps, plod-ding toward her captor. Blisters appear on her face. Emerging from the rays, she staggers toward the monster, grabs the box, hurls it angrily away, wavers, then falls to the floor.

CLOSE-UP on her burned, bleeding hand as it twitches, then becomes motionless.

THE FRANTIC BEEP STOPS.

The monster stares down in bewilderment.

A section of the ceiling slides away, revealing another monster.

> MONSTER 2
> (distorted voice)

How unfortunate. She was particularly
entertaining.

MONSTER 1
After all this time . . . I still don't understand
their emotions . . . but . . .
   (lowers his head)
I suspect that I'm feeling . . . what do they call it?

MONSTER 2
Grief.

MONSTER 1
Yes. An unusual emotion. The experiment failed.

MONSTER 2
Not totally. We learned something.

MONSTER 1
What?

MONSTER 2
When we scanned her mind, we learned that her
species kept rodent-like creatures . . . hamsters?...
in similar cages. What they called 'habitats.'
Apparently her kind were hypocrites. They
enjoyed *having*... but didn't like . . . in fact, they
loathed... being pets.

FADE OUT.

Few writers have been as prolific as Stirling Silliphant, whose literate yet action-filled scripts for the classic TV series Route 66 (*1960–64*) *made me want to be a writer. Over the decades, we became friends. Indeed, thanks to his urging, NBC produced a miniseries of my novel,* The Brotherhood of the Rose. *A pleasant, stocky man with sandy hair, a boyish smile, and a wonderful tenor voice, he was seventy when I last saw him. During our final dinner together, he confided in me that he was being offered fewer and fewer writing assignments. 'In a youth-oriented industry, I'm perceived as too old,' he told me. It didn't matter that he had received an Academy Award for 1967's* In the Heat of the Night, *or that his script for 1968's* Charly *had given Cliff Robertson the opportunity to deliver an Oscar-winning performance, or that Stirling had written some of the most financially successful movies of the 1970s* (The Poseidon Adventure and The Towering Inferno). *All the industry cared about was the young, new flavor of the month. In fact, most of the executives with whom Stirling had meetings were so young (in their mid-twenties) that they had never seen* In the Heat of the Night, Charly, *or* The Towering Inferno. *As for* Route 66, *the series had been on TV so long ago that it was rerun as a nostalgia series on* Nick at Nite. *Hardly the 'with-it' factor that executives worship. The intelligence of the industry had so declined that Stirling's agent advised him not to take a complete list of his credits to a studio interview because (a) the executive wouldn't believe that anyone could write that much, and (b) the executive would feel intimidated.*

Stirling eventually decided to chuck it all and move to Thailand, where he believed that in a past incarnation he had been an Oriental.

He had what he called 'a Beverly Hills garage sale', relocated to Bangkok, and became a Buddhist. We exchanged letters and tried to make plans for me to visit him, but something always interfered. In 1996, at the age of seventy-eight, he died from prostate cancer.

Front Man

'**T**ell me that again,' I said. 'He must have been joking.'

'Mort, you know what it's like at the networks these days.' My agent sighed. 'Cost-cutting. Lay-offs. Executives so young they think *Seinfeld* is nostalgia. He wasn't joking. He's willing to take a meeting with you, but he's barely seen your work, and he wants a list of your credits.'

'All *two hundred and ninety* of them? Steve, I like to think I'm not vain, but how can this guy be in charge of series development and not know what I've written?'

This conversation was on the phone. Mid-week, mid-afternoon. I'd been revising computer printouts of what I'd written in the morning, but frustration at what Steve had told me made me press my pencil down so hard I broke its tip. Rising from my desk, I clutched the phone tighter.

Steve hesitated before he replied. 'No argument. You and I know how much you contributed to television. The Golden Age. *Playhouse 90. Kraft Theater. Alcoa Presents.* You and Rod Serling and Paddy Chayefsky practically invented TV drama. But that was then. This executive just started his job three months ago. He's only twenty-eight, for Christ's sake. He's been clawing his way to network power since he graduated from business school. He doesn't actually *watch* television. He's too damned busy to watch it, except for current in-house projects. What he does is program, check the ratings, and read the trades. If you'd won your Emmys for something this season, he might be impressed. But *The Sidewalks of New York*? That's something they show on Nickolodeon cable reruns, a company he doesn't work for, so what does he care?'

I stared out my study window. From my home on top of the Hollywood Hills, I had a view of rushing traffic on smoggy Sunset Boulevard, of Spago, Tower Records, and Chateau Marmont. But at the moment, I saw none of them, indignation blinding me.

'Steve, am I nuts, or are the scripts I sent you good?'

'Don't put yourself down. They're better than good. They don't only grab me. They're fucking smart. I *believe* them, and I can't say that for . . .' He named a current hit series about a female detective that made him a fortune in commissions but was two thirds tits and ass and one third car chases.

'So what's the real problem?' I asked, unable to suppress the stridency in my voice. 'Why can't I get any work?'

'The truth?'

'Since when did I tolerate lies?'

'You won't get pissed off?'

'I *will* get pissed off if—'

'All right already. The truth is, it doesn't matter how well you write. The fact is, you're too old. The networks think you're out of touch with their demographics.'

'*Out of*—'

'You promised you wouldn't get pissed off.'

'But after I shifted from television, I won an Oscar for *The Dead of Noon*.'

'Twenty years ago. To the networks, that's like the Dark Ages. You know the axiom – what have you done for us lately? The fact is, Mort, for the past two years you've been out of town, out of the country, out of the goddamn *industry*.'

My tear ducts ached. My hurried breathing made me dizzy. 'I had a good reason. The most important reason.'

'Absolutely,' Steve said. 'In your place I'd have done the same. And your friends respect that reason. But the movers and shakers, the new regime that doesn't give a shit about tradition, *they* think you died or retired, if they give you a moment's thought at all. *Then* isn't *now*. To them, last week's ratings are ancient history. What's next? they want to know. What's new? they keep asking. What they really mean is, What's *young*?'

'That sucks.'

'Of course. But young viewers are loose with their dough, my friend, and advertisers pay the bills. So the bottom line is, the networks feel unless you're under thirty-five, or better yet under *thirty*, you can't communicate with their target audience. It's an uphill grind for writers like you, of a certain age, no matter your talent.'

'Swell.' My knuckles ached as I squeezed the phone. 'So what do I do? Throw my word processor out the window, and collect on my Writers Guild pension?'

'It's not as bad as that. But bear in mind, your pension is the highest any Guild member ever accumulated.'

'But if I retire, I'll die like—'

'No, what I'm saying is be patient with this network kid. He needs a little educating. Politely, you understand. Just pitch your idea, look confident and dependable, show him your credits. He'll come around. It's not as if you haven't been down this path before.'

'When I was in my twenties.'

'There you go. You identify with this kid already. You're in his mind.'

My voice dropped. 'When's the meeting?'

'Friday. His office. I pulled in some favors to get you in so soon. Four p.m. I'll be at my house in Malibu. Call me when you're through.'

'Steve . . .'

'Yeah, Mort?'

'Thanks for sticking with me.'

'Hey, it's an honor. To me, you're a legend.'

'What I need to be is a *working* legend.'

'I've done what I can. Now it's up to you.'

'Sure.' I set down the phone, discovered I still had my broken pencil in one hand, dropped it, and massaged the aching knuckles of my other hand.

The reason I'd left LA two years ago, at the age of sixty-eight, was that my dear wife—

—Doris—

—my best friend—

—my cleverest editor—

87

—my exclusive lover—

—had contracted a rare form of leukemia.

As her strength had waned, as her sacred body had gradually failed to obey her splendid mind, I'd disrupted my workaholic's habit of writing every day and acted as her constant attendant. We'd traveled to every major cancer research center in the United States. We'd gone to specialists in Europe. We'd stayed in Europe because their hospice system is humane about pain-relieving drugs. We'd gotten as far as Sweden.

Where Doris had died.

And now, struggling with grief, I'd returned to my career. What other meaning did I have? It was either kill myself or write. So I wrote. And wrote. Even faster than in my prime when I'd contributed every episode in the four-year run of *The Sidewalks of New York*.

And now a network yuppy bastard with the cultural memory of a four-year-old had asked for my credits. Before I gulped a stiff shot of Scotch, I vowed I'd show this town that *this* old fuck still had more juice than when I'd first started.

Century City. Every week, you see those monoliths of power behind the credits on this season's hit lawyer show, but I remembered, bitterly nostalgic, when the land those skyscrapers stood upon had been the back lot for Twentieth-Century Fox.

I parked my leased Audi on the second level of an underground garage and took an elevator to the seventeenth floor of one of the buildings. The network's reception room was wide and lofty, with plentiful leather couches where actors, writers, and producers made hurried phone calls to agents and assistants while they waited to be admitted to the Holy of Holies.

I stopped before a young, attractive woman at a desk. Thin. No bra. Presumably she wanted to be an actress and was biding her time, waiting for the right connections. She finished talking to one of three phones and studied me, her boredom tempered by the fear that, if she wasn't respectful, she might lose a chance to make an important contact.

I'm not bad-looking. Although seventy, I keep in shape. Sure, my hair's receding. I have wrinkles around my eyes. But my family's genes are spectacular. I look ten years younger than I am, especially when I'm tanned, as I was after recent daily half-hour laps in my swimming pool.

My voice has the resonance of Ed McMahon's. 'Mort Davidson to see Arthur Lewis. I've got a four o'clock appointment.'

The would-be-actress receptionist scanned a list. 'Of course. You're expected. Unfortunately Mr Lewis has been detained. If you'll please wait over there.' She pointed toward a couch and picked up a Judith Krantz novel. Evidently she'd decided that I couldn't promote her career.

So I waited.

And waited.

An hour later, the receptionist gestured for me to come over. Miracle of miracles, Arthur Lewis was ready to see me.

He wore an Armani linen suit, fashionably wrinkled. No tie. Gucci loafers. No socks. His skin was the color of bronze. His thick, curly black hair had a calculated, wind-blown look. Photographs of his blonde wife and infant daughter stood on his glass-topped desk. His wife seemed even younger and thinner than he was. Posters of various current hit series hung on the wall. A tennis racket was propped in a corner.

'It's an honor to meet you. I'm a fan of everything you've done,' he lied.

I made an appropriate humble comment.

His next remark contradicted what he'd just said. 'Did you bring a list of your credits?'

I gave him a folder and sat on a leather chair across from him while he flipped through the pages. His expression communicated a mixture of boredom and stoic endurance.

Finally his eyebrows narrowed. 'Impressive. I might add, astonishing. Really, it's hard to imagine anyone writing this much.'

'Well, I've been in the business quite a while.'

'Yes. You certainly have.'

I couldn't tell if he referred to my age or my numerous credits. 'There used to be a joke,' I said.

'Oh?' His eyes were expressionless.

' "How can Mort Davidson be so prolific?" This was back in the early sixties. The answer was, "He uses an electric typewriter".'

'Very amusing,' he said as if I'd farted.

'These days, of course, I use a word processor.'

'Of course.' He folded his hands on the desk and sat straighter. 'So. Your agent said you had an idea that might appeal to us.'

'That's right.'

The phone rang.

'Excuse me a moment.' He picked up the phone. Obviously, if he'd been genuinely interested in my pitch, he'd have instructed his secretary that he didn't want any calls.

An actor named Sid was important enough for Arthur Lewis to gush with compliments. And by all means, Sid shouldn't worry about the rewrites that would make his character more 'with it' in today's generation. The writer in charge of the project was under orders to deliver the changes by Monday morning. If he didn't, that writer would never again work on something called *The Goodtime Guys*. Sid was a helluva talent, Arthur Lewis assured him. Next week's episode would get a thirty ratings share at least. Arthur chuckled at a joke, set down the phone, and narrowed his eyebrows again. 'So your idea that you think we might like.' He glanced at his Rolex.

'It's about an at-risk youth center, a place where troubled kids can go and get away from their screwed-up families, the gangs, and the drug dealers on the streets. There's a center in the Valley that I see as our model – an old Victorian house that has several additions. Each week we'd deal with a special problem – teenage pregnancy, substance abuse, runaways – but mostly this would be a series about emotions, about people, the kids, but also the staff, a wide range of interesting, committed professionals, an elderly administrator, a female social worker, an Hispanic who used to be in the gangs, a priest, whatever mix works. I call it—'

The phone rang again.

'Just a second,' Arthur Lewis said.

Another grin. A producer this time. A series about a college sorority next to a fraternity, *Crazy 4 U*, had just become this season's new hit. Arthur Lewis was giving its cast and executives a party at Le Dome tomorrow evening. Yes, he guaranteed. Ten cases of Dom Perignon would arrive at the producer's home before the party. And beluga caviar? Enough for an after-party power party? No problem. And yes, Arthur Lewis was having the same frustrations as the producer. It was mighty damned hard to find a pre-school for gifted children.

He set down the phone. His face turned to stone. 'So that's your idea?'

'Drama, significance, emotion, action, and realism.'

'But what's the hook?'

I shook my head in astonishment.

'Why would anyone want to watch it?' Arthur Lewis asked.

'To feel what it's like to help kids in trouble, to *understand* those kids.'

'Didn't you have a stroke a while ago?'

'*What?*'

'I believe in honesty, so I'll be direct. You put in your time. You paid your dues. So why don't you back away gracefully?'

'I *didn't* have a stroke.'

'Then why did I hear—'

'My wife had cancer. She died . . .' I caught my breath. 'Six months ago.'

'I see. I'm sorry. I mean that sincerely. But television isn't the same as when you created . . .' He checked my list of credits. '*The Sidewalks of New York.* A definite classic. One of my absolute personal favorites. But times have changed. The industry's a lot more competitive. The pressure's unbelievable. A series creator has to act as one of the producers, to oversee the product, to guarantee consistency. I'm talking thirteen hours a day minimum, and ideally the creator ought to contribute something to every script.'

'That's what I did on *The Sidewalks of New York.*'

'Oh?' Arthur Lewis looked blank. 'I guess I didn't notice that in your credits.' He straightened. 'But my point's the same. Television's a pressure cooker. A game for people with energy.'

'Did I need a wheelchair when I came in here?'

'You've lost me.'

'Energy's not my problem. I'm full to bursting with the need to work. What matters is, what do you think of my idea?'

'It's . . .'

The phone rang.

Arthur Lewis looked relieved. 'Let me get back to you.'

'Of course. I know you're busy. Thanks for your time.'

'Hey, *any*time. I'm always here and ready for new ideas.' Again he checked his Rolex.

The phone kept ringing.

'Take care,' he said.

'You too.'

I took my list of credits off his desk.

The last thing I heard when I left was, 'No, that old fuck's wrong for the part. He's losing his hair. A rug? Get real. The audience can tell the difference. For God's sake, a hairpiece is death in the ratings.'

Steve had said to phone him when the meeting was over. But I felt so upset I decided to hell with phoning him and drove up the Pacific Coast Highway toward his place in Malibu. Traffic was terrible – rush hour, Friday evening. For once, though, it had an advantage. After an hour, my anger began to abate enough for me to realize that I wouldn't accomplish much by showing up unexpectedly in a fit at Steve's. He'd been loyal. He didn't need my aggravation. As he'd told me, 'I've done what I can. Now it's up to you.' But there wasn't much I *could* do if my age and not my talent was how I was judged. Certainly that wasn't Steve's fault.

So I stopped at something called the Pacific Coast Diner and took the advice of a bumper sticker on a car I'd been stuck behind – CHILL OUT. Maybe a few drinks and a meditative dinner would calm me down. The restaurant had umbrella-topped tables on a balcony that looked toward the ocean. I had to wait a half-hour, but a Scotch and soda made the time go quickly, and the crimson reflection of the setting sun on the ocean was spectacular.

Or would have been if I'd been paying attention. The truth was, I couldn't stop being upset. I had another Scotch and soda, ordered poached salmon, tried to enjoy my meal, and suddenly couldn't swallow, suddenly felt about as lonely as I'd felt since Doris had died. Maybe the network executives are right, I thought. Maybe I *am* too old. Maybe I *don't* know how to relate to a young audience. Maybe it's time I packed it in.

'Mort Davidson,' a voice said.

'Excuse me?' I blinked, distracted from my thoughts.

My waiter was holding the credit card I'd given him. 'Mort Davidson.' He looked at the name on the card, then at me. 'The screenwriter?'

I spared him a bitter 'used to be' and nodded with what I hoped was a pleasant manner.

'Wow.' He was tall and thin with sandy hair and a glowing tan. His blue eyes glinted. He had the sort of chiseled, handsome face that made me think he was yet another would-be actor. He looked to be about twenty-three. 'When I saw your name, I thought, no, it couldn't be. Who knows how many Mort Davidsons there are? The odds against this being . . . But it *is* you. The screenwriter.'

'Guilty,' I managed to joke.

'I bet I've seen everything you ever wrote. I must have watched *The Dead of Noon* twenty-five times. I really learned a lot.'

'Oh?' I was puzzled. What would my screenplay have taught him about acting?

'About structure. About pace. About not being afraid to let the characters talk. That's what's wrong with movies today. The characters don't have anything important to say.'

At once, it hit me. He wasn't a would-be actor.

'I'm a writer,' he said. 'Or trying to be. I mean, I've still got a lot to learn. That I'm working here proves it.' The glint went out of his eyes. 'I still haven't sold anything.' His enthusiasm was forced. 'But hey, nothing important is easy. I'll just keep writing until I crack the market. The boss is . . . I'd better not keep chattering at you. He doesn't like it. For sure, you've got better things to do than listen to me. I just wanted to say how much I like your work, Mr Davidson. I'll bring your credit card right back. It's a pleasure to meet you.'

As he left, it struck me that the speed with which he talked suggested not only energy but insecurity. For all his good looks, he felt like a loser.

Or maybe I was just transferring my own emotions onto him. This much was definite – getting a compliment was a hell of a lot better than a sharp stick in the eye or the meeting I'd endured.

When he came back with my credit card, I signed the bill and
gave him a generous tip.

'Thanks, Mr Davidson.'

'Hang in there. You've got one important thing on your side.'

'What's that?'

'You're young. You've got plenty of time to make it.'

'Unless . . .'

I wondered what he meant.

'Unless I don't have what it takes.'

'Well, the best advice I can give you is never doubt yourself.'

As I left the restaurant and passed beneath hissing arc lamps
toward my car, I couldn't ignore the irony. The waiter had youth
but doubted his ability. I had confidence in my ability but was
penalized because of my age. Despite the roar of traffic on the
Pacific Coast Highway, I heard waves on the beach.

And that's when the notion came to me. A practical joke of
sorts, like stories you hear about frustrated writers submitting
Oscar-winning screenplays, *Casablanca*, for example, but the frustrated writers change the title and the characters' names. The notes
they get back from producers as much as say the screenplays are
the lousiest junk the producers ever read. So then the frustrated
writers tell the trade papers what they've done, the point being that
the writers are trying to prove it doesn't matter *how* good a writer
you are if you don't have connections.

Why not? I thought. It would be worth seeing the look on those
bastards' faces.

'What's your name?'

'Ric Potter.'

'Short for Richard?'

'No. For Eric.'

I nodded. Breaking-the-ice conversation. 'The reason I came
back is I have something I want to discuss with you, a way that
might help your career.'

His eyes brightened.

At once, they darkened, as if he thought I might be trying to
pick him up.

'Strictly business,' I said. 'Here's my card. If you want to talk about writing and how to make some money, give me a call.'

His suspicion persisted, but his curiosity was stronger. 'What time?'

'Eleven tomorrow?'

'Fine. That's before my shift starts.'

'Come over. Bring some of your scripts.'

That was important. I had to find out if he could write or if he was fooling himself. My scheme wouldn't work unless he had a basic feel for the business. So the next morning, when he arrived exactly on time at my home in the hills above West Hollywood, we swapped: I let him see a script I'd just finished while I sat by the pool and read one of his. I finished around one o'clock. 'Hungry?'

'Starved. Your script is wonderful,' Ric said. 'I can't get over the pace. The sense of reality. It didn't feel like a story.'

'Thanks.' I took some tuna salad and Perrier from the refrigerator. 'Wholewheat bread and kosher dills okay? Or maybe you'd rather go to a restaurant.'

'After working in one every night?' Ric laughed.

But I could tell that he was marking time, that he was frustrated and anxious to know what I thought of his script. I remembered how I had felt at his age, the insecurity when someone important was reading my work. I got to the point.

'I like your story,' I said.

He exhaled.

'But I don't think it's executed properly.'

His cheek muscles tensed.

'Given what they're paying A-list actors these days, you have to get the main character on screen as quickly as possible. *Your* main character doesn't show up until page fifteen.'

He sounded embarrassed. 'I couldn't figure out a way to . . .'

'And the romantic element is so familiar it's tiresome. A shower scene comes from a washed-up imagination.'

That was tough, I knew, but I waited to see how he'd take it. If he turned out to be the sensitive type, I wasn't going to get anywhere.

'Yeah. Okay. Maybe I did rely on a lot of other movies I'd seen.'

His response encouraged me. 'The humorous elements don't work. I don't think comedy is your thing.'

He squinted.

'The ending has no focus,' I continued. 'Was your main character right or not? Simply leaving the dilemma up in the air is going to piss off your audience.'

He studied me. 'You said you liked the story.'

'Right. I did.'

'Then why do I feel like I'm on the *Titanic*?'

'Because you've got a lot of craft to learn, and it's going to take you quite a while to master it. If you ever do. There aren't any guarantees. The average Guild member earns less than six thousand dollars a year. Writing screenplays is one of the most competitive enterprises in the world. But I think I can help you.'

'Why?'

'Excuse me?'

'We met just last night. I was your waiter, for God's sake. Now suddenly I'm in your house, having lunch with you, and you're saying you want to help me. It can't be because of the force of my personality. You want something.'

'Yes, but not what you're thinking. I told you last night – this is strictly business. Sit down and eat while I tell you how we can both make some money.'

'This is Ric Potter,' I said. We were at a reception in one of those mansions in the hills near the Hollywood Bowl. Sunset. A string quartet. Champagne. Plenty of movers and shakers. 'Fox is very hot on one of his scripts. I think it'll go for a million.'

The man to whom I'd introduced Ric was an executive at Warner's. He couldn't have been over thirty. 'Oh?'

'Yeah, it's got a youth angle.'

'Oh?' The executive looked Ric up and down, confused, never having heard of him, at the same time worried because he didn't want to be out of the loop, fearing he *ought* to have heard of him.

'If I sound a little proud,' I said, 'it's because I discovered him. I found him last May when I was giving a talk to a young screenwriters' workshop at the American Film Institute. Ric convinced me to look at some things and . . . I'm glad I did. My *agent's* glad I did.' I chuckled.

The executive tried to look amused, although he hated like hell to pay writers significant money. For his part, Ric tried to look modest but unbelievably talented, young, young, young, and hot, hot, hot.

'Well, don't let Fox tie you up,' the executive told Ric. 'Have your agent send me something.'

'I'll do that, Mr Ballard. Thanks,' Ric said.

'Do I look old enough to be a "mister"? Call me Ed.'

We made the rounds. While all the executives considered me too old to be relevant to their 16–25 audience, they still had reverence for what they thought of as an institution. Sure, they wouldn't buy anything from me, but they were more than happy to talk to me. After all, it didn't cost them any money, and it made them feel like they were part of a community.

By the time I was through introducing Ric, my rumors about him had been accepted as fact. Various executives from various studios considered themselves in competition with executives from other studios for the services of this hot, new young writer who was getting a million dollars a script.

Ric had driven with me to the reception. On the way back, he kept shaking his head in amazement. 'And that's the secret? I just needed the right guy to give me introductions? To be anointed as a successor?'

'Not quite. Don't let their chumminess fool you. They only care if you can deliver.'

'Well, tomorrow I'll send them one my scripts.'

'No,' I said. 'Remember our agreement. Not one of your scripts. One of *mine*. By Eric Potter.'

So there it was. The deal Ric and I had made was that I'd give him ten percent of whatever my scripts earned in exchange for his being my front man. For his part, he'd have to take calls and go to meetings and behave as if he'd actually written the scripts. Along the way, we'd inevitably talk about the intent and technique of the scripts, thus providing Ric with writing lessons. All in all, not a bad deal for him.

Except that he had insisted on *fifteen* percent.

'Hey, I can't go to meetings if I'm working three-to-eleven at the restaurant,' he'd said. 'Fifteen percent. And I'll need an advance.

You'll have to pay me what I'm earning at the restaurant so I can be free for the meetings.'

I wrote him a check for a thousand dollars.

The phone rang, interrupting the climactic speech of the script I was writing. Instead of picking up the receiver, I let my answering machine take it, but I answered anyhow when I heard my agent talking about Ric.

'What about him, Steve?'

'Ballard over at Warner's likes the script you had me send him. He wants a few changes, but basically he's happy enough to offer seven hundred and fifty thousand.'

'Ask for a million.'

'I'll ask for nothing.'

'I don't understand. Is this a new negotiating tactic?'

'You told me not to bother reading the script, just to do the kid a favor and send it over to Warner's because Ballard asked for it. As you pointed out, I'm too busy to do any reading anyhow. But I made a copy of the script, and for the hell of it, last night I looked it over. Mort, what are you trying to pull? Ric Potter didn't write that script. *You* did. Under a different title, you showed it to me a year ago.'

I didn't respond.

'Mort?'

'I'm making a point. The only thing wrong with my scripts is an industry bias against age. Pretend somebody young wrote them, and all of a sudden they're wonderful.'

'Mort, I won't be a part of this.'

'Why not?'

'It's misrepresentation. I'd be jeopardizing my credibility as an agent. You know how the clause in the contract reads – the writer guarantees that the script is solely his or her own work. If somebody else was involved, the studio wants to know about it – to protect it against a plagiarism suit.'

'But if you tell Ballard I wrote that script, he won't buy it.'

'You're being paranoid, Mort.'

'Facing facts and being practical. Don't screw this up.'

'I told you, I won't go along with it.'

'Then if you won't make the deal, I'll get somebody else who will.'

A long pause. 'Do you know what you're saying?'

'Ric Potter and I need a new agent.'

I'll say this for Steve – even though he was furious about my leaving him, he finally swore, for old time's sake, at my insistence, that he wouldn't tell anybody what I was doing. He was loyal to the end. It broke my heart to leave him. The new agent I selected knew squat about the arrangement I had with Ric.

She believed what I told her – that Ric and I were friends and by coincidence we'd decided simultaneously to get new representation. I could have chosen one of those superhuge agencies like CAA, but I've always been uncomfortable when I'm part of a mob, and in this case especially, it seemed to me that small and intimate were essential. The fewer people who knew my business, the better.

The Linda Carpenter Agency was located in a stone cottage just past the gates to the old Hollywoodland subdivision. Years ago, the 'land' part of that subdivision's sign collapsed. The 'Hollywood' part remained, and you see that sign all the time in film clips about Los Angeles. It's a distance up past houses in the hills. Nonetheless, from outside Linda Carpenter's stone cottage, you feel that the sign's looming over you.

I parked my Audi and got out with Ric. He was wearing sneakers, jeans, and a blue cotton pullover. At my insistence. I wanted his outfit to be selfconsciously informal and youthful in contrast with my own mature, conservative slacks and sport coat. When we entered the office, Linda – who's thirty, with short red hair, and loves to look at gorgeous young men – sat straighter when I introduced Ric. His biceps bulged at the sleeves of his pullover. I was reminded again of how much – with his sandy hair, blue eyes, and glowing tan – he looked like an actor.

Linda took a moment before she reluctantly shifted her attention away from him, as if suddenly realizing that I was in the room. 'Good to see you again, Mort. But you didn't have to come all this way. I could have met you for lunch at Le Dome.'

'A courtesy visit. I wanted to save you the long drive, not to mention the bill.'

I said it as if I was joking. The rule is that agents always pick up the check when they're at a restaurant with clients.

Linda's smile was winning. Her red hair seemed brighter. 'Any time. I'm still surprised that you left Steve.' She tactfully didn't ask what the problem had been. 'I promise I'll work hard for you.'

'I know you will,' I said. 'But I don't think you'll have to work hard for my friend here. Ric already has some interest in a script of his over at Warner's.'

'Oh?' Linda raised her elegant eyebrows. 'Who's the executive?'

'Ballard.'

'My, my.' She frowned slightly. 'And Steve isn't involved in this? Your ties are completely severed?'

'Completely. If you want, call him to make sure.'

'That won't be necessary.'

But I found out later that Linda did phone Steve, and he backed up what I'd said. Also he refused to discuss why we'd separated.

'I have a hunch the script can go for big dollars,' I continued.

'How big is big?'

'A million.'

Linda's eyes widened. 'That certainly isn't small.'

'Ballard heard there's a buzz about Ric. Ballard thinks that Ric might be a young Joe Eszterhas.' The reference was to the screen-writer of *Basic Instinct*, who had become a phenomenon for writing sensation-based scripts on speculation and intriguing so many producers that he'd manipulated them into a bidding war and collected megabucks. 'I have a suspicion that Ballard would like to make a preemptive bid and shut out the competition.'

'Mort, you sound more like an agent than a writer.'

'It's just a hunch.'

'And Steve doesn't want a piece of this?'

I shook my head no.

Linda frowned harder.

But her frown dissolved the moment she turned again toward Ric and took another look at his perfect chin. 'Did you bring a copy of the script?'

'Sure.' Ric grinned with becoming modesty, the way I'd taught him. 'Right here.'

Linda took it and flipped to the end to make sure it wasn't

longer than 115 pages – a shootable size. 'What's it about?'

Ric gave the pitch that I'd taught him – the high concept first, then the target audience, the type of actor he had in mind, and ways the budget could be kept in check. The same as when we'd clocked it at my house, he took four minutes.

Linda listened with growing fascination. She turned to me. 'Have you been coaching him?'

'Not much. Ric's a natural.'

'He must be to act this polished.'

'And he's young,' I said.

'You don't need to remind me.'

'And Ballard *certainly* doesn't need reminding,' I said.

'Ric,' Linda said, 'from here on in, whatever you do, don't get writer's block. I'm going to make you the highest-paid new kid in town.'

Ric beamed.

'And Mort,' Linda said, 'I think you're awfully generous to help your friend through the ropes like this.'

'Well' – I shrugged – 'isn't that what friends are for?'

I had joked with Linda that our trip to her office was a courtesy visit – to save her a long drive and the cost of buying us lunch at an expensive restaurant. That was partly true. But I also wanted to see how Ric made his pitch about the script. If he got nerves and screwed up, I didn't want it to be in Le Dome, where producers at neighboring tables might see him get flustered. We were trying out the show on the road, so to speak, before we brought it to town. And I had to agree with Linda – Ric had done just fine.

I told him so, as we drove along Sunset Boulevard. 'I won't always be there to back you up. In fact, it'll be rare that I am. We have to keep training you so you give the impression there's very little about writing or the business you don't understand. Most of getting along with studio executives is making them have confidence in you.'

'You really think I impressed her?'

'It was obvious.'

Ric thought about it, peering out of the window, nodding. 'Yeah.'

★　★　★

So we went back to my home in the hills above West Hollywood, and I ran him through more variations of questions he might be asked – where he'd gotten the idea, what actors would be good in the roles, who he thought could direct the material, that sort of thing. At the start of a project, producers pay a lot of attention to a screenwriter, and they promise to keep consulting him the way they're consulting him now. It's all guff, of course. As soon as a director and a name actor are attached to a project, the producers suddenly get amnesia about the original screenwriter. But at the start, he's king, and I wanted Ric to be ready to answer any kind of question about the screenplay so he could be convincing that he'd actually written it.

Ric was a fast study. At eight, when I couldn't think of any more questions he might have to answer, we took a drive to dinner at a fish place near the Santa Monica pier. Afterward, we strolled to the end of the pier and watched the sunset.

'So this is what it's all about,' Ric said.

'I'm not sure what you mean.'

'The action. I can feel the action.'

'Don't get fooled by Linda's optimism. Nothing might come of this.'

Ric shook his head. 'I'm close.'

'I've got some pages I want to do tomorrow, but if you'll come around at four with your own new pages, I'll go over them for you. I'm curious to see how you're revising that script you showed me.'

Ric kept staring out at the sunset and didn't answer for quite a while. 'Yeah, my script.'

As things turned out, I didn't get much work done the next day. I had just managed to solve a problem in a scene that was running too long when my phone rang. That was around ten o'clock, and rather than be interrupted, I let my answering machine take it. But when I heard Ric's excited voice, I picked up the phone.

'Slow down,' I said. 'Take it easy. What are you so worked up about?'

'They want the script!'

I wasn't prepared. 'Warner's?'

'Can you believe that this is happening so fast?'

'Ballard's actually taking it? How did you find this out?'

'Linda just phoned me!'

'Linda?' I frowned. 'But why didn't Linda . . .' I was about to say 'Why didn't Linda phone *me*?' Then I realized my mistake. There wasn't any reason for Linda to phone me, except maybe to tell me the good news about my friend. But she definitely had to phone Ric. After all, he was supposedly the author of the screenplay.

Ric kept talking excitedly. 'Linda says Ballard wants to have lunch with me.'

'Great.' The truth is, I was vaguely jealous. 'When?'

'Today.'

I was stunned. Any executive with power was always booked several weeks in advance. For Ballard to decide to have lunch with Ric this soon, he would have had to cancel lunch with someone else. It definitely wouldn't have been the other way around. No one cancels lunch with Ballard.

'Amazing,' I said.

'Apparently he's got big plans for me. By the way, he likes the script as is. No changes. At least, for now. Linda says when they sign a director, the director always asks for changes.'

'Linda's right,' I said. 'And then the director'll insist that the changes aren't good enough and ask to bring in a friend to do the rewrite.'

'No fucking way,' Ric said.

'A screenwriter doesn't have any clout against a director. You've still got a lot to learn about industry politics. School isn't finished yet.'

'Sure.' Ric hurried on. 'Linda got Ballard up to a million and a quarter for the script!'

For a moment, I had trouble breathing.

'Great.' And this time I meant it.

Ric phoned again in thirty minutes. He was nervous about the meeting and needed reassurance.

Ric phoned thirty minutes after that, saying that he didn't feel comfortable going to a power lunch in the sneakers, jeans, and pullover that I had told him were necessary for the role he was playing.

'You have to,' I said. 'You've got to look like you don't belong to the Establishment or whatever the hell it is they call it these days. If you look like every other writer trying to make an impression, Ballard will *treat* you like every other writer. We're selling nonconformity. We're selling youth.'

'I still say I'd feel more comfortable in a jacket by . . .' Ric mentioned the name of the latest trendy designer.

'Even assuming that's a good idea, which it isn't, how on earth are you going to pay for it? A jacket by that designer costs fifteen hundred dollars.'

'I'll use my credit card,' Ric said.

'But a month from now, you'll still have to pay the bill. You know the whopping interest rates those credit card companies charge.'

'Hey, I can afford it. I just made a million and a quarter bucks.'

'No, Ric. You're getting confused.'

'All right, I know Linda has to take her ten percent commission.'

'You're still confused. *You* don't get the bulk of that money. *I* do. What *you* get is fifteen percent of it.'

'That's still a lot of cash. Almost two hundred thousand dollars.'

'But remember, you probably won't get it for at least six months.'

'*What?*'

'On a spec script, they don't simply agree to buy it and hand you a check. The fine points on the negotiation have to be completed. Then the contracts have to be drawn up and reviewed and amended. Then their business office drags its feet before issuing the check. I once waited a year to get paid for a spec script.'

'But I can't wait that long. I've got . . .'

'Yes?'

'Responsibilities. Look, Mort, I have to go. I need to get ready for this meeting.'

'And I need to get back to my pages.'

'With all this excitement, you mean you're actually writing today?'

'*Every* day.'

'No shit.'

But I was too preoccupied to get much work done.

Ric finally phoned around five. 'Lunch was fabulous.'

I hadn't expected to feel so relieved. 'Ballard didn't ask you any tricky questions? He's still convinced you wrote the script?'

'Not only that. He says I'm just the talent he's been looking for. A fresh imagination. Someone in tune with today's generation. He asked me to do a last-minute rewrite on an action picture he's starting next week.'

'*The Warlords?*'

'That's the one.'

'I've been hearing bad things about it,' I said.

'Well, you won't hear anything bad anymore.'

'Wait a . . . Are you telling me you accepted the job?'

'Damned right.'

'Without talking to me about it first?' I straightened in shock. 'What in God's name did you think you were doing?'

'Why would I need to talk to you? You're not my agent. Ballard called Linda from our table at the restaurant. The two of them settled the deal while I was sitting there. Man, when things happen, they happen. All those years of trying, and now, wham, pow, all of a sudden I'm there. And the best part is, since I'm a writer on hire for this job, they have to pay some of the money the minute I sit down to work, even if the contracts aren't ready.'

'That's correct,' I said. 'On work for hire, you have to get paid on a schedule. The Writers Guild insists on that. You're learning fast. But Ric, before you accepted the job, don't you think it would have been smart to read the script first – to see if it *can* be fixed?'

'How bad can it be?' Ric chuckled.

'You'd be surprised.'

'It doesn't matter *how* bad. The fee's a hundred thousand dollars. I need the money.'

'For *what*? You don't live expensively. You can afford to be patient and take jobs that build a career.'

'Hey, I'll tell you what I can afford. Are you using that portable phone in your office?'

'Yes. But I don't see why that matters.'

'Take a look out your front window.'

Frowning, I left my office, went through the TV room and the living room, and peered past the blossoming rhododendron outside my front window. I scanned the curving driveway, then focused on the gate.

Ric was wearing a designer linen jacket, sitting in a red Ferrari, using a car phone, waving to me when he saw me at the window. 'Like it?' he asked over the phone.

'For God's sake.' I broke the connection, set down the phone, and stalked out the front door.

'Like it?' Ric repeated when I reached the gate. He gestured toward his jacket and the car.

'You didn't have time to . . . Where'd you get . . .?'

'This morning, after Linda phoned about the offer from Ballard, I ordered the car over the phone. Picked it up after my meeting with Ballard. Nifty, huh?'

'But you don't have any assets. You mean they just let you drive the car off the lot?'

'Bought it on credit. I made Linda sign as the guarantor.'

'You made Linda . . .' I couldn't believe what I was hearing. 'Damn it, Ric, why don't you let me finish coaching you before you run off and . . . After I taught you about screenplay technique and industry politics, I wanted to explain to you how to handle your money.'

'Hey, what's to teach? Money's for spending.'

'Not in *this* business. You've got to put something away for when you have bad years.'

'Well, I'm certainly not having any trouble earning money so far.'

'What happened today is a fluke! This is the first script I've sold in longer than I care to think about. There aren't any guarantees.'

'Then it's a good thing I came along, huh?' Ric grinned.

'Before you accepted the rewrite job, you should have asked me if I wanted to do it.'

'But you're not involved in this. Why should I divide the money with you? *I'm* going to do it.'

'In that case, you should have asked yourself another question.'

'What?'

'Whether you've got the *ability* to do it.'

Ric flushed with anger. 'Of course I've got the ability. You've read my stuff. All I needed was a break.'

I didn't hear from Ric for three days. That was fine by me. I'd accomplished what I'd intended. I'd proven that a script with my name on it had less chance of being bought than the same script with a youngster's name on it. And to tell the truth, Ric's lack of discipline was annoying me. But after the third day, I confess I got curious. What was he up to?

He called at nine in the evening. 'How's it going?'

'Fine,' I said. 'I had a good day's work.'

'Yeah, that's what I'm calling about. Work.'

'Oh?'

'I haven't been in touch lately because of this rewrite on *The Warlords*.'

I waited.

'I had a meeting with the director,' Ric said. 'Then I had a meeting with the star.' He mentioned the name of the biggest action hero in the business. He hesitated. 'I was wondering. Would you look at the material I've got?'

'You can't be serious. After the way you talked to me about it? You all but told me to get lost.'

'I didn't mean to be rude. Honestly. This is all new to me, Mort. Come on, give me a break. As you keep reminding me, I don't have the experience you do. I'm young.'

I had to hand it to him. He'd not only apologized. He'd used the right excuse.

'Mort?'

At first I didn't want to be bothered. I had my own work to think about, and *The Warlords* would probably be so bad that it would contaminate my mind.

But then my curiosity got the better of me. I couldn't help wondering what Ric would do to improve junk.

'Mort?'

'When do you want me to look at what you've done?'

'How about right now?'

'Now? It's after nine. It'll take you an hour to get here and—'

'I'm already here.'

'What?'

'I'm on my car phone. Outside your gate again.'

Ric sat across from me in my living room. I couldn't help noticing that his tan was darker, that he was wearing a different designer jacket, a more expensive one. Then I glanced at the title page on the script he'd handed me.

THE WARLORDS
revisions by Eric Potter

I flipped through the pages. All of them were typed on white paper. That bothered me. Ric's inexperience was showing again. On last-minute rewrites, it's always helpful to submit changed pages on different-colored paper. That way, the producer and director can save time and not have to read the entire script to find the changes.

'These are the notes the director gave me,' Ric said. He handed me some crudely typed pages. 'And these' – Ric handed me pages with scribbling on them – 'are what the star gave me. It's a little hard to decipher them.'

'More than a little. Jesus.' I squinted at the scribbling and got a headache. 'I'd better put on my glasses.' They helped a little. I read what the director wanted. I switched to what the star wanted.

'These are the notes the producer gave me,' Ric said.

I thanked God that they were neatly typed and studied them as well. Finally I leaned back and took off my glasses.

'Well?'

I sighed. 'Typical. As near as I can tell, these three people are each talking about a different movie. The director wants more action and less characterization. The star has decided to be serious – he wants more characterization and less action. The producer wants it funny and less expensive. If they're not careful, this movie will have multiple personalities.'

Ric looked at me anxiously.

'Okay,' I said, feeling tired. 'Get a beer from the refrigerator and watch television or something while I go through this. It would help if I knew where you'd made changes. Next time you're in a situation like this, identify your work with colored paper.'

Ric frowned.

'What's the matter?' I asked.

'The changes.'

'So? What about them?'

'Well, I haven't started to make them.'

'You *haven't*? But on this title page it says "revisions by Eric Potter".'

Ric looked sheepish. 'The title page is as far as I got.'

'Sweet Jesus. When are these revisions due?'

'Ballard gave me a week.'

'And for the first three days of that week, you didn't work on the changes? What have you been doing?'

Ric glanced away.

Again I noticed that his tan was darker. 'Don't tell me you've just been sitting in the sun?'

'Not exactly.'

'Then *what* exactly?'

'I've been thinking about how to improve the script.'

I was so agitated I had to stand. 'You don't *think* about changes. You *make* changes. How much did you say you were being paid? A hundred thousand dollars?'

Ric nodded, uncomfortable.

'And the Writers Guild insists that on work for hire you get a portion of the money as soon as you start.'

'Fifty thousand.' Ric squirmed. 'Linda got the check by messenger the day after I made the deal with Ballard.'

'What a mess.'

Ric lowered his head, more uncomfortable.

'If you don't hand in new pages four days from now, Ballard will want his money back.'

'I know,' Ric said, then added, 'But I can't.'

'What?'

'I already spent the money. A deposit on a condo in Malibu.'

I was stunned.

'And the money isn't the worst of it,' I said. 'Your reputation. *That's* worse. Ballard gave you an incredible break. He decided to take a chance on the bright new kid in town. He allowed you to jump over all the shit. But if you don't deliver, he'll be furious. He'll spread the word all over town that you're not dependable. You won't be hot anymore. We won't be able to sell another script as easily as we did this one.'

'Look, I'm sorry, Mort. I know I bragged to you that I could do the job on my own. I was wrong. I don't have the experience. I admit it. I'm out of my depth.'

'Even on a piece of shit like this.'

Ric glanced down, then up. 'I was wondering . . . Could you give me a hand?'

My mouth hung open in astonishment.

Before I could tell him *no damned way*, Ric quickly added, 'It would really help both of us.'

'How do you figure that?'

'You just said it yourself. If I don't deliver, Ballard will spread the word. No producer will trust me. You won't be able to sell another script through me.'

My head began to throb. He was right, of course. If I wanted to keep selling my scripts, if I wanted to see them produced, I needed him. There was no doubt in my mind that as old as I was, I would never be able to sell another script with my name on it. I finally had to admit that all along, secretly, I had never intended the deception with Ric to be a one-time-only arrangement.

I swallowed and finally said, 'All right.'

'Thank you.'

'But I won't clean up your messes for nothing.'

'Of course not. The same arrangement as before. All I get out of this is fifteen percent.'

'By rights, you shouldn't get anything.'

'Hey, without me, Ballard wouldn't have offered the job.'

'Since you already spent the first half of the payment, how do I get that money?'

Ric made an effort to think of a solution. 'We'll have to wait until the check comes through on the spec script we sold. I'll give

110

you the money out of the two hundred thousand that's owed to me.'

'But you owe the Ferrari dealer a bundle. Otherwise Linda's responsible for your debt.'

'I'll take care of it.' Ric gestured impatiently. 'I'll take care of all of it. What's important now is that you make the changes on *The Warlords*. Ballard has to pay the remaining fifty thousand dollars when I hand in the pages. That money's yours.'

'Fine.'

It wasn't until later that I realized how Ric had set a precedent for restructuring our deal. Regardless of his promise to pay me what I was owed, the reality was that he had pocketed half the fee. Instead of getting fifteen percent, he was now getting *fifty* percent.

The script for *The Warlords* was even worse than I'd feared. How do you change bad junk into good junk? In the process, how do you please a director, a star, and a producer who ask for widely different things? One of the rules I've learned over the years is that what people say they want isn't always what they mean. Sometimes it's a matter of interpretation. And after I endured reading the script for *The Warlords*, I thought I had that interpretation.

The director said he wanted more action and less characterization. In my opinion, the script already had more than enough action. The trouble was that some of the action sequences were redundant, and others weren't paced effectively. The biggest stunts occurred two-thirds of the way into the story. The last third had stunts that suffered by comparison. So the trick here was to do some pruning and restructuring – to take the good stunts from the end and put them in the middle, to build on them and put the great stunts at the end, all the while struggling to retain the already feeble logic of the story.

The star said he wanted less action and more characterization. As far as I could tell, what he really wanted was to be sympathetic, to make the audience like the character he was playing. So I softened him a little, threw in some jokes, had him wait for an old lady to cross a street before he blew away the bad guys, basic things like that. Since his character was more like a robot than a

111

human being, any vaguely human thing he did would make him sympathetic.

The producer said he wanted more humor and a less expensive budget. Well, by making the hero sympathetic, I added the jokes the producer wanted. By restructuring the sequence of stunts, I managed to eliminate some of the weaker ones, thus giving the star his request for less action and the producer his request for holding down the budget since the preponderance of action scenes had been what inflated the budget in the first place.

I explained this to Ric as I made notes. 'They'll all be happy.'

'Amazing,' Ric said.

'Thanks.'

'No, what I mean is, the ideas you came up with, *I* could have thought of them.'

'Oh?' My voice hardened. 'Then why didn't you?'

'Because, well, they seem so obvious.'

'*After* I thought of them. Good ideas always seem obvious in retrospect. The real job is putting them on paper. I'm going to have to work like crazy to get this job done in four days. And then there's a further problem. I have to teach you how to pitch these changes to Ballard, so he'll be convinced you're the one who wrote them.'

'You can count on me,' Ric said.

'I want you to . . .' Suddenly I found myself yawning and looked at my watch. 'Three a.m.? I'm not used to staying up this late. I'd better get some sleep if I'm going to get this rewrite done in four days.'

'I'm a night person myself,' Ric said.

'Well, come back tomorrow at four in the afternoon. I'll take a break and start teaching you what to say to Ballard.'

Ric didn't show up, of course. When I phoned his apartment, I got his answering machine. I couldn't get in touch with him the next day, or the day after that.

But the day the changes were due, he certainly showed up. He phoned again from his car outside the gate, and when I let him in, he was so eager to see the pages that he barely said hello to me.

'Where the hell have you been?'

'Mexico.'

'*What?*'

'With all this stress, I needed to get away.'

'What have you done to put you under stress? *I'm* the one who's been doing all the work.'

Instead of responding, Ric sat on my living room sofa and quickly leafed through the pages. I noticed he was wearing yet another designer jacket. His tan was even darker.

'Yeah,' he said. 'This is good.' He quickly came to his feet. 'I'd better get to the studio.'

'But I haven't coached you about what to say to Ballard.'

Ric stopped at the door. 'Mort, I've been thinking. If this partnership is going to work, we need to give each other more space. You take care of the writing. Let me worry about what to say in meetings. Ballard likes me. I know how to handle him. Trust me.'

And Ric was gone.

I waited to hear about what happened at the meeting. No phone call. When I finally broke down and phoned *him*, an electronic-sounding voice told me that his number was no longer in service. It took me a moment to figure out that he must have moved to the condo in Malibu. So I phoned Linda to get the new number, and she awkwardly told me that Ric had ordered her to keep it secret.

'Even from me?'

'Especially from you. Did you guys have an argument or something?'

'No.'

'Well, he made it sound as if you had. He kept complaining about how you were always telling him what to do.'

'Of all the . . .' I almost told Linda the truth – that Ric hadn't written the script she had sold but rather *I* had. Then I realized that she'd be conscience-bound to tell the studio. The deception would make the studio feel chilly about the script. After all, as far as they were concerned, an old guy couldn't possibly write a script that appealed to a young generation. They would reread the script with a new perspective, prejudiced by knowing the true identity of the author. The deal would fall through. I'd lose the biggest fee I'd ever been promised.

So I mumbled something about intending to talk with him and straighten out the problem. Then I hung up and cursed.

After I didn't hear from Ric for a week, it became obvious that Linda would long ago have forwarded to him the check for the rewrite on *The Warlords*. He'd had ample time to send me my money. He didn't intend to pay me.

That made me furious, partly because he'd betrayed me, partly because I didn't like being made to feel naïve, and partly because I'm a professional. To me, it's a matter of honor that I get paid for what I write. Ric had violated one of my most basic rules.

My arrangement with him was finished. When I read about him in *Daily Variety* and *Hollywood Reporter* – about how Ballard was delighted with the rewrite and predicting that the script he had bought from Ric would be next year's smash hit, not to mention that Ric would win an Oscar for it – I was apoplectic. Ric was compared to Robert Towne and William Goldman, with the advantage that he was young and had a powerful understanding of today's generation. Ric had been hired for a half-million dollars to do another rewrite. Ric had promised that he would soon deliver another original script, for which he hinted that his agent would demand an enormous price. 'Quality is always worth the cost,' Ballard said.

I wanted to vomit.

As I knew he would have to, Ric eventually came to see me. Again the car phone at the gate. Three weeks later. After dark. A night person, after all.

I made a pretense of reluctance, feigned being moved by his whining, and let him in. Even in the muted lights of my living room, he had the most perfect tan I had ever seen. His clothes were even more expensive and trendy. I hated him.

'You didn't send me my money for the rewrite on *The Warlords*.'

'I'm sorry about that,' Ric said. 'That's part of the reason I'm here.'

'To pay me?'

'To explain. My condo at Malibu. The owners demanded more money as a down payment. I couldn't give up the place. It's too fabulous. So I had to . . . Well, I knew you'd understand.'

'But I don't.'

'Mort, listen to me. I promise – as soon as the money comes through on the script we sold, I'll pay you everything I owe.'

'You went to fifteen percent on the fee, to fifty percent, to one hundred percent. Do you think I work for nothing?'

'Mort, I can appreciate your feelings. But I was in a bind.'

'You *still* are. I've been reading about you in the trade papers. You're getting a half-million for a rewrite on another script, and you're also promising a new original script. How are you going to manage all that?'

'Well, I tried to do it on my own. I handed Ballard the script I showed you when we first met.'

'Jesus, no.'

'He didn't like it.'

'What a surprise.'

'I had to cover my tracks and tell him it was something I'd been fooling with but that I realized it needed a lot of work. I told him I agreed with his opinion. From now on, I intended to stick to the tried and true – the sort of thing I'd sold him.'

I shook my head.

'I guess you were right,' Ric said. 'Good ideas seem obvious after somebody's thought of them. But maybe I don't have what it takes to come up with them. I've been acting like a jerk.'

'I couldn't agree more.'

'So what do you say?' Ric offered his hand. 'Let's let bygones be bygones. I screwed up, but I've learned from my mistake. I'm willing to give our partnership another try if you are.'

I stared at his hand.

Suddenly beads of sweat burst out on his brow. He lifted his hand and wiped them away.

'What's the matter?' I asked.

'Hot in here.'

'Not really. Actually, I thought it was getting chilly.'

'Feels stuffy.'

'The beer I gave you. Maybe you drank it too fast.'

'Maybe.'

'You know, *I've* been thinking,' I said.

★ ★ ★

The beer was drugged, of course. After the nausea wore off, giddiness set in, as it was supposed to. The drug, which I'd learned about years ago when I was working on a TV crime series, left its victim open to suggestion. It took me only ten minutes to convince him it was a great idea to do what I wanted. As I instructed, Ric giddily phoned Linda and told her that he was feeling stressed out and intended to go back down to Mexico. He told her he suddenly felt trapped by materialism. He needed a spiritual retreat. He might be away for as long as six months.

Linda was shocked. Listening to the speakerphone, I heard her demand to know how Ric intended to fulfill the contracts he'd signed. She said his voice was slurred and accused him of being drunk or high on something.

I picked up the phone, switched off the speaker, and interrupted to tell Linda that Ric was calling from my house and that we'd made up our differences, that he'd been pouring out his soul to me. He was drunk, yes, but what he had told her was no different than what he had told *me* when he was sober. He was leaving for Mexico tonight and might not be back for quite a while. How was he going to fulfill his contracts? No problem. Just because he was going on a retreat in Mexico, that didn't mean he wouldn't be writing. Honest work was what he thrived on. It was food for his soul.

By then, Ric was almost asleep. After I hung up, I roused him, made him sign a document that I'd prepared, then made him tell me where he was living in Malibu. I put him in his car, drove over to his place, packed a couple of his suitcases, crammed them into the car, and set out for Mexico.

We got there shortly after dawn. He was somewhat conscious when we crossed the border at Tijuana, enough to be able to answer a few questions and to keep the Mexican immigration officer from becoming suspicious. After that, I drugged him again.

I drove until mid-afternoon, took a back road into the desert, gave him a final lethal amount of the drug, and dumped his body into a sinkhole. I drove back to Tijuana, left Ric's suitcases minus identification in an alley, left his Ferrari minus identification in another alley, the key in the ignition, and caught a bus back to Los

Angeles. I was confident that neither the suitcases nor the car would ever be reported. I was also confident that by the time Ric's body was discovered, if ever, it would be in such bad shape that the Mexican authorities, with limited resources, wouldn't be able to identify it. Ric had once told me that he hadn't spoken to his parents in five years, so I knew *they* wouldn't wonder why he wasn't in touch with them. As far as his friends went, well, he didn't have any. He'd ditched them when he came into money. They wouldn't miss him.

For an old guy, I'm resilient. I'd kept up my energy, driving all night and most of the day. I finally got some sleep on the bus. Not shabby, although toward the end I felt as if something had broken in me and I doubt I'll ever be able to put in that much effort again. But I had to, you see. Ric was going to keep hounding me, enticing me, using me. And I was going to be too desperate to tell him to get lost. Because I knew that no matter how well I wrote, I would never be able to sell a script under my own name again.

When I first started as a writer, the money and the ego didn't matter to me as much as the need to work, to tell stories, to teach and delight, as the poet Horace said. But when the money started coming in, I began to depend on it. And I grew to love the action of being with powerful people, of having a reputation for being able to deliver quality work with amazing speed. Ego. That's why I hated Ric the most. Because producers stroked his ego over scripts that I had written.

But not anymore. Ric was gone, and his agent had heard him say that he'd be in Mexico, and I had a document, with his signature on it, saying that he was going to mail in his scripts through me, that I was his mentor and that he wanted me to go to script meetings on his behalf. The document also gave me his power of attorney, with permission to oversee his income while he was away.

And that should have been the end of it. Linda was puzzled but went along. After all, she'd heard Ric on the phone. Ballard was even more puzzled, but he was also enormously pleased with the spec script that I pulled out of a drawer and sent in with Ric's name on it. As far as Ballard was concerned, if Ric wanted to be eccentric, that was fine as long as he kept delivering. Really, his speed and the quality of his work were amazing.

So in a way I got what I wanted – the action and the pleasure of selling my work. But there's a problem. When I sit down to do rewrites, when I type 'revisions by Eric Potter,' I suddenly find myself gazing out the window, wanting to sit in the sun. At the same time, I find that I can't sleep. Like Ric, I've become a night person.

I've sold the spec scripts that I wrote over the years and kept in a drawer. All I had to do was change the titles. Nobody remembered reading the original stories. But I couldn't seem to do the rewrites, and now that I've run out of old scripts, now that I'm faced with writing something new . . .

For the first time in my life, I've got writer's block. All I have to do is think of the title page and the words 'by Eric Potter,' and my imagination freezes. It's agony. All my life, every day, I've been a writer. For thirty-five years of married life, except for the last two when Doris got sick, I wrote every day. I sacrificed everything to my craft. I didn't have children because I thought it would interfere with my schedule. Nothing was more important than putting words on a page. Now I sit at my desk, stare at my word processor, and . . .

Mary had a little . . .

I can't bear this anymore.

I need rest.

The quick brown fox jumped over . . .

I need to forget about Ric.

Now is the time for all good men to . . .

The relationship between fathers and sons (metaphoric or actual) is a frequent theme in my work. Because I never adjusted to my father's death in World War II, I grew up craving the attention of a positive male authority figure. Eventually, I found three of them: Stirling Silliphant (whom I've spoken about), Philip Young (the great Hemingway scholar), and Philip Klass (under the pen name William Tenn, he was part of the Golden Age of science fiction in the 1950s). In Black Evening *and* Lessons from a Lifetime of Writing, *I discussed at length the many things Philip Klass taught me about writing. Given his specialty, I found it interesting that, of the many genres in which I've worked, I hadn't tried anything in science fiction. After three decades, that changed when writer/editor/anthologist Al Sarrantonio asked me to contribute a story to a science-fiction anthology he was putting together:* Redshift *(2001). I decided to move the parent–child relationship from algebra into something like quantum physics, exploring it in the most complex way I could imagine. Part of my impetus was that, after my son's death, I no longer identified with sons searching for fathers. Rather, I was a father searching for a son. In this story, reprinted in* Year's Best SF 7, *I was able to combine both approaches and even add a third. Philip Klass/William Tenn's collected fiction and non-fiction are now available in three gorgeous volumes from NESFA Press (www.nesfapress.com).*

Resurrection

Anthony was nine when his mother had to tell him that his father was seriously ill. The signs had been there – pallor and shortness of breath – but Anthony's childhood was so perfect, his parents so loving, that he couldn't imagine a problem they couldn't solve. His father's increasing weight loss was too obvious to be ignored, however.

'But . . . but what's wrong with him?' Anthony stared uneasily up at his mother. He'd never seen her look more tired.

She explained about blood cells. 'It's not leukemia. If only it were. These days, that's almost always curable, but the doctors have never seen anything like this. It's moving so quickly, even a bone marrow transplant won't work. The doctors suspect that it might have something to do with the lab, with radiation he picked up after the accident.'

Anthony nodded. His parents had once explained to him that his father was something called a maintenance engineer. A while ago, there'd been an emergency phone call, and Anthony's father had rushed to the lab in the middle of the night.

'But the doctors . . .'

'They're trying everything they can think of. That's why Daddy's going to be in the hospital for a while.'

'But can't I see him?'

'Tomorrow.' Anthony's mother sounded more weary. 'Both of us can see him tomorrow.'

When they went to the hospital, Anthony's father was too weak to recognize him. He had tubes in his arms, his mouth, and his nose.

121

His skin was gray. His face was thinner than it had been three days earlier, the last time Anthony had seen him. If Anthony hadn't loved his father so much, he'd have been frightened. As things were, all he wanted was to sit next to his father and hold his hand. But after only a few minutes, the doctors said that it was time to go.

The next day, when Anthony and his mother went to the hospital, his father wasn't in his room. He was having 'a procedure,' the doctors said. They took Anthony's mother aside to talk to her. When she came back, she looked even more solemn than the doctors had. Everything possible had been done, she explained. 'No results.' Her voice sounded tight. 'None. At this rate . . .' She could barely get the words out. 'In a couple of days . . .'

'There's nothing the doctors can do?' Anthony asked, afraid.

'Not now. Maybe not ever. But we can hope. We can try to cheat time.'

Anthony hadn't the faintest idea what she meant. He wasn't even sure that he understood after she explained that there was something called 'cryonics,' which froze sick people until cures were discovered. Then they were thawed and given the new treatment. In a primitive way, cryonics had been tried fifty years earlier, in the late years of the twentieth century, Anthony's mother found the strength to continue explaining. It had failed because the freezing method hadn't been fast enough and the equipment often broke. But over time, the technique had been improved sufficiently that, although the medical establishment didn't endorse it, they didn't reject it, either.

'Then why doesn't everybody do it?' Anthony asked in confusion.

'Because . . .' His mother took a deep breath. 'Because some of the people who were thawed never woke up.'

Anthony had the sense that his mother was telling him more than she normally would have, that she was treating him like a grownup, and that he had to justify her faith in him.

'Others, who did wake up, failed to respond to the new treatment,' she reluctantly said.

'Couldn't they be frozen again?' Anthony asked in greater bewilderment.

'You can't survive being frozen a second time. You get only one chance, and if the treatment doesn't work . . .' She stared down at the floor. 'It's so experimental and risky that insurance companies won't pay for it. The only reason we have it as an option is that the laboratory's agreed to pay for the procedure' – there was that word again – 'while the doctors try to figure out how to cure him. But if it's going to happen, it has to happen now.' She looked straight into his eyes. 'Should we do it?'

'To save Daddy? We have to.'

'It'll be like he's gone.'

'Dead?'

Anthony's mother reluctantly nodded.

'But he *won't* be dead.'

'That's right,' his mother said. 'We might never see him alive again, though. They might not ever find a cure. They might not ever wake him up.'

Only much later did Anthony understand the other issues his mother had to deal with. In the worst case, if his father died, at least his life insurance would allow his mother to support the two of them. In the unlikely event that she ever fell in love again, she'd be able to remarry. But if Anthony's father was frozen, in effect dead to them, they'd be in need of money, and the only way for her to remarry would be to get a divorce from the man who, a year after her wedding, might be wakened and cured.

'But it's the only thing we can do,' Anthony said.

'Yes.' His mother wiped her eyes and straightened. 'It's the only thing we can do.'

Anthony had expected that it would happen the next day or the day after that. But his mother hadn't been exaggerating that, if it was going to happen, it had to happen now. His unconscious father was a gray husk as they rode with him in an ambulance. At a building without windows, they walked next to his father's gurney as it was wheeled along a softly lit corridor and into a room where other doctors waited. There were glinting instruments and humming machines. A man in a suit explained that Anthony and his mother had to step outside while certain preparations were done to Anthony's father to make the freezing process safe. After that, they would be able to accompany him to his cryochamber.

Again, it wasn't what Anthony expected. In contrast with the humming machines in the preparation room, the chamber was only a niche in a wall in a long corridor that had numerous other niches on each side, metal doors with pressure gauges on them. Anthony watched his father's gaunt naked body being placed on a tray that went into the niche. But his father's back never actually touched the tray. As the man in the suit explained, a force field kept Anthony's father elevated. Otherwise, his back would freeze to the tray and cause infections when he was thawed. For the same reason, no clothes, not even a sheet, could cover him, although Anthony, thinking of how cold his father was going to be, dearly wished that his father had something to keep him warm.

While the man in the suit and the men who looked like doctors stepped aside, a man dressed in black but with a white collar arrived. He put a purple scarf around his neck. He opened a book and read, 'I am the Way, the Truth, and the Life.' A little later, he read, 'I am the Resurrection.'

Anthony's father was slid into the niche. The door was closed. Something hissed.

'It's done,' the man in the suit said.

'That *quickly?*' Anthony's mother asked.

'It won't work if it isn't instantaneous.'

'May God grant a cure,' the man with the white collar said.

Years earlier, Anthony's father had lost his parents in a fire. Anthony's mother had *her* parents, but without much money, the only way they could help was by offering to let her and Anthony stay with them. For a time, Anthony's mother fought the notion. After all, she had her job as an administrative assistant at the laboratory, although without her husband's salary she didn't earn enough for the mortgage payments on their house. The house was too big for her and Anthony anyhow, so after six months she was forced to sell it, using the money to move into a cheaper, smaller townhouse. By then, the job at the lab had given her too many painful memories about Anthony's father. In fact, she blamed the lab for what had happened to him. Her bitterness intensified until she couldn't make herself go into the lab's offices any longer. She quit, got a lesser paying job as a secretary at a real-estate firm, persuaded a sympathetic broker to sell her townhouse but not charge a commission, and went with Anthony to live with her parents.

She and Anthony spent all their free time together, even more than before the accident, so he had plenty of opportunity to learn what she was feeling and why she'd made those decisions. The times she revealed herself the most, however, were when they visited his father. She once complained that the corridor of niches reminded her of a mausoleum, a reference that Anthony didn't understand, so she explained it but so vaguely that he still didn't understand, and it was several years before he knew what she'd been talking about.

Visiting hours for the cryochambers were between eight and six during the day as long as a new patient wasn't being installed. At first, Anthony and his mother went every afternoon after she finished work. Gradually, that lessened to every second day, every third day, and once a week. But they didn't reach that point for at least a year. Sometimes there were other visitors in the corridor, solitary people or incomplete families, staring mournfully at niches, sometimes leaving small objects of remembrance on narrow tables in the middle of the corridor: notes, photographs, dried maple leaves, and small candles shaped like pumpkins, to mention a few. The company placed no names on any of the niches, so visitors used stick-on plaques that said who was behind the pressurized door, when he or she had been born, when they had gotten sick, of what, and when they had been frozen. Often there was a bit of a prayer or something as movingly simple as 'We love you. We'll see you soon.' Here and there, Anthony noticed just a name, but for the most part the plaques had acquired a common form, the same kind of information and in the same order as over the years a tradition had been established.

Over the years indeed. Some of the people in the niches had been frozen at least *twenty-five* years, he read. It made him fear that his father might never be wakened. His fear worsened each time his mother came back from visiting his father's doctors, who were no closer to finding a cure for his sickness. Eventually his mother took him along to see the doctors, although the visits grew wider apart, every other month, every six months, and then every year. The message was always depressingly the same.

By then, Anthony was fifteen, in his first year of high school. He decided that he wanted to become a doctor and find a way to cure his father. But the next year his grandfather had a heart attack, leaving a small life insurance policy, enough for his mother and his grandmother to keep the house going but hardly enough for Anthony's dreams of attending medical school.

Meanwhile, his mother began dating the sympathetic broker at the real-estate firm. Anthony knew that she couldn't be expected to be lonely forever, that after so much time it was almost as if his father was dead and not frozen, and that she had to get on with her life. But 'as if his father was dead' wasn't the same as actually being dead, and Anthony had trouble concealing his unhappiness when his mother told him that she was going to marry the broker.

'But what about Dad? You're still married to *him*.'

'I'm going to have to divorce him.'

'No.'

'Anthony, we did our best. We couldn't cheat time. It didn't work. Your father's never going to be cured.'

'No!'

'I'll never stop loving him, Anthony. But I'm not betraying him. He's the same as dead, and I need to live.'

Tears dripped from Anthony's cheeks.

'He'd have wanted me to,' his mother said. 'He'd have understood. He'd have done the same thing.'

'I'll ask him when he wakes up.'

When Anthony became eighteen, it struck him that his father had been frozen nine years, *half* of Anthony's life. If it hadn't been for pictures of his father, he feared that he wouldn't have been able to remember what his father had looked like. No, not *had* looked like, Anthony corrected himself. His father wasn't dead. Once a new treatment was discovered, once he was thawed and cured, he'd look the same as ever.

Anthony concentrated to remember his father's voice, the gentle tone with which his father had read bedtime stories to him and had taught him how to ride a bicycle. He remembered his father helping him with his math homework and how his father had come to his school every year on Career Day and proudly explained his job at the lab. He remembered how his father had hurried him to the emergency ward after a branch snapped on the backyard tree and Anthony's fall broke his arm.

His devotion to his father strengthened after his mother remarried and they moved to the broker's house. The broker turned out to be not as sympathetic as when he'd been courting Anthony's mother. He was bossy. He lost his temper if everything wasn't done exactly his way. Anthony's mother looked unhappy, and Anthony hardly ever talked to the man, whom he refused to think of as his stepfather. He stayed away from the house as much as possible, often lying that he'd been playing sports or at the library when actually he'd been visiting his father's chamber, which the broker didn't want him to do because he insisted it was disloyal to the new family.

The broker also said that he wasn't going to pay a fortune so that Anthony could go to medical school. He wanted Anthony to get a degree in business and that was the only education he was going to pay for. So Anthony studied extra hard, got nothing but A's, and applied for every scholarship he could find, eventually being accepted as a science major in a neighboring state. The university there had an excellent medical school, which he hoped to attend after his Bachelor of Science degree, and he was all set to go when he realized how much it would bother him not to visit his father. That almost made him change his plans until he reminded himself that the only way his father might be cured was if he himself became a doctor and *found* that cure. So, after saying goodbye to his mother, he told the broker to go to hell.

He went to college, and halfway through his first year he learned from his mother that the lab had decided that it was futile to hope for a cure. A number of recent deaths after patients were thawed had cast such doubt on cryonics that the lab had decided to stop the monthly payments the cryocompany charged for keeping Anthony's father frozen. For his part, the broker refused to make the payments, saying that it wasn't his responsibility, and anyway what was the point since the freezing process had probably killed Anthony's father anyhow.

Taking a job as a waiter in a restaurant, sometimes working double shifts even as he struggled to maintain his grades, Anthony managed to earn just enough to make the payments. But in his sophomore year, he received a notice that the cryocompany was bankrupt from so many people refusing to make payments for the discredited process. The contract that his mother had signed indemnified the company against certain situations in which it could no longer keep its clients frozen, and bankruptcy was one of those situations.

Smaller maintenance firms agreed to take the company's patients, but the transfer would be so complicated and hence so expensive that Anthony had to drop his classes and work full-time at the restaurant in order to pay for it. At school, he'd met a girl, who continued to see him even though his exhausting schedule gave him spare time only at inconvenient hours. He couldn't believe that he'd finally found some brightness in his life, and after he returned from making sure that his father was safely installed in a smaller facility, after he resumed his classes, completing his sophomore and junior year, he began to talk to her about marriage.

'I don't have much to offer, but . . .'

'You're the gentlest, most determined, most hardworking person I've ever met. I'd be proud to be your wife.'

'At the start, we won't have much money because I have to pay for my father's maintenance, but . . .'

'We'll live on what *I* earn. After you're a doctor, you can take care of *me*. There'll be plenty enough for us and our children *and* your father.'

'How many children would you like?'

'Three.'

Anthony laughed. 'You're so sure of the number.'

'It's good to hear you laugh.'

'You make me laugh.'

'By the time you're a doctor, maybe there'll be a cure for your father and you won't have to worry about him anymore.'

'Isn't it nice to think so?'

Anthony's mother died in a car accident the year he entered

128

medical school. Her remarriage had been so unsatisfying that she'd taken to drinking heavily and had been intoxicated when she veered from the road and crashed into a ravine. At the funeral, the broker hardly acknowledged Anthony and his fiancée. That night, Anthony cried in her arms as he remembered the wonderful family he had once been a part of and how badly everything had changed when his father had gotten sick.

He took his fiancée to the firm that now maintained his father. Since the transfer, Anthony had been able to afford returning to his home town to visit his father only sporadically. The distance made him anxious because the new firm didn't inspire the confidence that the previous one had. It looked on the edge of disrepair, floors not dirty but not clean, walls not exactly faded and yet somehow in need of painting. Rooms seemed vaguely underlit. The units in which patients were kept frozen looked cheap. The temperature gauges were primitive compared to the elaborate technology at the previous facility. But as long as they kept his father safe . . .

That thought left Anthony when he took another look at the gauge and realized that the temperature inside his father's chamber had risen one degree from when he'd last checked it.

'What's wrong?' his fiancée asked.

Words caught in his throat. All he could do was point.

The temperature had gone up yet another degree.

He raced along corridor after corridor, desperate to find a maintenance worker. He burst into the company's office and found only a secretary.

'My father . . .'

Startled, the secretary took a moment to react when he finished explaining. She phoned the control room. No one answered.

'It's almost noon. The technicians must have gone to lunch.'

'For God's sake, where's the control room?'

At the end of the corridor where his father was. As Anthony raced past the niche, he saw that the temperature gauge had gone up fifteen degrees. He charged into the control room, saw flashing red lights on a panel, and hurried to them, trying to figure out what was wrong. Among numerous gauges, eight temperature needles were rising, and Anthony was certain that one of them was for his father.

He flicked a switch beneath each of them, hoping to reset the controls.

The lights kept flashing.

He flicked a switch at the end of their row.

Nothing changed.

He pulled a lever. Every light on the panel went out. 'Jesus.'

Pushing the lever back to where it had been, he held his breath, exhaling only when all the lights came back on. The eight that had been flashing were now constant.

Sweating, he eased onto a chair. Gradually, he became aware of people behind him and turned to where his fiancée and the secretary watched in dismay from the open door. Then he stared at the panel, watching the temperature needles gradually descend to where they had been. Terrified that the lights would start flashing again, he was still concentrating on the gauges an hour later when a bored technician returned from lunch.

It turned out that a faulty valve had restricted the flow of freezant around eight of the niches. When Anthony had turned the power off and on, the valve had reset itself, although it could fail again at any time and would have to be replaced, the technician explained.

'Then do it!'

He would never again be comfortable away from his father. It made him nervous to return to medical school. He contacted the cryofirm every day, making sure there weren't any problems. He married, became a parent of a lovely daughter, graduated, and was lucky enough to be able to do his internship in the city where he'd been raised and where he could keep a close watch on his father's safety. If only his father had been awake to see him graduate, he thought. If only his father had been cured and could have seen his granddaughter being brought home from the hospital . . .

One night, while Anthony was on duty in the emergency ward, a comatose patient turned out to be the broker who'd married his mother. The broker had shot himself in the head. Anthony tried everything possible to save him. His voice tightened when he pronounced the time of death.

He joined a medical practice in his home town after he finished his internship. He started earning enough to make good on his promise and take care of his wife after she'd spent so many years taking care of *him*. She had said that she wanted three children, and she got them sooner than she expected, for the next time she gave birth, it was to twins, a boy and a girl. Nonetheless, Anthony's work prevented him from spending as much time with his family as he wanted, for his specialty was blood diseases, and when he wasn't seeing patients, he was doing research, trying to find a way to cure his father.

He needed to know the experiments that the lab had conducted and the types of rays that his father might have been exposed to. But the lab was obsessed with security and refused to tell him. He fought to get a court order to force the lab to cooperate. Judge after judge refused. Meanwhile, he was sadly conscious of all the family celebrations that his father continued to miss: the day Anthony's first daughter started grade school, the afternoon the twins began swimming lessons, the evening Anthony's second daughter played 'Chopsticks' at her first piano recital. Anthony was thirty-five before he knew it. Then forty. All of a sudden, his children were in high school. His wife went to law school. He kept doing research.

When he was fifty-five and his eldest daughter turned thirty (she was married, with a daughter of her own), the laboratory made a mistake and released the information Anthony needed among a batch of old data that the lab felt was harmless. It wasn't Anthony who discovered the information, but instead a colleague two thousand miles away who had other reasons to look through the old data and recognized the significance of the type of rays that Anthony's father had been exposed to. Helped by his colleague's calculations, Anthony devised a treatment, tested it on computer models, subjected rats to the same type of rays, found that they developed the same rapid symptoms as his father had, gave the animals the treatment, and felt his pulse quicken when the symptoms disappeared as rapidly as they had come on.

With his wife next to him, Anthony stood outside his father's cryochamber as arrangements were made to thaw him. He feared that the technicians would make an error during the procedure (the word echoed from his youth), that his father wouldn't wake up.

His muscles compacted as something hissed and the door swung open. The hatch slid out.

Anthony's father looked the same as when he'd last seen him: naked, gaunt, and gray, suspended over a force field.

'You thawed him that *quickly*?' Anthony asked.

'It doesn't work if it isn't instantaneous.'

His father's chest moved up and down.

'My God, he's alive,' Anthony said. 'He's actually . . .'

But there wasn't time to marvel. The disease would be active again, racing to complete its destruction.

Anthony hurriedly injected his father with the treatment. 'We have to get him to a hospital.'

He stayed in his father's room, constantly monitoring his father's condition, injecting new doses of the treatment precisely on schedule. To his amazement, his father improved almost at once. The healthier color of his skin made obvious what the blood tests confirmed – the disease was retreating.

Not that his father knew. One effect of being thawed was that the patient took several days to wake up. Anthony watched for a twitch of a finger, a flicker of an eyelid, to indicate that his father was regaining consciousness. After three days he became worried enough to order another brain scan, but as his father was being put in the machine, a murmur made everyone stop.

'. . . Where am I?' Anthony's father asked.

'In a hospital. You're going to be fine.'

His father strained to focus on him. '. . . Who . . .'

'Your son.'

'No . . . My son's . . . a child.' Looking frightened, Anthony's father lost consciousness.

The reaction wasn't unexpected. But Anthony had his own quite different reaction to deal with. While his father hadn't seen him age and hence didn't know who Anthony was, Anthony's father *hadn't* aged and hence looked exactly as Anthony remembered. The only problem was that Anthony's memory came from when he was nine, and now, at the age of fifty-five, he looked at his thirty-two-year-old father, who wasn't much older than Anthony's son.

132

'Marian's *dead*?'

Anthony reluctantly nodded. 'Yes. A car accident.'

'When?'

Anthony had trouble saying it. 'Twenty-two years ago.'

'No.'

'I'm afraid it's true.'

'I've been frozen *forty-six years*? No one told me what was going to happen.'

'We couldn't. You were unconscious. Near death.'

His father wept.

'Our house?'

'Was sold a long time ago.'

'My friends?'

Anthony looked away.

With a shudder, his father pressed his hands to his face. 'It's worse than being dead.'

'No,' Anthony said. 'You heard the psychiatrist. Depression's a normal part of coming back. You're going to have to learn to live again.'

'Just like learning to walk again,' his father said bitterly.

'Your muscles never had a chance to atrophy. As far as your body's concerned, no time passed since you were frozen.'

'But as far as my mind goes? Learn to live again? That's something nobody should have to do.'

'Are you saying that Mom and I should have let you die? Our lives would have gone on just the same. Mom would have been killed whether you were frozen or you died. Nothing would have changed, except that *you* wouldn't be here now.'

'With your mother gone . . .'

Anthony waited.

'With my son gone . . .'

'*I'm* your son.'

'My son had his ninth birthday two weeks ago. I gave him a new computer game that I looked forward to playing with him. I'll never get to see him grow up.'

'To see *me* grow up. But I'm here now. We can make up for lost time.'

'Lost time.' The words seemed like dust in his father's mouth.

'Dad' – it was the last time Anthony used that term – 'this is your grandson Paul. These are your granddaughters Sally and Jane. And this is *Jane's* son Peter. Your *great*-grandson.'

Seeing his father's reaction to being introduced to grandchildren who were almost as old as *he* was, Anthony felt heartsick.

'*Forty-six years?* But everything changed in a *second*,' his father said. 'It makes my head spin so much . . .'

'I'll teach you,' Anthony said. 'I'll start with basics and explain what happened since you were frozen. I'll move you forward. Look, here are virtual videos of—'

'What are virtual videos?'

'Of news shows from back then. We'll watch them in sequence. We'll talk about them. Eventually, we'll get you up to the present.'

Anthony's father pointed toward the startlingly lifelike videos from forty-six years earlier. '*That's* the present.'

'Is there anything you'd like to do?'

'Go to Marian.'

So Anthony drove him to the mausoleum, where his father stood for a long time in front of the niche that contained her urn.

'One instant she's alive. The next . . .' Tears filled his father's eyes. 'Take me home.'

But when Anthony headed north of the city, his father put a trembling hand on his shoulder. 'No. You're taking the wrong direction.'

'But we live at—'

'Home. I want to go *home*.'

So Anthony drove him back to the old neighborhood, where his father stared at the run-down house that he had once been proud to keep in perfect condition. Weeds filled the yard. Windows were broken. Porch steps were missing.

'There used to be a lawn here,' Anthony's father said. 'I worked so hard to keep it immaculate.'

'I remember,' Anthony said.

'I taught my son how to do somersaults on it.'

'You taught *me*.'

'In an instant.' His father sounded anguished. 'All gone in an instant.'

Anthony peered up from his breakfast of black coffee, seeing his father at the entrance to the kitchen. It had been two days since they'd spoken.

'I want to tell you,' his father said, 'that I realize you made an enormous effort for me. I can only imagine the pain and sacrifice. I'm sorry if I'm . . . No matter how confused I feel, I want to thank you.'

Anthony managed to smile, comparing the wrinkle-free face across from him to the weary one that he'd seen in the mirror that morning. 'I'm sorry, too. That you're having such a hard adjustment. All Mom and I thought of was, you were so sick. We were ready to do *anything* that would help you.'

'Your mother.' Anthony's father needed a moment before he could continue. 'Grief doesn't last just a couple of days.'

It was Anthony's turn to need a moment. He nodded. 'I've had much of my life to try to adjust to Mom being gone, but I still miss her. You'll have a long hard time catching up to me.'

'I . . .'

'Yes?'

'I don't know what to do.'

'For starters, why don't you let me make you some breakfast.' Anthony's wife was defending a case in court. 'It'll be just the two of us. Do waffles sound okay? There's some syrup in that cupboard. How about orange juice?'

The first thing Anthony's father did was learn how to drive the new types of vehicles. Anthony believed this was a sign of improving mental health. But then he discovered that his father was using his mobility not to investigate his new world, instead to visit Marian's ashes in the mausoleum and to go to the once-pristine house that he'd owned forty-six years previously, a time period that to him was yesterday. Anthony had done something similar when he'd lied to his mother's second husband about being at the library when actually he'd been at the cryofirm visiting his father. It worried him.

'I found a "For Sale" sign at the house,' his father said one evening at dinner. 'I want to buy it.'

'But . . .' Anthony set down his fork. 'The place is a wreck.'

'It won't be after I'm finished with it.'

Anthony felt as if he argued not with his father but with one of his children when they were determined to do something that he thought unwise.

'I can't stay here,' his father said. 'I can't live with you for the rest of my life.'

'Why not? You're welcome.'

'A father and his grown-up son? We'll get in each other's way.'

'But we've gotten along so far.'

'I want to buy the house.'

Continuing to feel that he argued with his son, Anthony gave in as he always did. 'All right, okay, fine. I'll help you get a loan. I'll help with the down payment. But if you're going to take on this kind of responsibility, you'll need a job.'

'That's something else I want to talk to you about.'

His father used his maintenance skills to become a successful contractor whose specialty was restoring old-style homes to their former beauty. Other contractors tried to compete, but Anthony's father had an edge: he knew those houses inside and out. He'd helped build them when he was a teenager working on summer construction jobs. He'd maintained his when that kind of house was in its prime almost a half-century earlier. Most important, he loved that old style of house.

One house in particular – the house where he'd started to raise his family. As soon as the renovation was completed, he found antique furniture from the period. When Anthony visited, he was amazed by how closely the house resembled the way it had looked when he was a child. His father had arranged to have Marian's urn released to him. It sat on a shelf in a study off the living room. Next to it were framed pictures of Anthony and his mother when they'd been young, the year Anthony's father had gotten sick.

His father found antique audio equipment from back then. The only songs he played were from that time. He even found an old computer and the game that he'd wanted to play with Anthony, teaching his great-grandson how to play it just as he'd already taught the little boy how to do somersaults on the lawn.

Anthony turned sixty. The hectic years of trying to save his father were behind him. He reduced his hours at the office. He followed an interest in gardening and taught himself to build a greenhouse. His father helped him.

'I need to ask you something,' his father said one afternoon when the project was almost completed.

'You make it sound awfully serious.'

His father looked down at his callused hands. 'I have to ask your permission about something.'

'Permission?' Anthony's frown deepened his wrinkles.

'Yes. I . . . It's been five years. I . . . Back then, you told me that I had to learn to live again.'

'You've been doing a good job of it,' Anthony said.

'I fought it for a long time.' His father looked more uncomfortable.

'What's wrong?'

'I don't know how to . . .'

'Say it.'

'I loved your mother to the depth of my heart.'

Anthony nodded, pained with emotion.

'I thought I'd die without her,' his father said. 'Five years. I never expected . . . I've met somebody. The sister of a man whose house I'm renovating. We've gotten to know each other, and . . . Well, I . . . What I need to ask is, would you object, would you see it as a betrayal of your mother if . . .'

Anthony felt pressure in his tear ducts. 'Would I object?' His eyes misted. 'All I want is for you to be happy.'

Anthony was the best man at his father's wedding. His stepmother was the same age as his daughters. The following summer, he had a half-brother sixty-one years younger than himself. It felt odd to see his father acting toward the baby in the same loving manner that he had presumably acted toward Anthony when *he* was a baby.

At the celebration when the child was brought home from the

hospital, several people asked Anthony if his wife was feeling ill. She looked wan.

'She's been working hard on a big trial coming up,' he said.

The next day, she had a headache so bad that he took her to his clinic and had his staff do tests.

The day after that, she was dead. The viral meningitis that killed her was so virulent that nothing could have been done to save her. The miracle was that neither Anthony nor anybody else in the family had caught it, especially the new baby.

He felt drained. Plodding through his house, he tried to muster the energy to get through each day. The nights were harder. His father often came and sat with him, a young man next to an older one, doing his best to console him.

Anthony visited his wife's grave every day. On the anniversary of her death, while picking flowers for her, he collapsed from a stroke. The incident left him paralyzed on his left side, in need of constant care. His children wanted to put him in a facility.

'No,' his father said. 'It's *my* turn to watch over *him*.'

So Anthony returned to the house where his youth had been wonderful until his father had gotten sick. During the many hours they spent together, his father asked Anthony to fill in more details of what had happened as Anthony had grown up: the arguments he'd had with the broker, his double shifts as a waiter, his first date with the woman who would be his wife.

'Yes, I can see it,' his father said.

The next stroke reduced Anthony's intelligence to that of a nine-year-old. He didn't have the capacity to know that the computer on which he played a game with his father came from long ago. In fact, the game was the same one that his father had given him on his ninth birthday, two weeks before his father had gotten sick, the game that he'd never had a chance to play with his son.

One morning, he no longer had a nine-year-old's ability to play the game.

'His neurological functions are decreasing rapidly,' the specialist said.

'Nothing can be done?' Anthony's father asked.

'I'm sorry. At this rate . . . In a couple of days . . .'

Anthony's father felt as if he had a stone in his stomach.

'We'll make him as comfortable here as possible,' the specialist said.

'No. My son should die at home.'

Anthony's father sat next to the bed, holding his son's frail hand, painfully reminded of having taken care of him when Anthony had been sick as a child. Now Anthony looked appallingly old for sixty-three. His breathing was shallow. His eyes were open, glassy, not registering anything.

Anthony's children and grandchildren came to pay their last respects.

'At least he'll be at peace,' his second daughter said.

Anthony's father couldn't bear it. 'He didn't give up on me. I won't give up on *him*.'

'That theory's been discredited,' the specialist said.

'It works.'

'In isolated cases, but—'

'I'm one of them.'

'Of the few. At your son's age, he might not survive the procedure.'

'Are you refusing to make the arrangements?'

'I'm trying to explain that with the expense and the risk—'

'My son will be dead by tomorrow. Being frozen can't be worse than *that*. And as far as the expense goes, he worked hard. He saved his money. He can afford it.'

'But there's no guarantee a treatment will ever be developed for brain cells as damaged as your son's are.'

'There's no guarantee it *won't* be developed, either.'

'He can't give his permission.'

'He doesn't need to. He made me his legal representative.'

'All the same, his children need to be consulted. There are issues of estate, a risk of a law suit.'

'*I'll* take care of his children. *You* take care of the arrangements.'

They stared at him.

Anthony's father suspected they resisted the idea because they didn't want to drain money from their inheritance. 'Look, I'm begging. He'd have done this for you. He did it for *me*. For God's sake, you can't give up on him.'

They stared harder.

'It's not going to cost you anything. I'll work harder and pay for it myself. I'll sign control of the estate over to you. All I want is, don't try to stop me.'

Anthony's father stood outside the cryochamber, studying the stick-on plaque that he'd put on the hatch. It gave Anthony's name, his birthdate, when he'd had his first stroke, and when he'd been frozen. 'Sweet dreams,' it said at the bottom. 'Wake up soon.'

'Soon' was a relative word, of course. Anthony had been frozen six years, and there was still no progress in a treatment. But that didn't mean there wouldn't be progress tomorrow or next month. There's always hope, Anthony's father thought. You've got to have hope.

On a long narrow table in the middle of the corridor, there were tokens of affection left by loved ones of other patients: family photographs, a baseball glove, and a guitar pick. Anthony's father had left the disk of the computer game that he and Anthony had been playing. 'We'll play it again,' he promised.

It was Anthony's father's birthday. He was forty-nine. He had gray in his sideburns, wrinkles in his forehead. I'll soon look like Anthony did when I woke up from being frozen and saw him leaning over me, he thought.

He couldn't subdue the discouraging notion that one of these days he'd be the same age as Anthony when he'd been frozen. But now that he thought about it, maybe that notion wasn't so discouraging. If they found a treatment that year, and they woke Anthony up, and the treatment worked . . . We'd both be sixty-six. We could grow old together.

I'll keep fighting for you, Anthony. I swear you can count on me. I couldn't let you die before me. It's a terrible thing for a father to outlive his son.

Douglas E. Winter is a fiction writer (Run), *critic* (*books about Stephen King and Clive Barker*), *anthologist, and attorney. His first anthology,* Prime Evil (*1988*), *is one of the great collections of the macabre. In the mid-1990s, he phoned to tell me about a second anthology he was planning:* Millennium. *When published in 1997, the book was retitled* Revelations *because of a conflict with a TV series that had the same name, but the original title* Millennium *gives you a sense of what Doug had in mind. He invited various writers to choose a decade in the twentieth century and write an apocalyptic story about it, one that would be rooted in history and give a sense of the ultimate issues that the decade had faced. I was immediately intrigued. As many of my novels show, the professor in me has always loved working with history. The forties, fifties, and sixties had already been taken, Doug said, so which of the remaining decades did I want? The teens, I said. Because of World War I? No, although the war would be in the story. The subject I wanted to dramatize had been potentially more apocalyptic than the war and foreshadowed later similar global threats. It gave me nightmares.*

If I Should Die Before I Wake

I t wasn't the first case, but it was Dr Jonas Bingaman's first case, although he would not realize that until two days later. The patient, a boy with freckles and red hair, lay listlessly beneath the covers of his bed. Bingaman, who had been leaving his office for the evening when the boy's anxious mother telephoned, paused at the entrance to the narrow bedroom and assessed immediately that the boy had a fever. It wasn't just that Joey Carter, whom Bingaman had brought into the world ten years earlier, was red in the face. After all, the summer of 1918 had been uncommonly hot, and even now, at the end of August, the doctor was treating cases of sunburn. No, what made him conclude so quickly that Joey had a fever was that, despite the lingering heat, the boy was shivering under a sheet and two blankets.

'He's been like this since he came home just before supper,' Joey's mother, Rebecca, said. A slim, plain woman of thirty-five, she entered Joey's room ahead of the doctor and gestured urgently for him to follow. 'I found his wet bathing suit. He'd been swimming.'

'At the creek. I warned him about that creek,' Joey's father, Edward, said. Elmdale's best carpenter, the gangly man still wore his coveralls and work boots and had traces of sawdust in his thick dark hair. 'I told him to stay away from it.'

'The creek?' Bingaman turned toward Edward, who waited anxiously in the hallway.

'The water's no good. Makes you sick. I know 'cause Bill Kendrick's boy got sick swimming in it last summer. Breathed wrong. Swallowed some of the water. Threw up all night long. I

143

warned Joey not to go near it, but he wouldn't listen.'

'The creek through Larrabee's farm?'

'That's the one. The cattle mess in the water. The stuff flows downstream and into the swimming hole.'

'Yes, I remember Bill Kendrick's boy getting sick from the water last summer,' Bingaman said. 'Has Joey been vomiting?'

'No.' Rebecca's voice was strained.

'I'd better take a look.'

As Bingaman went all the way into the room, he noted a baseball bat in a corner. A balsawood model of one of the Curtiss biplanes that the American Expeditionary Force was using against the Germans hung above the bed, attached by a cord to the ceiling.

'Not feeling well, Joey?'

It took an obvious effort for the boy to shake his head 'no.' His eyelids were barely open. He coughed.

'Been swimming in the creek?'

Joey had trouble nodding. 'Shoulda listened to Dad,' he murmured hoarsely.

'Next time you'll know the right thing to do. But for now, I want you to concentrate on getting better. I'm going to examine you, Joey. I'll try to be as gentle as I can.'

Bingaman opened his black bag and leaned over Joey, feeling heat come off the boy. Joey's mother and father stepped closer, watching intently. Joey's cough deepened.

Ten minutes later, Bingaman put his stethoscope back into his bag and straightened.

'Is that what it is?' Edward asked quickly. 'Bad water from Larrabee's farm?'

Bingaman hesitated. 'Why don't we talk somewhere else and let Joey rest?'

Downstairs, the evening's uneaten dinner of potatoes, carrots, and pork chops cooled in pots and a frying pan on the stove.

'But what do you think it is?' Rebecca asked the moment they were seated at the kitchen table.

'How serious *is* this?' Edward demanded.

'His temperature's a hundred and two. His glands are swollen. He has congestion in his lungs.'

'My God, you don't think he has diphtheria from the water?'

Rebecca's anxiety was nearing a quiet panic.

Edward stared at the floor and shook his head. 'I was afraid of this.'

'No, I don't think it's diphtheria,' Bingaman said.

Joey's father peered up, hoping.

'Some of the symptoms are those of diphtheria. But diphtheria presents bluish-white lesions that have the consistency of leather. The lesions are surrounded by inflammation and are visible near the tonsils and in the nostrils.'

'But Joey—'

'Doesn't have the lesions,' Bingaman said. 'I think he may have bronchitis.'

'Bronchitis?'

'I'll know more when I examine him again tomorrow. In the meantime, let's treat his symptoms. Give him one-half an adult dose of aspirin every six hours. Give him a sponge bath with rubbing alcohol. Both will help to keep down his fever. When his pajamas and bedding get sweaty, change them. Keep his window open. The fresh air will help chase the germs from his chest.'

'And?' Joey's father asked.

Bingaman didn't understand.

'That's all? That's the most you can do?'

'That and tell you to make certain he drinks plenty of water.'

'If he can keep it down. It's water that got him into this trouble.'

'Possibly. Did Joey tell you if any other boys went swimming with him?'

'Yes. Pete Williams. Ben Slocum.'

Bingaman nodded. He not only knew them; he had delivered them, just as he had delivered Joey. 'Take Joey's temperature every couple of hours. Telephone me if it gets higher or if other symptoms appear.'

'Mrs Williams, this is Dr Bingaman calling. This might sound strange, but I was wondering – is your son, Pete, feeling all right? No fever? No swollen glands? No congestion?'

He made another call.

'Nothing like that at all, Mrs Slocum? Your son's as fit as can be? Good. Thank you. Give my regards to your husband. Why did

I telephone to ask? Just a random survey. You know how I like to make sure Elmdale's students are all in good health before they go back to school. Good night. Thanks again.'

Bingaman set the long-stemmed ear piece onto the wooden wall phone in the front corridor of his home. Troubled, he shut off the overhead light and leaned against the wall, peering out his front-door window. Twilight was dimming. In the yard, fireflies began to twinkle. A Model T rattled past. On a porch across the street, illuminated by a glow of light from the living room window over there, Harry Webster sat in his rocking chair, smoking his pipe.

'Jonas, what's wrong?'

Bingaman turned to his wife, Marion, whose broad-shouldered outline approached him in the shadows of the hallway. The daughter of a German immigrant, an ancestry that she avoided mentioning given the war in Europe, Marion had been raised on a farm in upstate New York before she received her nurse's training, and her robust appearance had been one of the reasons that Bingaman was initially attracted to her. Twenty-five years ago. Now, at the age of fifty-two, she was as robust as ever, and he loved her *more* than ever. True, the honey-colored hair that he enjoyed stroking had acquired streaks of silver. But then his own hair had not only turned silvery but had thinned until he was almost bald. Marion called it 'distinguished.'

'Wrong?' Bingaman echoed. 'I'm not sure anything's wrong.'

'You've been pensive since you came home for dinner after visiting Joey Carter.'

'It's a problem I've been mulling over. Joey seems to have bronchitis. His father thinks he got it from swimming in infected water this afternoon. But bronchitis takes several days to develop, and none of the boys Joey went swimming with is sick.'

'What are you thinking?'

'Whatever it is, Joey must have gotten it somewhere else. But usually I don't see just one case of bronchitis. It spreads around. So where did he catch it if no one else in town has it?'

Rebecca Carter fidgeted at the open screen door, impatient for Bingaman to climb the front steps and enter the house. 'I was afraid I wouldn't be able to reach you.'

'Actually, when you telephoned, I was just about to drive over. Joey's the first patient on my list this morning.'

Feeling burdened by the weight he had put on recently, Bingaman started up the stairs to the second level, then paused, frowning when he heard labored coughing from the bedroom directly at the top. 'Has Joey been coughing like that all night?'

'Not as bad.' Rebecca's face was haggard from lack of sleep. 'This started just before dawn. I've been giving him aspirin and sponge baths like you told me, but they don't seem to do any good.'

The doctor hurried up the stairs, alarmed by what he saw when he entered the bedroom. Joey looked smaller under the covers. His face was much redder, but he also had a dark blue color around his lips. His chest heaved, as if he was coughing even when he wasn't.

Bingaman went urgently to work, removing instruments from his bag, noting that Joey's temperature had risen to a hundred and four, that his lungs sounded more congested, that the inside of his throat was inflamed, that his glands were more swollen, and that the boy didn't have the energy to respond to questions. The day before, Joey's pulse and respiration rate had been 85 and 20. Now they were 100 and 25.

'I'm sorry to tell you this, Mrs Carter.'

'What's *wrong* with him?'

'It might be pneumonia.'

Rebecca Carter gasped.

'I know you'd prefer to keep him at home,' Bingaman said, 'but what's best for Joey right now is to admit him to the hospital.'

Rebecca looked as if she doubted her sanity, as if she couldn't possibly be hearing what the doctor had just told her. '*No. I can take care of him.*'

'I'm sure you can, but Joey needs special treatment that isn't available here.'

Rebecca looked more frightened. 'Like what?'

'I'll explain after I telephone the hospital and make the arrangements.' Hoping that he had distracted her, Bingaman hurried downstairs to the wall phone near the front door. What he didn't want to tell her was that the dark blue color around Joey's mouth was an indication of cyanosis. The congestion in the boy's lungs

147

was preventing him from getting enough oxygen. If Joey wasn't hooked up to an oxygen tank at the hospital, he might asphyxiate from the fluid in his lungs.

'It certainly has the symptoms of pneumonia,' the Elmdale hospital's chief of staff told Bingaman. His name was Brian Powell, and his wiry frame contrasted with Bingaman's portly girth. The two physicians had been friends for years, and Powell, who happened to be in the emergency ward when Joey Carter was admitted, had invited Bingaman to his office for a cup of coffee afterward. In his mind, Bingaman kept hearing Mrs Carter sob.

'But if it *is* pneumonia, how did he get it?' Bingaman ignored the steaming cup of coffee on the desk in front of him. 'Do *you* have any patients who present these symptoms?'

Powell shook his head. 'During the winter, the symptoms wouldn't be unusual. Colds and secondary infections leading to pneumonia. But in summer? I'd certainly remember.'

'It just doesn't make any sense.' Bingaman sweated under his suit coat. 'Why is *Joey* the only one?'

'No.' Rebecca Carter waited outside Joey's hospital room in the hope that she'd be allowed to enter. Her eyes were red from tears. 'Nothing different. It was just an ordinary summer. We did what we always do.'

'And what would that be?' Bingaman asked.

Rebecca dabbed a handkerchief against her eyes. 'Picnics. Joey likes to play baseball. We go to the park, and Edward teaches him how to pitch. And the movies. Sometimes we go to the movies. Joey likes Charlie Chaplin.'

'That's it? That's all?'

'Just an ordinary summer. I have my sewing club. We don't often get a chance to do things as a family because Edward works late, taking advantage of the good weather. Why do you ask? Didn't Joey get sick from the water in the creek?'

'Can you think of anything else that Joey did this summer? Anything even the slightest bit unusual?'

'No. I'm sorry. I—'

She was interrupted by her husband hurrying along the hospital corridor. 'Rebecca.' Edward Carter's lean face glistened with sweat. 'I decided to come home for lunch and check on Joey. Mrs Wade next door said you and he had gone to . . . My God, Doctor, what's wrong with Joey?'

'We're still trying to find that out. It might be pneumonia.'

'*Pneumonia?*'

The door to Joey's room opened. For a moment, the group had a brief glimpse of Joey covered by sheets in a metal bed, an oxygen mask over his face. Then a nurse came out and shut the door.

'How is he?' Joey's mother asked.

'Light-headed,' the nurse answered. 'He keeps talking about feeling as if he's on a Ferris wheel.'

'Ferris wheel?' Bingaman asked.

'He's probably remembering the midway,' Joey's father said.

'Midway?'

'In Riverton. Last week I had to drive over there to get some special lumber for a job I'm working on. Joey went with me. We spent an hour at the midway. He really loved the Ferris wheel.'

'Yes, patients with fever, swollen glands, and congestion,' Bingaman explained, using the telephone in Dr Powell's office.

'A possible diagnosis of pneumonia.' He was speaking to the chief of staff at Riverton's hospital, fifty miles away. 'Nothing? Not one case? Why am I . . . I'm trying to understand how one of my patients came down with these symptoms. He was in Riverton last week. I thought perhaps the midway you had there . . . If you remember anything, would you please call me? Thank you.'

Bingaman hooked the earpiece onto the telephone and rubbed the back of his neck.

Throughout the conversation, Powell had remained seated behind his desk, studying him. 'Take it easy. Pneumonia can be like pollen in the wind. You'll probably *never* know where the boy caught the disease.'

Bingaman stared out a window toward a robin in an elm tree. 'Pollen in the wind?' He exhaled. 'You know what I'm like. I'm compulsive. I think too much. I can't leave well alone, and in this case, my patient isn't doing well at all.'

Marion watched him stare at his plate. 'You don't like the pot roast?'

'What?' Bingaman looked up. 'Oh . . . I'm sorry. I guess I'm not much company tonight.'

'You're still bothered?'

Bingaman raised some mashed potatoes on his fork. 'I don't like feeling helpless.'

'You're *not* helpless. This afternoon you did a lot of good for the patients who came to your office.'

Without tasting the potatoes, Bingaman set down the fork. 'Because their problems were easy to correct. I can stitch shut a gash in an arm. I can prescribe bicarbonate of soda for an upset stomach. I can recommend a salve that reduces the itch of poison ivy and stops the rash from spreading. But aside from fighting the symptoms, there is absolutely nothing I can do to fight pneumonia. We try to reduce Joey's fever, keep him hydrated, and give him oxygen. After that, it's all a question of whether the boy is strong enough to fight the infection. It's out of *my* hands. It's in *God's* hands. And sometimes God can be cruel.'

'The war certainly shows that,' Marion said. She was American, stoutly loyal, but her German ancestry made her terribly aware that good men were dying on *both* sides of the Hindenburg line.

'All those needless deaths from infected wounds.' Bingaman tapped his fork against his plate. 'In a way, it's like Joey's infection. Lord, how I wish I were young again. In medical school again. I keep up with the journals, but I can't help feeling I'm using outmoded techniques. I wish I'd gone into research. Microbiology. I'd give anything to be able to attack an infection at its source. Maybe some day someone will invent a drug that tracks down infectious microbes and kills them.'

'It would certainly make your job easier. But in the meantime . . .'

Bingaman nodded solemnly. 'We do what we can.'

'You've been putting in long hours. Why don't you do something for yourself? Go up to your study. Try out the wireless radio you bought.'

'I'd almost forgotten about that.'

'You certainly were determined when you spent that Sunday

afternoon installing the antenna on the roof.'

'And you were certainly determined to warn me I was going to fall off the roof and break my neck.' Bingaman chuckled. 'That radio seemed like an exciting thing when I bought it. A wonder of the twentieth century.'

'It still is.'

'The ability to talk to someone in another state. In another country. Without wires. To listen to a ship at sea. Or a report from a battlefield.' Bingaman sobered. 'Well, that part isn't wonderful. The rest of it, though . . . Yes, I believe I will do something for myself tonight.'

But the telephone rang as he walked down the hallway to go upstairs. Wearily, he unhooked the earpiece and leaned toward the microphone.

'Hello.' He listened. 'Oh.' His voice dropped. 'Oh.' His tone became somber. 'I'm on my way.'

'An emergency?' Marion asked.

Bingaman felt pressure in his chest. 'Joey Carter is dead.'

Marion turned pale. 'Dear Lord.'

'With oxygen, I thought he had a chance to . . . How terrible.' He felt paralyzed and struggled to rouse himself. 'I'd better go see the parents.'

But after Bingaman put on his suit coat and reached for his black bag, the telephone rang again. He answered, listened, and when he replaced the earpiece, he felt older and more tired.

'What is it?' Marion touched his arm.

'That was the hospital again. Joey's father just collapsed with a hundred-and-two fever. He's coughing. His glands are swollen. The two boys Joey went swimming with now have Joey's symptoms also. Their parents just brought them into the emergency ward.'

'If it was only Joey's two friends, I'd say, yes, they might all have gotten sick from swimming in Larrabee's creek,' Bingaman told Dr Powell, who had returned to the hospital in response to Bingaman's urgent summons. It was midnight. They sat across from each other in Powell's office, a pale desk lamp making their faces look sallow. 'The trouble is, Joey's father didn't go anywhere near that creek, and he's got the infection too.'

'You're still thinking of Riverton?'

'It's the only answer that makes sense. Joey probably got infected at the midway. Maybe a worker sneezed on him. Maybe it was a passenger on the Ferris wheel. However it happened, he then passed the infection on to his father and his two friends. *They* showed symptoms a day after *he* did because they'd been infected later than Joey was.'

'Infected *by* Joey. It's logical except for one thing.'

'What's that?'

'Why hasn't Joey's mother—'

Someone knocked on the door. Without waiting for an answer, a nurse rushed in. 'I'm sorry to disturb you, but I was certain you'd want to know. Mrs Carter just collapsed with the same symptoms as her son and husband.'

Both doctors sprang to their feet.

'We'll have to implement quarantine precautions.' Bingaman rushed from the office.

'Yes.' Powell hurried next to him. 'No visitors. Mandatory gauze masks for medical personnel, anybody who goes into those rooms. The emergency ward should be disinfected.'

'Good idea.' Bingaman moved faster. 'And the room where Joey died. The nurses who treated him had better scrub down. They'd better put on clean uniforms in case they've been contaminated.'

'But we still don't know how to treat this, aside from what we've already tried.'

'And that didn't work.' Bingaman's chest felt hollow.

'If you're right about how the infection started, why haven't there been cases in Riverton?' Powell sounded out of breath.

'I don't know. In fact, there's almost nothing I *do* know. When do we get the results from Joey Carter's autopsy?'

The stoop-shouldered man peeled off his rubber gloves, dropped them into a medical waste bin, then took off his gauze mask, and leaned against a locker. His name was Peter Talbot. A surgeon, he also functioned as Elmdale's medical examiner. He glanced from Bingaman to Powell and said, 'The lungs were completely filled with fluid. It would have been impossible for the boy to breathe.'

Bingaman stepped closer. 'Could the fluid have accumulated subsequent to his death?'

'What are you suggesting?'

'Another cause of death. Did you examine the brain?'

'Of course.'

'Was there any sign of—'

'What exactly are you looking for?'

'Could the cause of death have been something as highly contagious as meningitis?'

'No. No sign of meningitis. What killed this boy attacked his lungs.'

'Pneumonia,' Powell said. 'There's no reason to discount the initial diagnosis.'

'Except that pneumonia doesn't normally spread this fast.'

'Spread this fast?' Talbot straightened. 'You have other cases?'

'Four since the boy died.'

'Good Lord.'

'I know. This sounds like the start of an epidemic.'

'But caused by what?' Bingaman rubbed his forehead.

'I'll try to find out.' Talbot pointed toward a table. 'I have tissue samples ready to be cultured. I'll do my best to identify the microorganism responsible. What else can we—'

Bingaman started toward the door. 'I think it's time to make another telephone call to the Riverton hospital.'

Blood drained from Bingaman's face as he listened to the doctor in charge of the emergency room at the Riverton hospital.

'But I asked your chief of staff to get in touch with me if any cases were reported.' Damn him, Bingaman thought. 'Too busy? No time? Yes. And I'm very much afraid we're *all* going to get a lot busier.'

As he turned from the telephone, he couldn't help noticing the apprehension on Powell's face.

'How many cases do they have?'

'Twelve,' Bingaman answered.

'*Twelve?*'

'They were all admitted within the past few hours. Two of the patients have died.'

153

★ ★ ★

He parked his Model T in his driveway and extinguished the headlights. The time was after three a.m., and he had hoped that the chug-chug, rattle-rattle of the automobile would not waken his wife, but he saw a pale yellow glow appear in the window of the master bedroom, and he shook his head, discouraged, wishing he still owned a horse and buggy. The air had a foul odor from the car's exhaust fumes. Too many inventions. Too many complications. Even so, he thought, there's one invention you do wish for – a drug that eliminates infectious microbes.

Exhausted, he got out of the car. Marion had the front door open, waiting for him, as he climbed the steps onto the porch.

'You look awful.' She took his bag and put an arm around him, guiding him into the house.

'It's been that kind of night.' Bingaman explained what was happening at the hospital, the new patients he'd examined and the treatment he'd prescribed. 'In addition to aspirin, we're using quinine to control the fever. We're rubbing camphor oil on the patients' chests and having them breathe through strips of cloth soaked in it, to try to keep their bronchial passages open.'

'Is that working?'

'We don't know yet. I'm so tired I can hardly think straight.'

'Let me put you to bed.'

'Marion . . .'

'What?'

'I'm not sure how to say this.'

'Just go ahead and say it.'

'If this disease is as contagious as it appears to be . . .'

'Say it.'

'I've been exposed to the infection. Maybe you ought to keep your distance from me. Maybe we shouldn't sleep in the same bed.'

'After twenty-five years? I don't intend to stop sleeping with you now.'

'I love you.'

The patient, Robert Wilson, was a forty-two-year-old blue-eyed carpenter who worked with Edward Carter. The man had swollen glands and congested lungs. He complained of a headache and soreness in his muscles. His temperature was a hundred and one.

'I'm afraid I'm going to have to send you to the hospital,' Bingaman said.

'Hospital?' Wilson coughed.

Bingaman stepped back.

'But I can't afford the time off work,' the heavyset carpenter said. 'Can't you just give me a pill or something?'

Don't I wish, Bingaman thought, saying, 'Not in this case.'

Wilson raised a hand to his mouth and coughed again. His blue eyes were glassy. 'But what do I have?'

'I'll need to do more tests on you at the hospital,' Bingaman said, his professional tone cloaking the truth. What do you have? he thought. Whatever killed Joey Carter.

And killed Joey's father, Bingaman learned after he finished with his morning's patients and arrived at the hospital. Joey's mother and the boy's two friends weren't doing well either, struggling to breathe despite the oxygen they were being given. And eight more cases had been admitted.

'We're still acting on the assumption that this is pneumonia,' Powell said as they put on gauze masks and prepared to enter the quarantined ward.

'Are the quinine and camphor oil having any effect?'

'Marginally. Some of the patients feel better for a time. Their temperatures go down briefly. For example, Rebecca Carter's dropped from one hundred and four to one hundred and two. I thought we were making progress. But then her temperature shot up again. Some of these patients would have died without oxygen, but I don't know how long our supply will last. I've sent for more, but our medical distributor in Albany is having a shortage.'

Conscious of the tight mask on his face, Bingaman surveyed the quarantined ward, seeing understaffed, overworked nurses doing their best to make their patients comfortable, hearing the hiss of oxygen tanks and the rack of coughing. In a corner, a curtain had been pulled around a bed.

'Some of the patients are coughing up blood,' Powell said.

'What did you just say?'

'Blood. They're—'

'Before that. Your medical distributor in Albany is having a shortage of oxygen?'

'Yes.'

'Why?'

'Their telegram didn't say.'

'Could it be that too many other places need it?'

'What are you talking about?'

'The midway had to have come from somewhere to reach Riverton. After Riverton, it had to have *gone* somewhere.'

'Jonas, you're not suggesting—'

'Do you suppose this whole section of the state is infected?'

'I'm sorry,' the operator said. 'I can't get through to the switchboard in Albany. All the lines are busy.'

'*All* of them?'

'It's the state capital. So much business gets done there. If everybody's trying to call the operator at once—'

'Try Riverton. Try the hospital there.'

'Just a moment . . . I'm sorry, sir. I can't get through to the operator there, either. The lines are busy.'

Bingaman gave the operator the names of three other major towns in the area.

The operator couldn't reach her counterparts in those districts. All the lines were in use.

'*They're* not the state capital,' Bingaman said. 'What's going on that so many calls are being made at the same time?'

'I really have no idea, sir.'

'Well, can't you interrupt and listen in?'

'Only locally. As I explained, I don't have access to the other operators' switchboards. Besides, I'm not supposed to eavesdrop unless it's an emergency.'

'That's what this is.'

'An emergency?' The operator coughed. 'What sort of emergency?'

Bingaman managed to stop himself from telling her. If I'm not careful, he thought, I'll cause a panic.

'I'll try again later.'

He hung up the telephone's earpiece. His head started aching.

'No luck?' Powell asked.

'This is so damned frustrating.'

'But even if we do find out that this section of the state is affected, that still won't help us to fight what we've got here.'

'It might if we knew what we were fighting.' Bingaman massaged his throbbing temples. 'If only we had a way to get in touch with . . .' A tingle rushed through him. 'I *do* have a way.'

The wireless radio sat on a desk in Bingaman's study. It was black, two feet wide, a foot and a half tall and deep. There were several dials and knobs, a Morse code key, and a microphone. From the day Marconi had transmitted the first transatlantic wireless message in 1901, Bingaman had been fascinated by the phenomenon. With each new dramatic development in radio communications, his interest had increased until finally, curious about whether he'd be able to hear radio transmissions from the war in Europe, he had celebrated his fifty-second birthday in March by purchasing the unit before him. He had studied for and successfully passed the required government examination to become an amateur radio operator. Then, having achieved his goal, he had found that the demands of his practice, not to mention middle age, left him little energy to stay up late and talk to amateur radio operators around the country.

Now, however, he felt greater energy than he could remember having felt in several years. Marion, who was astonished to see her husband come home in the middle of the afternoon and hurry upstairs with barely a 'hello' to her, watched him remove his suit coat, sit before the radio, and turn it on. When she asked him why he had come home so early, he asked her to please be quiet. He said he had work to do.

'Be quiet? Work to do? Jonas, I know you've been under a lot of strain, but that's no excuse for—'

'*Please.*'

Marion watched with greater astonishment as Bingaman turned knobs and spoke forcefully into a microphone, identifying himself by name and the operator number that the government had given to him, repeatedly trying to find someone to answer him. Static crackled. Sometimes Marion heard an electronic whine. She stepped closer, feeling her husband's tension. In surprise, she heard a voice from the radio.

With relief, Bingaman responded. 'Yes, Harrisburg, I read you.' He had hoped to raise an operator in Albany or somewhere else in New York State, but the capital city of neighboring Pennsylvania was near enough, an acceptable substitute. He explained the reason he was calling, the situation in which Elmdale found itself, the information he needed, and he couldn't repress a groan when he received an unthinkable answer, far worse than anything he'd been dreading. 'Forty thousand? No. I can't be receiving you correctly, Harrisburg. Please repeat. Over.'

But when the operator in Harrisburg repeated what he had said, Bingaman still couldn't believe it. '*Forty thousand?*'

Marion gasped when, for only the third time in their marriage, she heard him blaspheme.

'Dear sweet Jesus, help us.'

'Spanish influenza.' Bingaman's tone was bleak, the words a death sentence.

Powell looked startled.

Talbot leaned tensely forward. 'You're quite certain?'

'I confirmed it from two other sources on the wireless.'

The hastily assembled group, which also consisted of Elmdale's other physician, Douglas Bennett, and the hospital's six-member nursing staff, looked devastated. They were in the largest non-public room in the hospital, the nurses' rest area, which was barely adequate to accommodate everyone, the combined body heat causing a film of perspiration to appear on brows.

'Spanish influenza,' Powell murmured, as if testing the ominous words, trying to convince himself that he'd actually heard them.

'Spanish . . . I'd have to check my medical books,' Bennett said, 'but as I recall, the last outbreak of influenza was in—'

'Eighteen eighty-nine,' Bingaman said. 'I did some quick research before I came back to the hospital.'

'Almost thirty years.' Talbot shook his head. 'Long enough to have hoped that the disease wouldn't be coming back.'

'The outbreak before that was in the winter of 1847–48,' Bingaman said.

'In that case, *forty* years apart.'

'Resilient.'

'*Spanish* influenza?' a pale nurse said. 'Why are they calling it . . . Did this outbreak come from Spain?'

'They don't know *where* it came from,' Bingaman said. 'But they're comparing it to an outbreak in 1647 that *did* come from Spain.'

'*Wherever it came from doesn't matter,*' Powell said, standing. 'The question is, what are we going to do about it? Forty thousand?' Bewildered, he turned toward Bingaman. 'The wireless operator you spoke to confirmed that? Forty thousand patients with influenza in Pennsylvania?'

'No, that isn't correct. You misunderstood me.'

Powell relaxed. 'I hoped so. That figure is almost impossible to believe.'

'It's much worse than that.'

'Worse?'

'Not forty thousand *patients* with influenza. Forty thousand *deaths*.'

Someone inhaled sharply. The room became very still.

'Deaths,' a nurse whispered.

'That's only in Pennsylvania. The figures for New York City aren't complete, but it's estimated that they're getting two thousand new cases a day. Of those, a hundred patients are dying.'

'Per *day?*'

'A conservative estimate. As many as fifteen thousand patients may have died there by now.'

'In New York State.'

'No, in New York *City.*'

'But this is beyond imagination!' Talbot said.

'And there's more.' Bingaman felt the group staring at him. 'The wireless operators I spoke to have been in touch with other parts of the country. Spanish influenza has also broken out in Philadelphia, Boston, Chicago, Denver, San Francisco and—'

'A fully-fledged epidemic,' Bennett said.

'Why haven't we heard about it until now?' a nurse demanded.

159

'Exactly. Why weren't we warned?' Powell's cheeks were flushed. 'Albany should have warned us! They left us alone out here, without protection! If we'd been alerted, we could have taken precautions. We could have stockpiled medical supplies. We could have . . . could have . . .' His words seemed to choke him.

'You want to know why we haven't heard about it until now?' Bingaman said. 'Because the telephone and the telegraph aren't efficient. How many people in Elmdale have telephones? A third of the population. How many of those make long-distance calls? Very few, because of the expense. And who would they call? Most of their relatives live right here in town. Our newspaper isn't linked to Associated Press, so the news we get is local. Until there's a national radio network and news can travel instantly across the country, each city's more isolated than we like to think. But as for why the authorities in Albany didn't warn communities like Elmdale about the epidemic, well, the wireless operators I spoke to have a theory that the authorities *didn't want* to warn anyone about the disease.'

'Didn't . . .'

'To avoid panic. There weren't any public announcements. The newspapers printed almost nothing about the possibility of an influenza outbreak.'

'But that's totally irresponsible.'

'The idea seems to have been to stop everyone from losing control and fleeing into the countryside. Each day, the authorities evidently hoped that the number of new cases would dwindle, that the worst would be over. When things got back to normal, order would have been maintained.'

'But things *haven't* gone back to normal, have they?' Talbot said. 'Not at all.'

Talbot's comment echoed ominously in Bingaman's mind as the meeting concluded and the doctors and nurses went out to the public part of the hospital. What the medical personnel faced as they went to their various duties was the beginning of Elmdale's own chaos. During the half-hour of the meeting, twenty new patients had shown up with what the staff now recognized as the symptoms of influenza: high fever, aching muscles, severe headaches, sensitive vision, dizziness, difficulty in breathing. The litany of coughing made Bingaman terribly selfconscious about the air he breathed. He hurriedly reached for his gauze mask. He had a mental vision of germs, thousands and thousands of them, spewing across the emergency room. The mental image was so powerful that Bingaman feared he was hallucinating.

'Mrs Brady,' he told one of the untrained volunteer nurses who'd been watching the emergency room while the meeting was in progress, 'your mask. You forgot to put on your mask. And all these new patients need masks also. We can't have them coughing over each other.'

And over *us*, Bingaman thought in alarm.

The end of normalcy, the chaos that had burst upon them, wasn't signaled only by the welter of unaccustomed activity or by the dramatic increase in new patients. What gave Bingaman the sense of the potential scope of the unfolding nightmare was that Elmdale's hospital, which was intended to serve the medical needs of the entire county, now had more patients than its thirty-bed capacity.

'What are we going to do?' Powell asked urgently. 'We can put patients on mattresses and cots in the corridors, but at this rate we'll soon use up *those* spaces. The same applies to my office and the nurses' rest area.'

The head nurse, Virginia Keel, a strawberry blond with a notoriously humorless personality, turned from administering to a patient. 'This won't do. We need to establish an emergency facility, a place big enough to accommodate so many patients.'

'The high-school gymnasium,' Bingaman said.

The head nurse and the chief of staff looked at him as if he'd lost his mind.

'With school about to start, you want to turn the gymnasium into a pest house?' Powell asked in amazement.

'Who said anything about school starting?'

Powell looked shocked, beginning to understand.

'A third of our patients are children,' Bingaman said. 'At the moment, I don't see any reason not to assume that we'll soon be receiving even more patients, and a great many of *them* will be children. It would be criminal to allow school to start. That would only spread infection faster. We need to speak to the school board. We need to ask them to postpone school for several weeks until we realize the scope of what we're dealing with. Maybe the epidemic will abate.'

'The look on your face tells me you don't think so,' Powell said.

'Postpone the start of school?' Mayor Halloway, who was also the head of the country's board of education, blinked. 'That's preposterous. School is scheduled to start four days from now. Can you imagine the response I'd have to suffer from angry parents? The ones who had telephones wouldn't stop calling me. The ones who didn't would form a mob outside my office. Those parents want their lives to get back to normal. They've had enough of their children lollygagging around town all summer. They want them in front of a blackboard again, learning something.'

'A week from now, if this epidemic keeps growing at the present rate, those parents will be begging you to close the schools,' Bingaman said.

'Then that'll be the time to close them,' Halloway said, blinking again. 'When the people who elected me tell me what they want.'

'You're not listening to me.' Bingaman put both hands on the mayor's desk. 'People are dying. You need to take the initiative on this.'

Halloway stopped blinking. 'I'm not prepared to make a hasty decision.'

'Well, make *some* kind of decision. Will you allow the high-school gymnasium to be turned into another hospital?'

'I'll have to consult with the other members of the school board.'

'That's fine,' Bingaman said angrily. 'While you're consulting, I'll be setting up beds in the gym.'

'This is really as serious as you say it is?'

'Serious enough that you're going to have to think about closing any places where people form crowds – the restaurants, the movie theater, the stores, the saloons, the—'

'Close the business district?' Halloway jerked his head back so sharply that his spectacles almost fell off his nose. 'Close the . . .

Maybe the saloons. I've been getting more and more complaints from church groups about what goes on in them. This prohibition movement is becoming awfully powerful. But the restaurants and the stores? All the uproar from the owners because of the business they would lose.' Mayor Halloway guffawed. 'You might as well ask me to close the churches.'

'It might come to that.'

Mayor Halloway suddenly wasn't laughing any longer.

He's worried about the epidemic's effect on business? Bingaman thought in dismay as he drove his Model T along Elmdale's deceptively sleepy street toward the hospital. Well, there's one business whose prosperity the mayor won't have to worry about: the undertaker's.

This premonition was confirmed when Bingaman reached the hospital's gravel parking area, alarmed to find it crammed with vehicles and buggies, evidence of new patients. He was further alarmed by Powell's distraught look when they met at the entrance to the noisy, crowded emergency room.

'Eighteen more cases,' Powell said. 'Three more deaths, including Joey Carter's mother.'

For a moment, Bingaman couldn't catch his breath. His headache, which had persisted from yesterday, had also worsened. The emergency room felt unbearably hot, sweat making his heavily starched shirt stick to him under his suit coat. He wanted to unbutton his strangling shirt collar but knew that his position of authority prohibited such public informality.

'Has anybody warned Ballard and Standish?' he managed to ask. He referred to Elmdale's two morticians.

Powell nodded, guiding Bingaman into a corner, away from the commotion in the emergency room. His manner indicated that he didn't want to be overheard. 'They didn't need to be told,' he whispered. 'Each has been here several times. I'm still adjusting to what Ballard said to me.'

'What was that?'

Powell dropped his voice even lower. 'He said, "My God, where am I going to get enough gravediggers? Where am I going to find enough coffins?" '

'We're out of oxygen.' Virginia Keel, the head nurse, stopped next to them. 'We're extremely low on aspirin, quinine, and camphor oil.'

'We'll have to get everything we can from the pharmacists downtown,' Powell said.

'Before the townsfolk panic and start hoarding,' Bingaman said.

'But without medical supplies—'

'Try to get fluids into them,' Bingaman told the nurse. 'Do your best to keep them nourished. Soups. Custard. Anything bland and easy to digest.'

'But we don't have anyone to cook for the patients.'

'The Women's League,' Powell said. 'We'll ask *them* to do the cooking.'

'And to help my nurses,' Keel said. 'Even with the volunteers who arrived this morning, I'm hopelessly understaffed.'

'Who else can we ask to help us?' Bingaman tried desperately to think. 'Has anyone spoken to the police department? What about the volunteer fire department? And the ministers? They can spread the word among their congregations.'

It was almost two a.m. before Bingaman managed to get home. Again he extinguished the headlights of his Model T. Again a pale yellow light appeared in the bedroom window. Despite his weariness, he managed to smile as Marion met him at the door.

'You can't keep going like this,' she said.

'No choice.'

'Have you eaten?'

'A sandwich on the go. A cup of coffee here and there.'

'Well, you're going to sit at the kitchen table. I'll heat up the chicken and dumplings I made for supper.'

'Not hungry.'

'You're not listening to what I said. You're going to sit at the kitchen table.'

Bingaman laughed. 'If you insist.'

'And tomorrow I'm going with you. I should have done it today.'

He suddenly became alert. 'Marion, I'm not sure—'

'Well, *I* am. I'm a trained nurse, and I'm needed.'

'But this is different from what you think it is. This is—'

164

'What?'

'One of our nurses collapsed today. She has all the symptoms.'

'And the other nurses?'

'They're exhausted, but so far they haven't gotten sick, thank God.'

'Then the odds are in my favor.'

'No. I don't want to lose you, Marion.'

'I can't stay barricaded in this house. And what about you? Look at the risk *you're* taking. I don't want to lose you, either. But if *you* can take the risk, so can *I*.'

Bingaman almost continued to argue with her, but he knew she was right. The townsfolk needed help, and neither of them would be able to bear the shame if they didn't fulfill their moral obligation. He'd seen amazing things today, people whom he had counted on to volunteer telling him that he was crazy if he thought they would risk their lives to help patients with the disease, others who never went to church or participated in community functions showing up to help without needing to be asked. The idea had occurred to him that the epidemic was God's way of testing those who didn't die, of determining who was worthy to be redeemed.

The idea grew stronger after he ate the chicken and dumplings that Marion warmed up for him, his favorite meal, although he barely tasted it. He went upstairs, but instead of proceeding into the bedroom, he entered his study, sat wearily at his desk, and turned on the wireless radio.

'Jonas?'

'In a moment.'

Hearing crackles and whines, he turned knobs and watched dials. Periodically, he spoke into the microphone, identifying himself.

Finally he contacted another operator, this one in Boston, but as the operator described what was happening there – the three thousand new cases per day, a death toll so fierce that the city's 291 hearses were kept constantly busy – Bingaman brooded again about God. According to the radio operator in Boston, there wasn't a community in the United States that hadn't been hit. From Minneapolis to New Orleans, from Seattle to Miami, from north to south and west to east and everywhere in between, people

165

were dying at a sanity-threatening rate. In Canada and Mexico, in Argentina and Brazil, England and France, Germany and Russia, China and Japan . . . Not an epidemic. A *pan*demic. It wasn't just in the United States. It was *everywhere*. Horrified, Bingaman thought about the bubonic plague known as the Black Death that had ravaged Europe in the Middle Ages, but what he was hearing about now was far more widespread than the Black Death had been, and if the mortality figures being given to him were accurate, the present scourge had the potential to be far more lethal. Lord, the cold weather hadn't arrived yet. What would happen when the worst of winter aggravated the symptoms of the disease? Bingaman had a nightmarish image of millions of frozen corpses strewn around the world with no one to bury them. Yes, the Spanish influenza was God's way of testing humanity, of judging how the survivors reacted, he thought. Then a further dismaying thought occurred to him, making him shiver. Or could it possibly be the end of the world?

'It appears to have started in Kansas,' Bingaman told the medical team. They had agreed to meet every morning at eight in the nurses' rest area in the hospital: to relay information and subdue rumors. After the meeting, they would disperse to inform volunteers about what had been discussed.

'Kansas?' Powell furrowed his brow in confusion. 'I assumed it would have started somewhere more exotic.'

'At Fort Riley,' Bingaman continued. He had gotten only two hours' sleep the night before and was fighting to muster energy. His head throbbed. 'That Army facility is one of the main training areas for the Allied Expeditionary Force. In March, it had a dust storm of unusual force.'

'Dust,' Talbot said. 'I've been formulating a theory that dust is the principal means by which the disease is carried over distances.' He turned to the nurses. 'We have to take extra precautions. Close every window. Eliminate the slightest dust.'

'In this heat?' Virginia Keel said. As head nurse, she never failed to speak her mind, even to a doctor. 'And with the patients' high temperatures? They won't be able to bear it.'

Talbot's eyes flashed with annoyance that he'd been contradicted.

Before angry words could be exchanged, Bingaman distracted them. 'There might be another agent responsible for the initial transmission. I spoke to a wireless operator in Kansas early this morning, and he told me the theory at the camp is that the dust storm, which turned the day into night for three hours, left not only several inches of dust over everything in the camp but also ashes from piles of burned manure.'

Bennett's nostrils twitched. 'Burned manure?'

Bingaman nodded. 'I realize that it's an indelicate subject. My apologies to the ladies. But we can't stand on niceties during the present emergency. There's a considerable cavalry detachment at Fort Riley. Thousands of mules and horses. It's estimated that those animals deposit nine thousand tons of manure a month in the camp, an obvious hygiene problem that the fort's commander attempted to alleviate by ordering his men to burn the droppings. The smoke from the fires and then the ashes blown by the dust storm apparently spread infectious microbes throughout the entire camp. Subsequent to the storm, so many soldiers came down with influenza symptoms that the surgeon-general for the fort was afraid they'd take up all three thousand beds in the fort's hospital. Fortunately, the outbreak abated after five weeks.'

'And then?' Powell frowned. He seemed to have a premonition about what was coming.

'Two divisions were sent from the fort to join the rest of our expeditionary forces in Europe. Influenza broke out on the troop ships. When the soldiers arrived in France, they spread it to our units and the British and the French. Presumably also to the Germans. At last count, the Royal Navy alone has over ten thousand cases of influenza. Of course, the civilian population has been affected too. After that, the disease spread from Europe throughout Asia and Africa and everywhere else, including of course back to America. An alternate theory about the pandemic's origin is that it started among farm animals in China and was introduced into France by Chinese coolies whom the Allies used to dig trenches. Perhaps the *true* origin will never be known.'

'But what about the death rate?' a nurse asked, obviously afraid of the answer.

'In three months, the flu has killed more people in Europe,

soldiers and civilians, than have died in military operations on both sides during the entire four years of the war.'

For several moments, the group was speechless.

'But you're talking about *millions* of deaths,' Virginia Keel said.

'And many *more* millions who continue to suffer from the disease.'

'Then . . .'

'Yes?' Bingaman turned to a visibly troubled nurse.

'There's no hope.'

Bingaman shook his throbbing head. 'If we believe that, then there truly won't be any. We *must* hope.'

The nurse raised a hand to her mouth and coughed. Everyone else in the room tensed and leaned away from her.

Bingaman helped finish admitting twenty-five patients to the gymnasium that had been converted into a hospital. As he and Dr Bennett left the spacious building – which was rapidly being filled with occupied beds – they squinted from the brilliant September sunlight and noticed corpses being loaded onto horse-drawn wagons.

'How many died last night?'

'Fifteen.'

'It keeps getting worse.'

Bingaman faltered.

'What's the matter?' Bennett asked. 'Aren't you feeling well?'

Bingaman didn't reply but instead took labored steps toward one of the wagons. The corpse of a woman in a nurse's uniform was being lifted aboard.

'But I saw her only yesterday. How could this have happened so quickly?'

'I've been hearing reports that the symptoms are taking less time to develop,' Bennett said behind him. 'From the slightest hint of having been infected, a person might suddenly have a full-blown case within twenty-four hours. I heard a story this morning about a man, apparently healthy, who left his home to go to work. He wasn't coughing. None of his family noticed a fever. He died on the street a block from the factory where he worked. I heard another story.'

'Yes?'

'Four women were playing bridge last night. The game ended at eleven. None of them was alive in the morning.'

Bingaman's chest felt heavy. His shoulders ached. His eyes hurt – from lack of sleep, he tried to assure himself. He removed his gauze mask from his pocket, having taken it off when he left the hospital. 'From now on, I think we're going to have to wear our masks all the time, even when we're not with patients. Day or night. At home or on duty. Everywhere.'

'At home? Isn't that a little extreme?' Bennett asked.

'Is it?' Bingaman gave the dead nurse, in her twenties with long brown hair, a final look as the wagon clattered away. So young, so much to live for, he thought. 'None of us is immune. The disease is all around us. There's no telling who might give it to us.' He glanced at Bennett. 'I keep remembering she was the nurse who coughed in the room with us yesterday.'

'Don't touch me! Get away!

The outburst made Bingaman look up from the patient he was examining. He was in the middle of a row of beds in the gymnasium, surrounded by determined activity as nurses and volunteers moved from patient to patient, giving them water, or soup if they were capable of eating, then rubbing their feverish brows with ice wrapped in towels. Another team of volunteers took care of the unsavory, hazardous problem of what to do with the bodily wastes from so many helpless people. A stench of excrement, sweat, and death filled the now hopelessly small area. Contrary to Dr Talbot's theories about dust and closed windows, Bingaman had ordered that all the windows in the gymnasium be opened. Nonetheless, the foul odor inside the building made him nauseous.

'I told you, damn it, get your filthy hands off me!'

The objectionable language attracted Bingaman's attention as much as the sense of outrage. The man responsible coughed hoarsely. There, Bingaman saw. To the right. Three rows over. Nurses, volunteers, and those few patients with a modicum of strength looked in that direction also.

'You bitch, if you touch me again—' The man's raspy voice

disintegrated into a paroxysm of coughing.

Such language could absolutely not be tolerated. Bingaman left the patient he'd been examining, veered between beds, reached another row, and veered between other beds, approaching the commotion. Three men had evidently carried in a fourth, who was sprawled on a cot, resisting the attentions of a nurse. Bingaman's indignation intensified at the thought of a nurse being called such things, but what he heard next was even more appalling. His emotions made it difficult for him to breathe.

'You goddamn German!'

Marion. The nurse the patient shouted at was Bingaman's wife. The three men who had carried in the patient were pushing her away.

Outraged, Bingaman reached the commotion. 'Don't you touch her! What's going on here?'

The patient's face reddened from the fury with which he coughed. Spittle flew. Bingaman stepped back reflexively, making sure that he stayed protectively in front of Marion.

'Put these masks on. No one comes in here without one. What's the matter with you?'

'*She's* what's the matter,' one man said. His voice was slurred. He was tall, wore work clothes, and had obviously been drinking. 'Lousy German.'

'Watch what you're saying.'

'Hun! Kraut!' a second man said, more beefy than the first. 'Yer not foolin' anybody.' He, too, was obviously drunk. 'Yer the one who did it! Made my friend sick! Gave everybody the influenza!'

'What kind of nonsense . . .'

'Spanish nothing.' The man on the bed coughed again. He was losing strength. Despite his feverish cheeks, he had alarming black circles around his eyes. 'It's the *German* influenza.'

The first man took a tottering step toward Marion. 'How much did the Kaiser pay you, Kraut?'

'Pay her?' the second man said. 'Didn't need to pay the bitch. She's a German, ain't she? Germans *love* killing Americans.'

'I've heard *enough*.' Bingaman shook with rage. 'Get out of this hospital. Now. I swear I'll send for a policeman.'

'And leave *her*?' The third man pointed drunkenly past Bingaman toward Marion. 'Leave *her* to kill more Americans? *She's* the one brought the influenza here. The *German* influenza. This is how the Kaiser thinks he's gonna win the war. Damned murderous Kraut.'

'I won't tell you again! Leave this instant or I'll—'

Bingaman stepped toward the men, urging them toward the door. The first man braced himself, muttered, 'The Huns killed my son in France, you goddamn Kraut-lover,' and struck the doctor's face.

Time seemed to stop. At once, it began again. Hearing exclamations around him, Bingaman lurched back, distantly aware of blood spewing from his lips beneath his mask. Then something struck his nose, and he saw double. Blood spurted from his nostrils. He lost control of his legs. He seemed to float. When he struck the floor, he heard far-away screaming.

Then everything was a blur. He had a vague sense of being lifted, carried. He heard distant, urgent voices. His mind reeled as he was set on something.

A cot. In a shadowy supply room at the rear of the gymnasium.

'Jonas, are you all right? Jonas?'

He recognized Marion's voice. Each anxious word sounded closer, as if she was leaning down.

'Jonas?'

'Yes. I think I'm all right.'

'Let me get your face mask off so you can breathe.'

'No. Can't risk contamination. Leave it on.'

She was wiping blood from his face. 'I'll give you a clean one.'

'Jonas?' A man's voice. Worried. Powell

'I'm only dazed,' Bingaman answered slowly. 'Caught me by surprise.' His words seemed to echo. 'I'll be all right in a moment.' He tried to sit up, but he felt as if he had ball bearings in his skull and they all rolled backward, forcing his head down. 'Those men. Are they . . .'

'Gone.'

'A policeman. Did you send for one?'

'What would be the point? When they closed the schools, the restaurants, and the stores, they also emptied the jail. There isn't any place to put those men.'

'Can't understand what got into them. Accusing Marion. Outrageous,' Bingaman said.

He managed to open his eyes and focus his aching vision. He saw Marion's worried face. And Powell's, which had a reluctant expression.

'What is it? What aren't you telling me?' Bingaman asked.

'This isn't the first time.'

'I don't understand.'

'People are frightened,' Powell said. 'They can't accept that it's random and meaningless. They want easy explanations. Something specific.'

'I still don't understand.'

'Someone to blame. The Germans. Marion.'

'But that's preposterous. How could they be so foolish as to think that Marion would . . .'

The discomfited look on Marion's face made Bingaman frown. 'You've been aware of this?'

'Yes.'

'How long has this been going on?'

'Several days.'

'And yet you still volunteered to come down here and help? I'm amazed.' But then Bingaman thought about it, and he *wasn't* amazed. Marion always did what was right, even when it was difficult.

'Don't get the wrong impression,' Powell said. 'It's not like everyone feels that way. Only a minority. A *small* minority. But they've certainly made their opinions known.'

'I'm going to have to stay home,' Marion said.

'No,' Powell said. 'You can't let them bully you.'

'It isn't because of them. I have a more important job. Feel Jonas's forehead. Touch the glands in his throat. Put your hand on his chest. You don't need a stethoscope. You can *feel* the congestion. He has it.'

The jolt of wheels into potholes and the noxious fumes of the Model T aggravated Bingaman's excruciating headache, making him nauseous as Marion drove him home. His injuries seemed to have broken the resolve with which he'd subdued the symptoms that he'd attributed only to fatigue. Now, as delirium took control of him, his last lucid thought was an echo of what he'd said to Dr

Bennett after seeing the nurse's corpse: *How could this have happened so quickly?* By the time Marion brought him home, the pain in his swollen lips and nostrils was insignificant compared to the soul-deep aching of his joints and limbs. He was so light-headed that he felt disassociated from himself, seeming to hover, watching Marion struggle to get him out of the car and up the steps into the house.

He did his best to cough away from her, grateful that he'd insisted she put a new mask on him. But the moment she eased him onto the bed, exhaling with effort, she loosened his shirt collar and took off the mask, which had become blood-soaked on the ride home.

'No', he murmured.

'Don't argue with me, Jonas. I have to get you cleaned up.'

'Should have left me in the hospital.'

'Not when you have a trained nurse to give you constant care at home.'

She took off his shoes, his socks, his pants, his bloody suit coat and vest and shirt. She stripped off his underwear. Shivering, naked on the bed, clutching his arms across his chest, teeth chattering, he watched the ceiling ripple as Marion bathed him from head to toe. She used warm water and soap, dried him thoroughly, then made him sit up and slipped his nightshirt over his head, pulling it down to his knees. She tugged long woolen socks over his feet. She covered him with a sheet and three blankets. When that still wasn't enough and his shivering worsened, she brought him a hot-water bottle and put on the down-filled comforter.

Bingaman coughed and murmured about a face mask.

'It interferes with your breathing,' Marion said.

'Might contaminate . . .'

'I don't think it does any good. Besides, I've already been exposed to it.' Working, Marion breathed harder.

Minutes, perhaps hours later, she was spooning hot tea into him, and when the chills suddenly turned into alarming amounts of sweat oozing from him, she tore off the covers, stripped him again, bathed him with rubbing alcohol, ignored his coughing, and eased him out of bed onto the floor. He had lost control of his bowels and fouled the bed. She had to change the sheets, then clean him and change his nightshirt, then tug him up onto the bed, and pull blankets over him again because the chills had returned. She covered his brow with a steaming washcloth and spooned more hot tea into him, trying to make him swallow pieces of warm bread soaked in the tea.

He lost all external impressions and floated away into darkness. His mind was like a boat on an increasingly choppy sea. A night sea. Storm-tossed. Spinning.

He had no idea how long he was away, but gradually the spinning stopped, the weather calmed, and when he came back, slowly, dimly, he didn't think that his throat had ever felt so dry or that he had ever been so weak. His eyes hurt as if they had sunk into his skull. His skin was tight from dehydration, greasy from repeated sweating frenzies. At the same time, it seemed loose, as if he had lost weight.

These sensations came to him gradually. He lay passively, watching a beam of sunlight enter the bedroom window on his left. Then it went away, and eventually the sunbeam entered through the window on his right, and he realized that he'd been in a semi-stupor while the sun passed from east to west. But he wasn't so stupefied that he failed to realize that nothing in the room had changed, that his nightshirt and covers were the same as in the morning, that no one had been in the room, that *Marion* hadn't been in the room.

He tried to call to her, but his lungs were too weak, his throat too dry, and nothing came out. He tried again and managed to produce only an animal-like whimper.

Marion! he thought desperately. His fear was not for himself, not that he had been left alone, helpless. His terror was for Marion. If she wasn't taking care of him, that meant she wasn't *able* to, and that meant . . .

The effort to move made him cough. Congestion rattled in his chest. Breath wheezed past his swollen bronchial passages and up his raw throat. But despite his pain and lethargy, he had the sense that he was better, not as feverish. His headache didn't threaten to cause his skull to explode. His muscles ached, but not as if he were being stretched on a rack.

When he squirmed to the side of the bed and tried to stand, his legs wobbled. He slumped on the floor. Marion! he kept thinking. He crawled. The hand-over-hand movement reminded him of the fear and determination he had felt when learning to swim. A pitcher on a table attracted his attention, and he grasped a chair beside the table, struggling to raise himself, to tilt the pitcher toward his lips. Water trickled into his mouth, over his scabbed, cracked, parched lips, down his chin, onto his nightshirt. He clumsily set the pitcher back down, apprehensive about dropping it, the water tasting too precious for him to risk wasting it. But as precious as it tasted, it was also tepid, stale, with a slight grit of dust. It had obviously been there a while, and with his premonition mounting, filling him with terror, he tried to call Marion's name, shuddered at the weak sound of his croaky voice, and crawled again.

He found her downstairs on the floor in the kitchen. His immediate panicked thought was that she was dead. But when he moaned, he thought he heard an echo, only to realize that the second moan had come from *her*, weak, faint, a moan nonetheless, and he fought to increase the effort with which he crawled to her. He touched her brow and felt the terrible heat coming off it. Yes! Alive! But the depth of her cough and the sluggishness of her response when he tried to rouse her filled him with dread, and he knew that his first priority was to get fluid into her. He gripped the top of the kitchen counter, pulled himself up, and sweated while he worked the pump handle in the sink, filling a bowl with water from the house's well. He almost spilled the bowl and barely remembered to bring a spoon, but at last he sat exhausted next to Marion on the kitchen floor, cradled her head, and spooned water between her dry, swollen lips. The heat coming off her was overwhelming. He struggled to the ice box, used an ice pick, and clumsily chipped off chunks from the half-melted block in the upper compartment. With the chunks of ice wrapped in a dish towel, he slumped yet again beside Marion and wiped the cool cloth over her beet-red face. He set the cloth on her forehead, spooned more water into her mouth, then gave in to his own thirst and drank from the bowl, only to have it slip from his grasp and topple onto the floor, soaking Marion and himself. He moaned, felt dizzy again, and lowered his head to the floor.

Time blurred. When he regained consciousness, he found himself on a chair in the parlor. Marion was on the couch across from him, a throwrug over her. Her chest rose and fell. She coughed. A plate of stale bread and a pitcher of water were on a side table. Someone found us, Bingaman thought, coughing. Someone came in and helped. But during the next few effort-filled hours, he was forced to realize that he was mistaken, that no one had come, that somehow *he* had shifted Marion into the parlor, that *he* had brought the bread and the pitcher of water.

The bread was so old and hard that he had to soak it in the water before he could gently insert it into Marion's mouth and encourage her to eat. He breathed a prayer of thanks when she swallowed. When she coughed, he feared that she would expel the food, but it stayed down, and then he, too, was eating, rinsing a crust of bread down with the unbelievably delicious water.

Again time blurred. It wasn't bread but strawberry jam and a spoon that he now found on the table beside the couch. He remembered having seen the jam in the ice box. Marion was coughing. He was rubbing her fiery brow with a towel that held the last of the ice. He was spooning the jam into her mouth. He was raising a glass to her lips. He was drinking from another glass, feeling his parched mouth and throat seeming to absorb the water.
Darkness. Light.

Darkness again. The cellar. Stumbling. Opening the door to the root cellar. Despite the coolness, sweating. Groping for two jars of Marion's preserves on a shelf. Coughing. Swaying. Stumbling up the cellar steps, reaching the kitchen, squinting from the painful brilliance of blazing sunset, discovering that the preserves he had expended so much effort to get were dill pickles.
Darkness. Light.

Darkness. Light.

★ ★ ★

Light again. Marion was no longer coughing. Bingaman later concluded that what saved her life was her robust constitution, although when she was alert enough she insisted that *he* had been the reason she stayed alive. Because of his ministrations, she called them. She told him not to be so modest.

'Hush,' he told her lovingly. 'Don't waste your strength.'

In the reverse, however, he had no doubt that Marion's own ministrations in the initial stage of *his* illness had been what saved *him*. The ruthless disease could be attacked only on the basis of its symptoms. After that, the patient would live or die strictly on the basis of his or her own resources, and now that Bingaman had endured the intimate experience of the influenza's devastating power, he marvelled that *anyone* had the strength to resist it.

Perhaps strength was not the determining factor. Perhaps it was luck. Or Fate. Or God's will. But if the latter was indeed the case, God certainly must have turned against a great many people. To a Presbyterian such as Bingaman, who believed in a contract that linked hard work and prosperity with salvation, the notion that the influenza might be God's display of worldwide disapproval was disquieting. Surely, even taking the war into account, the world couldn't be that bad a place. Or was the so-called *world* war, with its machine-guns and tear gas, chlorine gas, phosgene gas, mustard gas, the mounting horrors, the millions of needless casualties, in fact the problem?

But in that case, did it make sense for God in turn to inflict millions of other casualties?

'*Dr Bingaman.*' The nurse stepped back in fear, her face suddenly drained of color, almost as white as her uniform. 'It can't be!'

'What on earth . . .'

'I was told you were dead!'

'*Dead?*' Bingaman took another step toward the nurse in the hospital corridor.

She almost backed away. 'After Dr Powell died and Dr Talbot, I—'

'Wait a second. Dr *Powell* is dead?'

'Yes, and Dr Talbot and—'

'Dead.' Shock overwhelmed him. Dizzy, he feared that he was

having a relapse and placed a hand against the wall to steady himself. He took a deep breath, repressed a cough, and studied her. 'What made you think *I* was dead?'

'That's what I was told!'

'*Who* told you?'

'A lot of people. I don't know. I don't remember. It's been so terrible. So many people have gotten sick. So many people have died. I can't remember who's alive and who isn't. I can't remember when I slept last or when . . .'

Bingaman's fatigue and his preoccupation when he entered the hospital had prevented him from realizing how exhausted the nurse looked. 'Sit down,' he said, realizing something else – the reason no one had come to his house to find out if he needed help. Why would anyone have bothered if everyone thought I was dead? And there must be a *lot* of people who have died.

'You need to go home,' Bingaman said. 'Get some food. Rest.'

'I can't. So many patients. I can't keep the living straight from the dying. They keep going out and others come in. There's so much to do. I . . .'

'It's all right. I'm giving you permission. Go home. I'll speak to Virginia.' He referred to the head of the nursing staff. 'I'm sure she'll agree.'

'You can't.'

'What?'

'Speak to her.'

'I don't understand.'

'Virginia's dead.'

He found himself speechless, staring at her, horrified by the thought of being told that whoever else he referred to would be dead. So much had happened so quickly. Stretcher bearers passed him, carrying the corpse of Mayor Halloway.

A further horrifying thought occurred to him. 'How long?' he managed to ask.

The weary nurse shook her head in confusion.

'What I mean is . . .' His brow felt warm again. 'What day is it?'

Confused, she answered, 'Wednesday.'

He rubbed his forehead. 'What I'm trying to ask is – the date?'

'October ninth.' The nurse frowned in bewilderment.

'October ninth?' He felt as he had when he'd been struck in the face. He lurched backward.

'Dr Bingaman, do you feel all right?'

'A month.'

'I don't understand.'

'The last thing I recall it was early September.'

'I still don't—'

'I've lost the rest of September and . . . A month. *I've lost a whole month.*' Frightened, he tried to explain, to give the nurse a sense of what it was like to spend so many weeks fighting to breathe through congested lungs, all the while enduring a storm-tossed black sea of delirium. He strained to describe the unbelievable thirst, the torture of aching limbs, the suffocating heaviness on his chest.

The disturbed way the nurse looked at him gave him the sense that he was babbling. He didn't care. Because all the time he struggled to account for how he'd lost a month of his life, he realized that if it had happened to him, it must have happened to others. Dear God, he thought, how many others are trapped inside their houses, too weak to answer their phone if they have one, or to respond to someone knocking on their door? When he'd left his house an hour earlier, he'd knocked on the doors of his neighbors to his right and left. No one had answered. He had been troubled by how deserted his elm-lined street looked, a cool breeze blowing leaves that had turned from green to autumnal yellow with amazing rapidity in just a few days – except that he now realized it had been a month. And those neighbors hadn't gone away somewhere. He had a heart-pounding, dreadful certainty that they were *inside*, helpless or dead.

'Jonas, you look terrible. You've got to rest,' Dr Bennett said. 'Go home. Take care of Marion.'

'She's doing fine. Others are worse. She insisted I help take care of them.'

'But—'

'You and I are the only physicians left in town! People are dying! I can't go home! I'm needed!'

Every church in town had been converted into a hospital. All of them were full. The cemeteries no longer had room for all the corpses. Gravediggers could not keep up the labor of shoveling dirt from fresh pits. Corpses lay in rows in a pasture at the edge of town. Armed sentries were posted to stop animals from eating them, each man wearing a gauze mask and praying that he wouldn't catch the disease from the corpses. Funerals were limited to family members wearing masks, ministers rushing as fast as dignity would allow while they read the prayers for the dead.

'We have to keep searching!' Bingaman organized teams. 'Who knows how many people need our help? Even if they're dead, we have to find them. There's too great a risk of cholera. Pestilence. The decomposing bodies will cause a secondary plague.'

Leading his own group, Bingaman marched along streets and banged on doors. Sometimes a trembling hand let them in, a bony, sunken-eyed face assuring Bingaman that everyone inside was over the worst, obviously not aware that Bingaman had reached them barely soon enough to try to save them. Other times, receiving no answer, Bingaman's team broke in. Weak coughing led them to a few survivors. Too often, the odor of sickness and decay made everyone gag. Whole families had been dead for quite a while.

> *I had a little bird.*
> *Its name was Enza.*
> *I opened the window*
> *And in-flu-Enza.*

The rhyme, which Bingaman happened to hear a gaunt-cheeked little girl sing hypnotically, almost insanely, as her parents were carted dead from her house, festered in his mind. He couldn't get rid of it, couldn't still it, couldn't smother it. I opened the window and in-flu-Enza. The rhythm was insidious – like the disease. It repeated itself in his thoughts until it made him dizzy and he feared that he would have another bout of Enza. Opened the window. Yes. The disease was everywhere. All around. In the sky. In the air. In every breath. Bingaman knew that after his ordeal he ought to follow Bennett's advice and rest, but no matter how dizzy he felt . . . in-flu-Enza . . . he persisted, as Marion urged him to do, struggling from home to home, performing the corporal works of mercy for the suffering and the dead. In-flu-Enza. He persisted because he had come to the firm conclusion that if this disease was God's punishment, it was also an opportunity that God was offering to make the world a better place, to eradicate evil and work for salvation.

Bingaman's team rammed the door open and searched through musty shadows, first floor, second floor, cellar, and attic. His apprehension had been needless. There was no one, alive or dead.

Grateful to return outside, scuffling their shoes through dead leaves, the team followed Bingaman along the wooden sidewalk.

'We haven't looked in *this* house.'

'No need,' Bingaman said.

'Why not?'

'It's mine.'

'But what's that smell?'

'I don't know what you mean.'

'It's coming from—'

'The house farther down,' Bingaman said.

'No, *this* house. *Your* house.'

'Nonsense. I don't smell anything.'

'I think we'd better take a look.'

'Stop.'

'The door's locked.'

'Stay away.'

'The smell's worse here on the porch. Give us the key.'

'Get off my property!'

'The drapes are closed. I can't see through the windows.'

'I'm telling you to leave!'

'That smell is . . . Somebody help me break in the door.'

Amid Bingaman's screaming protest, they crashed in, and the stench that made several men vomit came unmistakably from the parlor. Bingaman's wife had been dead for six weeks. Her gray-skinned, gas-bloated corpse was smeared with strawberry jam and camphor oil. Quinine and aspirin pills had been stuffed inside her mouth until her cheeks bulged and her teeth were parted. A dill pickle also protruded from her mouth. Her exposed back resembled a pin cushion, except that the pins were large hypodermics which the doctor had pressed between her ribs and inserted into her lungs, desperately trying to extract the fluid that had drowned her. Several pails contained foul-smelling, yellow liquid.

'Marion.' Bingaman stroked her hair. 'I'm sorry. I tried to keep them away. I know how much you like your naps. Why don't you try to go back to sleep?'

The pandemic's peak coincided with the armistice in Europe, the declaration of peace, 11 November 1918. Thereafter, as armies disbanded and exhausted soldiers began their long journey home, the flu did not return with them to reinforce the infectious microbes that were already in place. To the contrary, against all logic, the disease began to lose its strength, and by the end of 1919, during the dead of winter, when the symptoms of the flu – exacerbated by cold weather – should have been at their worst, the pandemic approached its end. A few remote areas – Pacific islands and jungle outposts – remained to suffer the onslaught. Otherwise, having scoured the entire world, making no distinction between Eskimo villages and European metropolises, the Spanish influenza came to an end.

Bingaman, whose face would never regain its former ruddy cheerfulness and whose already thinning, silvery hair had fallen completely out because of his intense fever, rested, as did his fellow survivors. Of Elmdale's population of twelve thousand, eight thousand had collapsed with symptoms. Of those, two thousand had died. The remaining four thousand had worked non-stop to care for the sick and to bury the dead. Some, of course, had refused to help under any circumstances, for fear of being infected. They would have to make their peace with God.

Humanity had been tested. During the major outbreaks of the Black Death in Europe during the Middle Ages, it was estimated that twenty-five million had died. The number of soldiers estimated to have been killed during the five years of the Great War was eight and a half million. The latter figure Bingaman learned from his increasingly long nights communicating with radio operators in America and Europe. But the estimated number of worldwide deaths caused by the influenza was perhaps as much as *fifty* million. Even more astonishing, the total number of those presumed to have been infected by the disease was *two hundred* million, one twentieth of the world's population. If the pandemic had continued at its exponential, devastating rate, the human race might have been exterminated by the spring of 1920. Listening to his fellow radio operators around the country and around the globe, Bingaman shared their sense of helplessness and loss. But he also sympathized with a latent hope in some of their comments. Yes, the cream of American and European youth had been eradicated in the war. What the war had failed to accomplish, the flu had taken care of among the other age groups. Society had been gutted.

But what if . . . and this idea was almost unthinkable, and yet a few had given it voice, based on their reading of Charles Darwin . . . what if the pandemic had been a means of natural selection and now that the strong had survived, humanity would be better for it, able to improve itself genetically? Such a materialistic way of thinking was repugnant to Bingaman. He had heard enough about Darwinism to know that it was based on a theory of random events, that at bottom it was atheistic and worshipped accident. For Bingaman, there was no such thing as randomness and accident. Everything was part of a cosmic plan and had an ultimate purpose, and any theory that did not include God was unacceptable. But another theory *was* acceptable, and it was this that gave him hope – that this plague, one of the horsemen of the Apocalypse, had been God's way of demanding humanity's attention, of warning the survivors about their sins, and of granting them an opportunity to learn from their transgressions, to make a fresh start.

'Like the war,' Bingaman said to Marion, who had walked into his study three weeks after her funeral. He had looked up from his tears and smiled. He'd been talking to her ever since.

'The flu was God's warning that there must never be another war like this one. Isn't that what they've been calling it? The War to End All Wars? I'm convinced this is an opportunity to look ahead.'

Marion didn't respond.

'Also, I've been reading about the movement to make prohibition an amendment to the Constitution,' Bingaman said. 'When the saloons were closed to help keep the flu from spreading, it was obvious how much better society was without them. People have seen the error of their ways. The saloons will stay closed.'

Still Marion didn't respond.

'And something else,' Bingaman said. 'You know I always try to be optimistic. I'm convinced that society will benefit in other ways from the flu's devastation. We came so close to dying, all of us, the world. So now we'll all learn to cherish life more, to respect it, to be better. This decade's ending. A new one's about to start. A fresh beginning. It's going to be fascinating to see how we recover from so much death.'

Marion continued to remain silent.

'One thing troubles me, though,' Bingaman said. 'On the wireless last night, I heard about a medical researcher in New York City who discovered that influenza isn't caused by a bacteria but by a virus. In theory, that information ought to make it easier to develop a cure. Normally.' He frowned. 'All things being equal, we should be able to develop a vaccine. But not in this case. Because the researcher also discovered that the influenza virus is constantly mutating. Any vaccine would be effective only for a limited time. Meanwhile the ever-changing virus could come back in an even more deadly form. Or a different and worse virus might come along.'

For the first time, Marion spoke. 'God help us.' She coughed. Blood-tinted saliva beaded her bluish-black lips.

Bingaman shuddered, afraid that he was going to lose her a second time, that the horror would be repeated, again and again. 'Yes, that's what it comes down to. An act of faith. God help us. Remember how fervently we tried to have children, how deeply disappointed we were to find that we couldn't? We told ourselves that it wasn't meant to be, that God had given us a burden to test our faith. Perhaps it was for the best.' He sobbed as Marion's image faded. 'I couldn't bear to lose anyone else.'

Outside the study window, snow had begun to fall. A chill wind swept through the skeletal elms, burying the last of their fungus-wilted yellow leaves.

This mini-novel was written for another Al Sarrantonio anthology: 999, New Stories of Horror and Suspense *(1999). I enjoy doing fiction that's intimately connected to the location in which it occurs. When I lived in Iowa City, I wrote a number of tales about the haunting expanse of the Midwest. When I moved to Santa Fe, New Mexico, I became interested in the fictional possibilities of what locals call the Land of Enchantment and the City Different. 'Rio Grande Gothic' begins a couple of blocks from my home and involves a phenomenon that I started noticing about ten years ago – shoes lying in the middle of the road, different ones each day. I later discovered that this isn't only a Santa Fe curiosity. Throughout the US, other communities started noticing the same thing – conspiracy theorists take note.*

Rio Grande Gothic

When Romero finally noticed the shoes on the road, he realized that he'd actually been seeing them for several days. Driving into town along Old Pecos Trail, passing the adobe-walled Santa Fe Woman's Club on the left, approaching the pueblo-style Baptist church on the right, he reached the crest of the hill, saw the jogging shoes on the yellow median line, and steered his police car onto the dirt shoulder of the road.

Frowning, he got out and hitched his thumbs onto his heavy gunbelt, oblivious to the roar of passing traffic, focusing on the jogging shoes. They were laced together, a Nike label on the back. One was on its side, showing how worn its tread was. But they hadn't been in the middle of the road yesterday, Romero thought. No, yesterday it had been a pair of leather sandals. He remembered having been vaguely aware of them. And the day before yesterday? Had it been a pair of women's high heels? His recollection wasn't clear, but there had been *some* kind of shoes – of that he was certain. What the . . .?

After waiting for a break in traffic, Romero crossed to the median and stared down at the jogging shoes as if straining to decipher a riddle. A pickup truck crested the hill too fast to see him and slow down, the wind it created ruffling his blue uniform. He barely paid attention, preoccupied by the shoes. But when a second truck sped over the hill, he realized that he'd better get off the road. He withdrew his nightstick from his gunbelt, thrust it under the tied laces, and lifted. Feeling the weight of the shoes dangling from the nightstick, he waited for a minivan to speed past, then returned to his police car, unlocked its trunk, and dropped the shoes into it. Probably that was what had happened to the other shoes, he decided. A sanitation truck or someone working for the city must have stopped and cleared what looked like garbage. This was the middle of May. The tourist season would soon be in full swing. It wasn't good to have visitors seeing junk on the road. I'll toss these shoes in the trash when I get back to the station, he decided.

The next pickup that rocketed over the hill was doing at least fifty. Romero scrambled into his cruiser, flicked on his siren, and stopped the truck just after it ran a red light at Cordova Street.

He was forty-two. He'd been a Santa Fe policeman for fifteen years, but the thirty thousand dollars he earned each year wasn't enough for him to afford a house in Santa Fe's high-priced real-estate market, so he lived in the neighboring town of Pecos, twenty miles northeast, where his parents and grandparents had lived before him. Indeed, he lived in the same house that his parents had owned before a drunk driver, speeding the wrong way on the Interstate, had hit their car head-on and killed them. The modest structure had once been in a quiet neighborhood, but six months earlier, a supermarket had been built a block away, the resultant traffic noise and congestion blighting the area. Romero had married when he was twenty. His wife worked for an Allstate Insurance agent in Pecos. Their twenty-two-year-old son lived at home and wasn't employed. Each morning, Romero argued with him about looking for work. That was followed by a different argument in which Romero's wife complained he was being too hard on the boy. Typically, he and his wife left the house not speaking to each other. Once trim and athletic, the star of his high-school football team, Romero was puffy in the face and stomach from too much takeout food and too much time spent behind a steering wheel. This morning, he'd noticed that his sideburns were turning gray.

By the time he finished with the speeding pickup truck, a house burglary he was sent to investigate, and a purse snatcher he managed to catch, Romero had forgotten about the shoes. A fight between two feuding neighbors who happened to cross paths with each other in a restaurant parking lot further distracted him. He completed his paperwork at the police station, attended an after-shift debriefing, and didn't need much convincing to go out for a beer with a fellow officer rather than muster the resolve to make the half-hour drive to the tensions of his home. He got in at ten, long after his wife and son had eaten. His son was out with friends. His wife was in bed. He ate leftover fajitas while watching a rerun of a situation comedy that hadn't been funny the first time.

The next morning, as he crested the hill by the Baptist church, he came to attention at the sight of a pair of loafers scattered along the median. After steering sharply onto the shoulder, he opened the door and held up his hands for traffic to stop while he went over, picked up the loafers, returned to the cruiser, and set them in the trunk beside the jogging shoes.

'Shoes?' his sergeant asked back at the station. 'What are you talking about?'

'Over on Old Pecos Trail. Every morning, there's a pair of shoes,' Romero said.

'They must have fallen off a garbage truck.'

'Every morning? And only shoes, nothing else? Besides, the ones I found this morning were almost new.'

'Maybe somebody was moving and they fell off the back of a pickup truck.'

'Every morning?' Romero repeated. 'These were Cole Hahns. Expensive loafers like that don't get thrown on top of a load of stuff in a pickup truck.'

'What difference does it make? It's only shoes. Maybe somebody's kidding around.'

'Sure,' Romero said. 'Somebody's kidding around.'

'A practical joke,' the sergeant said. 'So people will wonder why the shoes are on the road. Hey, *you* wondered. The joke's working.'

'Yeah,' Romero said. 'A practical joke.'

The next morning, it was a battered pair of Timberland work boots. As Romero crested the hill by the Baptist church, he wasn't surprised to see them. In fact, the only thing he'd been uncertain about was what type of footwear they would be.

If this is a practical joke, it's certainly working, he thought.

Whoever's doing it is awfully persistent. Who . . .

The problem nagged at him all day. Between investigating a hit-and-run on St Francis Drive and a break-in at an art gallery on Canyon Road, he returned to the crest of the hill on Old Pecos Trail several times, making sure that other shoes hadn't appeared. For all he knew, the joker was dumping the shoes during the daytime. If so, the plan Romero was thinking about would be worthless. But after the eighth time he returned and still didn't see more shoes, he told himself he had a chance.

The plan had the merit of simplicity. All it required was determination, and of that he had plenty. Besides, it would be a good reason to postpone going home. So after getting a quarter-pounder and fries, a Coke and two large containers of coffee from McDonald's, he headed toward Old Pecos Trail as dusk thickened. He used his private car, a five-year-old dark blue Jeep Cherokee – no sense in being conspicuous. He considered establishing his stakeout in the Baptist church's parking lot. That would give him a great view of Old Pecos Trail. But at night, with his car the only one in the lot, he'd be conspicuous. Across from the church, though, East Lupita Road intersected with Old Pecos Trail. It was a quiet residential area, and if he parked there, he couldn't be seen by anyone driving along Old Pecos. In contrast, he himself would have a good view of passing traffic.

It can work, he thought. There were street lights on Old Pecos Trail but not on East Lupita. Sitting in darkness, munching on his quarter-pounder and fries, using the caffeine in the Coke and the two coffees to keep him alert, he concentrated on the illuminated crest of the hill. For a while, the headlights of passing cars were frequent and distracting. After each vehicle passed, he stared toward the area of the road that interested him, but no sooner did he focus on that spot than more headlights sped past, and he had to stare harder to see if anything had been dropped. He had his right hand ready to turn the ignition key and yank the gearshift into forward, his right foot primed to stomp the accelerator. To relax, he turned on the radio for fifteen-minute stretches, careful that he didn't weaken the battery. Then traffic became sporadic, making it easy to watch the road. But after an eleven o'clock news report in which the main item was about a fire in a store at the De

Vargas mall, he realized the flaw in his plan. All that caffeine. The tension of straining to watch the road.

He had to go to the bathroom.

But I went when I picked up the food.

That was then. Those were two large coffees you drank.

Hey, I had to keep awake.

He squirmed. He tensed his abdominal muscles. He would have relieved himself into one of the beverage containers, but he had crumpled all three of them when he stuffed them into the bag the quarter-pounder and fries had come in. His bladder ached. Headlights passed. No shoes were dropped. He pressed his thighs together. More headlights. No shoes. He turned his ignition key, switched on his headlights, and hurried toward the nearest public restroom, which was five blocks away on St Michael's Drive at an all-night gas station.

When he got back, two cowboy boots were on the road.

"It's almost one in the morning. Why are you coming home so late?'

Romero told his wife about the shoes.

'Shoes? Are you crazy?'

'Haven't you ever been curious about something?'

'Yeah, right now I'm curious why you think I'm stupid enough to believe you're coming home so late because of some old shoes you found on the road. Have you got a girlfriend, is that it?'

'You don't look so good,' his sergeant said.

Romero shrugged despondently.

'You been out all night, partying?' the sergeant joked.

'Don't I wish.'

The sergeant became serious. 'What is it? More trouble at home?'

Romero almost told him the whole story, but remembering the sergeant's indifference when he'd earlier been told about the shoes, Romero knew he wouldn't get much sympathy. Maybe the opposite. 'Yeah, more trouble at home.'

After all, what he'd done last night was, he had to admit, a little strange. Using his free time to sit in a car for three hours, waiting for . . . If a practical joker wanted to keep tossing shoes on the road, so what? Let the guy waste his time. Why waste my own time trying to catch him? There were too many real crimes to be investigated. What am I going to charge the guy with? Littering?

Throughout his shift, Romero made a determined effort not to go near Old Pecos Trail. A couple of times during a busy day of interviewing witnesses about an assault, a break-in, another purse snatching, and a near-fatal car accident on Paseo de Peralta, he was close enough to have swung past Old Pecos Trail on his way from one incident to another, but he deliberately chose an alternate route. Time to change patterns, he told himself. Time to concentrate on what's important.

At the end of his shift, his lack of sleep the previous night caught up to him. He left work, exhausted. Hoping for a quiet evening at home, he followed congested traffic through the dust of the eternal construction project on Cerrillos Road, reached Interstate 25, and headed north. Sunset on the Sangre de Cristo mountains tinted them the blood color for which the early Spanish colonists had named them. In a half-hour I'll have my feet up and be drinking a beer, he thought. He passed the exit to St Francis Drive. A sign told him that the next exit, the one for Old Pecos Trail, was two miles ahead. He blocked it from his mind, continued to admire the sunset, imagined the beer he was going to drink, and turned on the radio. A weather report told him that the high for the day had been seventy-five, typical for mid-May, but that a cold front was coming in and that the night temperature could drop as much as forty degrees, with a threat of frost in low-lying areas. The announcer suggested covering any recently purchased plants and . . .

Romero took the Old Pecos Trail exit.

Just for the hell of it, he thought. Just to have a look and settle my curiosity. What can it hurt? As he crested the hill, he was surprised to notice that his heart was beating a little faster. Do I really expect to find more shoes? he asked himself. Is it going to annoy me that they were here all day and I didn't come over to check? Pressure built in his chest as that section came into view. He breathed deeply . . .

And exhaled when he saw that there wasn't anything on the road. There, he told himself. It was worth the detour. I proved that I'd have wasted my time if I drove over here during my shift. I can go home now without being bugged that I didn't satisfy my curiosity.

But all the time he and his wife sat watching television while they ate Kentucky Fried Chicken (their son was out with friends), Romero felt restless. He couldn't stop thinking that whoever was dumping the shoes would do so again. The bastard will think he's outsmarted me. You? What are you talking about? He doesn't have the faintest idea who you are. Well, he'll think he's outsmarted whoever's picking up the shoes. The difference is the same.

The beer Romero had looked forward to tasted like water.

And of course the next morning, damn it, there was a pair of women's tan pumps five yards away from each other along the median. Scowling, Romero blocked morning traffic, picked up the pumps, and set them in the trunk with the others. Where the hell is this guy getting the shoes? he thought. These pumps are almost new. So are the loafers I picked up the other day. Who throws out perfectly good shoes, even for a practical joke?

When Romero was done for the day, he phoned his wife to tell her, 'I have to work late. One of the guys on the evening shift got sick. I'm filling in.' He caught up on some paperwork he needed to do. Then he went to a nearby Pizza Hut and got a medium pepperoni with mushrooms and black olives, to go. He also got a large Coke and two large coffees, but this time he'd learned his lesson and came prepared with an empty plastic gallon jug he could urinate in. More, he brought a Walkman and earphones so he wouldn't have to use the car's radio and worry about wearing down the battery.

Confident that he hadn't forgotten anything, he drove to the stakeout. Santa Fe had its share of dirt roads, and East Lupita was one of them. Flanked by chamisa bushes and Russian olive trees, it had widely spaced adobe houses and got very little traffic. Parked near the corner, Romero saw the church across from him, its bell tower reminding him of a pueblo mission. Beyond were the pinon-dotted Sun Mountain and Atalaya Ridge, the sunset as vividly blood-colored as it had been the previous evening.

Traffic passed. Studying it, he put on his headphones and switched the Walkman from CD to radio. After finding a call-in show (Was the environment truly as threatened as ecologists claimed?), he sipped his Coke, dug into his pizza, and settled back to watch traffic.

An hour after dark, he realized that he had indeed forgotten something. The previous day's weather report had warned about low night temperatures, possibly even a frost, and now Romero felt a chill creep up his legs. He was grateful for the warm coffee. He hugged his chest, wishing he'd brought a jacket. His breath vapor clouded the windshield so much that he had to use a handkerchief to clear it. He rolled down his window, and that helped control his breath vapor, but it also allowed more cold to enter the vehicle, making him shiver. Moonlight reflected off lingering snow on the mountains, especially at the ski basin, and that made him feel even colder. He turned on the Jeep and used its heater to warm him. All the while, he concentrated on the dwindling traffic.

Eleven o'clock, and still no shoes. He kept reminding himself that it had been about this hour two nights earlier when he'd been forced to leave to find a restroom. When he'd returned twenty minutes later, he'd found the cowboy boots. If whoever was doing this followed a pattern, there was a good chance something would happen in the next half-hour.

Stay patient, he thought.

But the same as had happened two nights earlier, the Coke and the coffees finally had their effect. Fortunately, he had that problem taken care of. He grabbed the empty gallon jug from the seat beside him, twisted its cap off, positioned the jug beneath the steering wheel, and started to urinate, only to squint from the headlights of a car that approached behind him, reflecting in his rearview mirror.

His bladder muscles tensed, interrupting the flow of urine. Jesus, he thought. Although he was certain the driver wouldn't be able to see what he was doing, he felt selfconscious enough that he quickly capped the jug and set it on the passenger floor.

Come on, he told the approaching car. He needed to urinate as bad as ever and urged the car to pass him, to turn onto Old Pecos Trail and leave, so he could grab the jug again.

The headlights stopped behind him.

What in God's name? Romero thought.

Then rooflights began to flash, and Romero realized that what was behind him was a police car. Ignoring his urgent need to urinate, he rolled down his window and placed his hands on top of the steering wheel, where the approaching officer, not knowing who was in the car or what he was getting into, would be relieved to see them.

Footsteps crunched on the dirt road. A blinding flashlight scanned the inside of Romero's car, assessing the empty pizza box, lingering over the yellow liquid in the plastic jug. 'Sir, may I see your license and registration please?'

Romero recognized the voice. 'It's okay, Tony. It's me.'

'Who . . . Gabe?'

The flashlight beam hurt Romero's eyes.

'*Gabe?*'

'The one and only.'

'What the hell are you doing out here? We had several complaints about somebody suspicious sitting in a car, like he was casing the houses in the neighborhood.'

'It's only me.'

'Were you here two nights ago?'

'Yes.'

'We had complaints then, too, but when we got here, the car was gone. What are you doing?'

Trying not to squirm from the pressure of his abdomen, Romero said, 'I'm on a stakeout.'

'Nobody told me about any stakeout. What's going on?'

Realizing how long it would take to explain the odd-sounding truth, Romero said, 'They've been having some attempted break-ins over at the church. I'm watching to see if whoever's been doing it comes back.'

'Man, sitting out here all night – this is some piss-poor assignment they gave you.'

'You have no idea.'

'Well, I'll leave before I draw any more attention to you. Good hunting.'

'Thanks.'

'And next time, tell the shift commander to let the rest of us know what's going on so we don't screw things up.'

'I'll make a point of it.'

The officer got back in his cruiser, turned off the flashing lights, passed Romero's car, waved, and steered onto Old Pecos Trail. Instantly, Romero grabbed the plastic jug and urinated for what seemed a minute and a half. When he finished and leaned back, sighing, his sense of relaxation lasted only as long as it took him to study Old Pecos Trail again.

The next thing, he scrambled out of his car and ran cursing toward a pair of men's shoes – they turned out to be Rockports – lying laced together in the middle of the road.

'Did you tell Tony Ortega you'd been ordered to stake out the Baptist church?' his sergeant demanded.

Romero reluctantly nodded.

'What kind of bullshit? Nobody put you on any stakeout. Sitting in a car all night, acting suspicious. You'd better have a damned good reason for—'

Romero didn't have a choice. 'The shoes.'

'What?'

'The shoes I keep finding on Old Pecos Trail.'

His eyes wide, the sergeant listened to Romero's explanation. 'You don't put in enough hours? You want to donate a couple nights' free overtime on some crazy—'

'Hey, I know it's a little unusual.'

'A *little*?'

'Whoever's dumping those shoes is playing some kind of game.'

'And you want to play it with him.'

'What?'

'He leaves the shoes. You take them. He leaves more shoes. You take them. You're playing his game.'

'No, it isn't like that.'

'Well, what *is* it like? Listen to me. Quit hanging around that street. Somebody might shoot you for a prowler.'

When Romero finished his shift, he found a dozen old shoes piled in front of his locker. Somebody laughed in the lunch room.

★ ★ ★

'I'm Officer Romero, ma'am, and I guess I made you a little nervous last night and two nights earlier. I was in my car, watching the church across the street. We had a report that somebody might try to break in. It seems you thought *I'm* the one who might try breaking in. I just wanted to assure you the neighborhood's perfectly safe with me parked out there.'

'I'm Officer Romero, sir, and I guess I made you a little nervous last night and two nights earlier . . .'

This time, he had everything under control. No more large Cokes and coffees, although he did keep his plastic jug, just in case. He made sure to bring a jacket, although the frost danger had finally passed and the night temperature was warmer. He was trying to eat better, too, munching on a *burrito grande con pollo* from Felipe's, the best Mexican takeout in town. He settled back and listened to the radio call-in show on the Walkman. The program was still on the environmental theme: 'Hey, man, I used to be able to swim in the rivers when I was a kid. I used to be able to eat the fish I caught in them. I'd be nuts to do that now.'

It was just after dark. The headlights of a car went past. No shoes. No problem. Romero was ready to be patient. He was in a rhythm. Nothing would probably happen until it usually did – after eleven. The Walkman's earphones pinched his head. He took them off and readjusted them as headlights sped past, heading to the right, out of town. Simultaneously, a different pair of headlights rushed past, heading to the left, *into* town. Romero's window was down. Despite the sound of the engines, he heard a distinct *thunk*, then another. The vehicles were gone, and he gaped at two hiking boots on the road.

Holy . . .

Move! He twisted the ignition key and yanked the gearshift into drive. Breathless, he urged the car forward, its rear tires spewing stones and dirt, but as he reached Old Pecos Trail, he faced a hurried decision. Which driver had dropped the shoes? Which car? Right or left?

He didn't have any jurisdiction out of town. Left! His tires

squealing on the pavement, he sped towards the receding tail
lights. The road dipped, then rose toward the stop light at Cordova, which was red and which Romero hoped would stay that
way, but as he sped closer to what he now saw was a pickup truck,
the light changed to green, and the truck drove through the
intersection.

Shit.

Romero had an emergency light on the passenger seat. Shaped
like a dome, it was plugged into the cigarette lighter. He thrust it
out the window and onto the roof, where its magnetic base held it
in place. Turning it on, seeing the reflection of its flashing red
light, he pressed harder on the accelerator. He sped through the
intersection, rushed up behind the pickup truck, blared his horn,
and nodded when the truck went slower, angling toward the side of
the road.

Romero wasn't in uniform, but he did have his 9mm Beretta in a
holster on his belt. He made sure that his badge was clipped onto
the breast pocket of his denim jacket. He aimed his flashlight
toward a load of rocks in the back of the truck, then carefully
approached the driver. 'License and registration, please.'

'What seems to be the trouble, Officer?' The driver was Anglo,
young, about twenty-three. Thin. With short sandy hair. Wearing a
red-and-brown-checked work shirt. Even sitting, he was tall.

'You were going awfully fast coming over that hill by the
church.'

The young man glanced back, as if to remind himself that
there'd been a hill.

'License and registration.' Romero repeated.

'I'm sure I wasn't going more than the speed limit,' the young
man said. 'It's forty there, isn't it?' He handed over his license and
pulled the registration from a pouch on the sun visor above his
head.

Romero read the name. 'Luke Parsons.'

'Yes, sir.' The young man's voice was reedy, with a gentle
politeness.

'PO Box 25, Dillon, New Mexico?' Romero asked.

'Yes, sir. That's about fifty miles north. Up past Espanola and
Embudo and—'

'I know where Dillon is. What brings you down here?'

'Selling moss rocks at the roadside stand off the Interstate.'

Romero nodded. The rocks in the back of the truck were valued locally for their use in landscaping. The lichen that speckled them turned pleasant muted colors after a rain. Hardscrabble vendors gathered them in the mountains and sold them, along with home-made bird houses, self-planed roof-support beams, firewood, and vegetables in season, at a clearing off a country road that paralleled the Interstate.

'Awful far from Dillon to be selling moss rocks,' Romero said.

'Have to go where the customers are. Really, what's this all a—'

'You're selling after dark?'

'I wait until dusk in case folks coming out of Harry's Road House or the steak house farther along decide to stop and buy something. Then I go over to Harry's and get something to eat. Love his barbecued vegetables.'

This wasn't how Romero had expected the conversation to go. He'd anticipated that the driver would look uneasy because he'd lost the game. But the young man's politeness was disarming.

'I want to talk to you about those shoes you threw out of the car. There's a heavy fine for—'

'Shoes?'

'You've been doing it for several days. I want to know why—'

'Officer, honestly, I haven't the faintest idea what you're talking about.'

'The shoes I saw you throw onto the road.'

'Believe me, whatever you saw happen, it wasn't me doing it. Why would I throw shoes on the road?'

The young man's blue eyes were direct, his candid look disarming. Damn it, Romero thought, I went after the wrong car.

Inwardly, he sighed.

He gave back the license and registration. 'Sorry to bother you.'

'No problem, Officer. I know you have to do your job.'

'Going all the way back to Dillon tonight?'

'Yes, sir.'

'As I said, it's a long way to travel to sell moss rocks.'

'Well, we do what we have to do.'

'That's for sure,' Romero said. 'Drive safely.'

'I always do, Officer. Good night.'

'Good night.'

Romero drove back to the top of the hill, picked up the hiking shoes, and put them in the trunk of his car. It was about that time, a little before ten, that his son was killed.

He passed the crash site on the way home to Pecos. Seeing the flashing lights and the silhouettes of two ambulances and three police cars on the opposite section of the Interstate, grimacing at the twisted wrecks of two vehicles, he couldn't help thinking, poor bastards. God help them. But God didn't, and by the time Romero got home, the medical examiner was showing the state police the wallet that he'd taken from the mutilated body of what seemed to be a young Hispanic male.

Romero and his wife were arguing about his late hours when the phone rang.

'Answer it!' she yelled. 'It's probably your damned girlfriend.'

'I keep telling you I don't have a—' The phone rang again. 'Yeah, hello.'

'Gabe? This is Ray Becker with the state police. Sit down, would you?'

As Romero listened, he felt a cold ball grow inside him. He had never felt so numb, not even when he'd been told about the deaths of his parents.

His wife saw his stunned look. *'What is it?'*

Trembling, he managed to overcome his numbness enough to tell her. She screamed. She never stopped screaming until she collapsed.

Two weeks later, after the funeral, after Romero's wife went to visit her sister in Denver, after Romero tried going back to work (his sergeant advised against it, but Romero knew he'd go crazy just sitting around home), the dispatcher sent him on a call that forced him to drive up Old Pecos Trail by the Baptist church. Bitterly, he remembered how fixated he had been on this spot not long ago. Instead of screwing around wondering about those shoes, I should have stayed home and paid attention to my son, he thought. Maybe I could have prevented what happened.

There weren't any shoes on the road.

There weren't any shoes on the road the next day or the day after that.

Romero's wife never came back from Denver.

'You have to get out more,' his sergeant told him.

It was three months later, the middle Saturday of August. As a part of the impending divorce settlement and as a way of trying to stifle memories, Romero had sold the house in Pecos. With his share of the proceeds, he'd moved to Santa Fe and risked a down payment on a modest house in the El Dorado subdivision. It didn't make a difference. He still had the sense of carrying a weight on his back.

'I hope you're not talking about dating.'

'I'm just saying, you can't stay holed up in this house all the time. You have to get out and do something. Distract yourself. While I think of it, you ought to be eating better. Look at the crap in this fridge. Stale milk, a twelve-pack of beer, and some leftover Chicken McNuggets.'

'Most of the time, I'm not hungry.'

'With a fridge like this, I don't doubt it.'

'I don't like cooking for myself.'

'It's too much effort to make a salad? I tell you what. Saturdays, Maria and I go to the Farmers' Market. Tomorrow morning, you come with us. The vegetables don't come any fresher. Maybe if you had some decent food in this fridge, you'd—'

'What's wrong with me the Farmers' Market isn't going to cure.'

'Hey, I'm knocking myself out trying to be a friend. The least you can do is humor me.'

The Farmers' Market was near the old train station, past the tracks, in an open area the city had recently purchased, called the Rail Yard. Farmers drove their loaded pickups in and parked in spaces they'd been assigned. Some set up tables and put up awnings. Others just sold from the back of their trucks. There were taste samples of everything from pies to salsa. A blue-grass band played in a corner. Somebody dressed up as a clown wandered through the crowd.

'See, it's not so bad,' the sergeant said.

Romero walked listlessly past stands of cider, herbal remedies, free-range chicken, and sunflower sprouts. In a detached way, he had to admit, 'Yeah, not so bad.' All the years he'd worked for the police department, he'd never been here – another example of how he'd let his life pass him by. But instead of motivating him to learn from his mistakes, his regret only made him more depressed.

'How about some of these little pies?' the sergeant's wife asked. 'You can keep them in the freezer and heat one up when you feel like it. They're only one or two servings, so you won't have any leftovers.'

'Sure,' Romero said, not caring. 'Why not?' His dejected gaze drifted over the crowd.

'What kind?'

'Excuse me?'

'What kind? Peach or butter pecan?'

'It doesn't matter. Choose some for me.'

His gaze settled on a stand that offered religious icons made out of corn husks layered over carved wood: Madonnas, manger scenes, and crosses. The skillfully formed images were painted and covered with a protective layer of varnish. It was a traditional Hispanic folk art, but what caught Romero's attention wasn't the attractiveness of the images but rather that an Anglo instead of an Hispanic was selling them as if he'd made them.

'This apple pie looks good too,' the sergeant's wife said.

'Fine.' Assessing the tall, thin, sandy-haired man selling the icons, Romero added, 'I know that guy from somewhere.'

'What?' the sergeant's wife asked.

'Nothing. I'll be back in a second to get the pies.' Romero made his way through the crowd. The young man's fair hair was extremely short. His thin face emphasized his cheekbones, making him look as if he'd been fasting. He had an esthetic quality similar to that on the faces of the icons he was selling. Not that he looked ill. The opposite. His tan skin glowed.

His voice, too, seemed familiar. As Romero approached, he heard the reedy, gentle tone in which the young man explained to a customer the intricate care with which the icons were created.

Romero waited until the customer walked off with her purchase.

'Yes, sir?'

'I know you from somewhere, but I just can't seem to place you.'

'I wish I could help you, but I don't think we've met.'

Romero noticed the small crystal that hung from a woven cord on the young man's neck. It had a hint of pale blue in it, as if borrowing some of the blue in the young man's eyes. 'Maybe you're right. It's just that you seem so awfully—'

Movement to his right distracted him, a young man carrying a large basket of tomatoes from a pickup truck and setting it next to baskets of cucumbers, peppers, squash, carrots, on a stand next to this one.

But more than the movement distracted him. The young man was tall and thin, with short sandy hair, and a lean esthetic face. He had clear blue eyes that seemed to lend some of their color to the small crystal hanging from his neck. He wore faded jeans and a white tee-shirt, the same as the young man to whom Romero had been talking. The white of the shirt emphasized his glowing tan.

'You *are* right,' Romero told the first man. 'We haven't met. Your brother's the one I met.'

The newcomer looked puzzled.

'It's true, isn't it? Romero asked. 'The two of you are brothers? That's why I got confused. But I still can't remember where—'

'Luke Parsons.' The newcomer extended his hand.

'Gabe Romero.'

The young man's forearm was sinewy, his handshake firm.

Romero needed all his discipline and training not to react, his mind reeling as he remembered. Luke Parsons? Christ, this was the man he'd spoken to the night his son had been killed and his life had fallen apart. To distract himself from his memories, he had come to this market, only to find someone who reminded him of what he was desperately trying to forget.

'And this is my brother Mark.'

'. . . Hello.'

'Say, are you feeling all right?'

'Why? What do you—'

'You turned pale all of a sudden.'

'It's nothing. I just haven't been eating well lately.'

'Then you ought to try this.' Luke Parsons pointed toward a

small bottle filled with brown liquid.

Romero narrowed his eyes. 'What is it?'

'Home-grown echinacea. If you've got a virus, this'll take care of you. Boosts your immune system.'

'Thanks, but—'

'When you feel how dramatically it picks you up—'

'You make it sound like drugs.'

'God's drug. Nothing false. If it doesn't improve your well-being, we'll give you a refund.'

'There you are,' Romero's sergeant said. 'I've been looking all over for you.' He noticed the bottle in Romero's hand. 'What's *that*?'

'Something called home-grown . . .' The word eluded him.

'Echinacea,' Luke Parsons said.

'Sure,' the sergeant's wife said. 'I use it when we get colds. Boosts the immune system. Works like a charm. Lord, these tomatoes look wonderful.'

As she started buying, Luke told Romero, 'When your appetite's off, it can mean your body needs to be detoxified. These cabbage, broccoli, and cauliflower are good for that. Completely organic. No chemicals of any kind ever went near them. And you might try *this*.' He handed Romero a small bottle of white liquid.

'Milk thistle,' the sergeant's wife said, glancing at the bottle while selecting green peppers. 'Cleans out the liver.'

'Where on earth did you learn about this stuff?' the sergeant asked.

'Rosa down the street got interested in herbal remedies,' she explained later as the three of them crossed the train tracks, carrying sacks of vegetables. 'Hey, this is Santa Fe, the world's capital of alternate medicines and New Age religions. If you can't beat 'em, join 'em.'

'Yeah, those crystals around their necks. They're New Agers for sure,' Romero said. 'Did you notice their belts were made of hemp? No leather. Nothing from animals.'

'No fried chicken and takeout burgers for those guys.' The sergeant gave Romero a pointed look. 'They're as healthy as can be.'

'All right, okay, I get it.'
'Just make sure you eat your greens.'

The odd part was that he actually did start feeling better. Physically, at least. His emotions were still as bleak as midnight, but as one of the self-help books he'd read advised, 'One way to heal yourself is from the body to the soul.' The echinacea (ten drops in a glass of water, the typed directions said) tasted bitter. The milk thistle tasted worse. The salads didn't fill him up. He still craved a pepperoni pizza. But he had to admit, the vegetables at the Farmers' Market were as good as any he'd come across. No surprise. The only vegetables he'd eaten before came from a supermarket, where they'd sat for God knew how long, and that didn't count all the time they'd been in a truck on the way to the store. They'd probably been picked before they were ready so they wouldn't ripen until they reached the supermarket, and then there was the issue of how many pesticides and herbicides they'd been doused with. He remembered a radio call-in show that had talked about poisons in food. The program had dealt with similar problems in the environment and—

Romero shivered.

The program had been the one he'd listened to in his car the night he'd been waiting for the shoes to drop and his son had been killed.

Screw it. If I'm going to feel this bad, I'm going to eat what I want.

It took him only fifteen minutes to drive in from El Dorado and get a big takeout order of ribs, fries, coleslaw, and plenty of barbecue sauce. He never ate in restaurants anymore. Too many people knew him. He couldn't muster the energy for small talk. Another fifteen minutes, and he was back at home, watching a lawyer show, drinking beer, gnawing on ribs.

He was sick before the ten o'clock news.

'I swear, I'm keeping to my diet. Hey, don't look at me like that. I admit I had a couple of relapses, but I learned my lesson. I've never eaten more wholesome food in my life.'

★　★　★

207

'Fifteen pounds. That health club I joined really sweats the weight off.'

'Hi, Mark.'

The tall, thin, sandy-hair young man behind the vegetables looked puzzled at him.

'What's wrong?' Romero asked. 'I've been coming to this market every Saturday for the past six weeks. You don't recognize me by now?'

'You've confused me with my brother.' The man had blue eyes, a hint of their color in the crystal around his neck. Jeans, a white tee-shirt, a glowing tan, and the thin-faced, high-cheekboned esthetic look of a saint.

'Well, I know you're not Luke. I'm sure I'd recognize *him*.'

'My name is John.' His tone was formal.

'Pleased to meet you. I'm Gabe Romero. Nobody told me there were *three* brothers.'

'Actually—'

'Wait a minute. Let me guess. If there's a Mark, Luke and John, there's got to be a Matthew, right? I bet there are *four* of you.'

John's lips parted slightly, as if he wasn't accustomed to smiling. 'Very good.'

'No big deal. It's my business to deduce things.' Romero joked.

'Oh? And what business is—' John straightened, his blue eyes as cold as a star, watching Luke come through the crowd. 'You were told not to leave the stand.'

'I'm sorry. I had to go to the bathroom.'

'You should have gone before we started out.'

'I did. But I can't help it if—'

'That's right. You can't help me if you're not here. We're almost out of squash. Bring another basket.'

'I'm really sorry. It won't happen again.'

Luke glanced selfconsciously at Romero, then back at his brother, and went to get the squash.

'Are you planning to buy something?' John asked.

You don't exactly win friends and influence people, do you? Romero thought. 'Yeah, I'll take a couple of those squash. I guess with the early frost that's predicted, these'll be the last of the tomatoes and peppers, huh?'

John simply looked at him.

'I'd better stock up,' Romero said.

He'd hoped that the passage of time would ease his numbness, but each season only reminded him. Christmas, New Year's, then Easter, and too soon after that, the middle of May. Oddly, he'd never associated his son's death with the scene of the accident on the Interstate. Always the emotional connection was with that section of road by the Baptist church at the top of the hill on Old Pecos Trail. He readily admitted that it was masochism that made him drive by there so often as the anniversary of the death approached. He was so preoccupied that for a moment he was convinced that he'd willed himself into reliving the sequence, that he was hallucinating as he crested the hill and for the first time in almost a year saw a pair of shoes on the road.

Rust-colored, ankle-high hiking boots. They so surprised him that he slowed down and stared. The close look made him notice something so alarming that he slammed on his brakes, barely registering the squeal of tires behind him as the car that followed almost hit the cruiser. Trembling, he got out, crouched, stared even more closely at the hiking boots, and rushed toward his two-way radio.

The shoes had feet in them.

As an approaching police car wailed and officers motioned for traffic to go past on the shoulder of the road, Romero stood with his sergeant, the police chief, and the medical examiner, watching the lab crew do its work. His cruiser remained where he'd stopped it next to the shoes. A waist-high screen had been put up.

'I'll know more when we get the evidence to the lab,' the medical examiner said, 'but judging from the straight clean lines, I think something like a power saw was used to sever the feet from the legs.'

Romero bit his lower lip.

'Anything else you can tell us right away?' the police chief asked.

'There isn't any blood on the pavement, which means that the blood on the shoes and the stumps of the feet was dry before they were dropped here. The discoloration of the tissue suggests that at least twenty-four hours passed between the crime and the dis-posal.'

'Anybody notice anything else?'

'The size of the shoes,' Romero said.

They looked at him.

'Mine are tens. These look to be sevens or eights. My guess is, the victim was female.'

The same police officers who'd left the pile of old shoes in front of Romero's locker now praised his instincts. Although he had long since discarded the various shoes that he'd collected, no one blamed him. After all, so much time had gone by, who could have predicted the shoes would be important? Still, he remembered what kind they'd been, just as he remembered that he'd started noticing them almost exactly a year ago, around 15 May.

But there was no guarantee that the person who'd dropped the shoes a year ago was the person who'd left the severed feet. All the investigating team could do was deal with the little evidence they had. As Romero suspected, the medical examiner eventually deter-mined that the victim had indeed been a woman. Was the person responsible a tourist, someone who came back to Santa Fe each May? If so, would that person have committed similar crimes somewhere else? Inquiries to the FBI revealed that over the years numerous murders by amputation had been committed through-out the US, but none matched the profile that the team was dealing with. What about missing persons reports? Those in New Mexico were checked and eliminated, but as the search spread, it became clear that so many thousands of people disappeared in the US each month that the investigation team would need more staff than it could ever hope to have.

Meanwhile, Romero was part of the team staking out that area of Old Pecos Trail. Each night, he used a night-vision telescope to watch from the roof of the Baptist church. After all, if the killer stayed to his pattern, other shoes would be dropped, and perhaps – God help us, Romero thought – they too would contain severed feet. If he saw anything suspicious, all he needed to do was focus on the car's license plate and then use his two-way radio to alert police cars hidden along Old Pecos Trail. But night after night, there was nothing to report.

A week later, a current-model red Saturn with New Hampshire plates was found abandoned in an arroyo southeast of Albuquerque. The car was registered to a thirty-year-old woman named Susan Crowell, who had set out with her fiancé on a cross-country car tour three weeks earlier. Neither she nor her fiancé had contacted their friends and relatives in the past eight days.

May became June, then July. The Fourth of July pancake breakfast in the historic Plaza was its usual success. Three weeks later, the Spanish Market occupied the same space, local Hispanic artisans displaying their paintings, icons, and woodwork. Tourist attendance was down, the sensationalist publicity about the severed feet having discouraged some visitors from coming. But a month after that, the similar but larger Indian Market occurred, and memories were evidently short, for now the usual thirty thousand tourists thronged the Plaza to admire Native American jewelry and pottery.

Romero was on duty for all of these events, making sure everything proceeded in an orderly fashion. Still, no matter the tasks assigned to him, his mind was always back on Old Pecos Trail. Some nights, he couldn't stay away. He drove over to East Lupita, watched the passing headlights on Old Pecos Trail, and brooded. He didn't expect anything to happen, not as fall approached, but being there made him feel on top of things, helped focus his thoughts, and in an odd way gave him a sense of being close to his son. Sometimes, the presence of the church across the street made him pray.

One night, a familiar pickup truck filled with moss rocks drove by. Romero remembered it from the night his son had been killed and from so many summer Saturdays when he'd watched baskets of vegetables being carried from it to a stand at the Farmers' Market. He had never stopped associating it with the shoes. Granted, at the time he'd been certain he'd stopped the wrong vehicle. He didn't have a reason to take the huge step of suspecting that Luke Parsons had anything to do with the murders of Susan Crowell and her fiancé. Nonetheless, he'd told the investigation team about that night the previous year, and they'd checked Luke out as thoroughly as possible. He and his three brothers lived with their father on a farm in the Rio Grande gorge north of Dillon. They were hard workers, kept to themselves, and stayed out of trouble.

Seeing the truck pass, Romero didn't have a reason to make it stop, but that didn't mean he couldn't follow it. He pulled onto Old Pecos Drive and kept the truck's tail lights in view as it headed into town. It turned right at the state capitol building and proceeded along Paseo de Peralta until on the other side of town it steered into an Allsup's gas station.

Romero chose a pump near the pickup truck, got out of his Jeep, and pretended to be surprised by the man next to him.

'Luke, it's Gabe Romero. How are you?'

Then he *was* surprised, realizing his mistake. This wasn't Luke.

'*John?* I didn't recognize you.'

The tall, thin, sandy-haired, somber-eyed young man assessed him. He lowered his eyes to the holstered pistol on Romero's hip. Romero had never worn it to the Farmers' Market. 'I didn't realize you were a police officer.'

'Does it matter?'

'Only that it's reassuring to know my vegetables are safe when you're around.' John's stern features took the humor out of the joke.

'Or your moss rocks.' Romero pointed toward the back of the truck. 'Been selling them over on that country road by the Interstate? That's usually Luke's job.'

'Well, he has other things to do.'

'Yeah, now that I think of it, I haven't seen him at the market lately.'

'Excuse me. It's been a long day. It's a long drive back.'

'You bet. I didn't mean to keep you.'

Luke wasn't at the Farmers' Market the next Sunday, or the final one the week after that.

Late October. There'd been a killing frost the night before, and in the morning there was snow in the mountains. Since the Farmers'

Market was closed for the year and Romero had his Saturday free, he thought, Why don't I take a little drive?

The sunlight was cold, crisp, and clear as Romero headed north along Highway 285. He crested the hill near the modernistic Sante Fe Opera House and descended from the juniper-and-pinon-dotted slopes of town into a multicolored desert, its draws and mesas stretching dramatically away toward white-capped mountains on each side. No wonder Hollywood made so many westerns here, he thought. He passed the Camel Rock Indian Casino and the Cities of Gold Indian Casino, reaching what had once been another eternal construction project, the huge interchange that led west to Los Alamos.

But instead of heading toward the atomic city, he continued north, passing through Espanola, and now the landscape changed again, the hills on each side coming closer, the narrow highway passing between the ridges of the Rio Grande gorge. WATCH OUT FOR FALLING ROCK, a sign said. Yeah, I intend to watch out, he thought. On his left, partially screened by leafless trees, was the legendary Rio Grande, narrow, taking its time in the fall, gliding around curves, bubbling over boulders. On the far side of the river was Embudo Station, an old stagecoach stop the historic buildings of which had been converted into a microbrewery and a restaurant.

He passed it, heading farther north, and now the gorge began to widen. Farms and vineyards appeared on both sides of the road, where silt from melting during the Ice Age had made the soil rich. He stopped in Dillon, took care that his handgun was concealed by his zipped-up windbreaker, and asked at the general store if anybody knew where he could find the Parsons farm.

Fifteen minutes later, he had the directions he wanted. But instead of going directly to the farm, he drove to a scenic view outside town and waited for a state police car to pull up beside him. During the morning's drive, he'd used his cellular phone to contact the state police barracks farther north in Taos. After explaining who he was, he'd persuaded the dispatcher to send a cruiser down to meet him

'I don't anticipate trouble,' Romero told the burly trooper as they stood outside their cars and watched the Rio Grande flow through a chasm beneath them. 'But you never know.'

'So what do you want me to do?'

'Just park at the side of the highway. Make sure I come back out of the farm.'

'Your department didn't send you up here?'

'Self-initiative. I've got a hunch.'

The trooper looked doubtful. 'How long are you going to be in there?'

'Considering how unfriendly they are, not long. Fifteen minutes. I just want to get a sense of the place.'

'If I get a call about an emergency down the road . . .'

'You'll have to go. But I'd appreciate it if you came back and made sure I left the property. On my way to Santa Fe, I'll stop at the general store in Dillon and leave word that I'm okay.'

The state trooper still looked doubtful.

'I've been working on this case a long time,' Romero said. 'Please, I'd really appreciate the help.'

The dirt road was just after a sign that read TAOS, 20 MILES. It was on the left of the highway and led down a slope toward fertile bottom land. To the north and west, ridges bordered the valley. Well-maintained rail fences enclosed rich black soil. The Parsonses were certainly hard workers, he had to admit. With cold weather about to arrive, the fields had been cleared, everything ready for spring.

The road headed west toward a barn and outbuildings, all of them neat looking, their white appearing freshly painted. A simple wood frame house, it white also, had a pitched metal roof that gleamed in the autumn sun. Beyond the house was the river, about thirty feet wide, with a raised footbridge leading across to leafless aspen trees and scrub brush trailing up a slope.

As he drove closer, Romero saw movement at the barn, someone getting off a ladder, putting down a paint can. Someone else appeared at the barn's open doors. A third person came out of the house. They were waiting in front of the house as Romero pulled up and stopped.

This was the first time he'd seen three of the brothers together, their tall, lean, sandy-haired, blue-eyed similarities even more striking. They wore the same denim coveralls with the same blue wool shirts underneath.

But Romero was well enough acquainted with them that he could tell one from another. The brother on the left, about nineteen, must be the one he'd never met.

'I assume you're Matthew.' Romero got out of the car and walked toward them, extending his hand.

No one made a move to shake hands with him.

'I don't see Luke,' Romero said.

'He has things to do,' John said.

Their features were pinched.

'Why did you come here?' Mark asked.

'I was driving up to Taos. While I was in the neighborhood, I thought I'd drop by and see if you had any vegetables for sale.'

'You're not welcome.'

'What kind of attitude is that? For somebody who's been as good a customer as I have, I thought you might be pleased to see me.'

'Leave.'

'But don't you want my business?'

'Matthew, go in the house and bring me the phone. I'm going to call the state police.'

The young man nodded and turned toward the house.

'That's fine,' Romero said. 'I'll be on my way.'

The trooper was at the highway when Romero drove out.

'Thanks for the backup.'

'You'd better not thank me. I just got a call about you. Whatever you did in there, you really pissed them off. The dispatcher says, if you come back, they want you arrested for trespassing.'

'. . . the city's attorney,' the police chief said.

The man's handshake was unenthusiastic.

'And this is Mr Daly, the attorney for Mr Parsons,' the chief said.

An even colder handshake.

'Mr Parsons you've definitely met,' the chief said.

Romero nodded to John.

'I'll get right to the point,' Daly said. 'You've been harassing my client, and we want it stopped.'

'Harassing? Wait a minute. I haven't been harassing—'

'Detaining the family vehicle without just cause. Intimidating my client and his brothers at their various places of business. Following my client. Confronting him in public places. Invading his property and refusing to leave when asked to. You crowd him just about everywhere he goes, and we want it stopped, or we'll sue both you and the city. Juries don't like rogue cops.'

'Rogue cop? What are you talking about?'

'I didn't come here to debate this.' Daly stood, motioning for John to do the same. 'My client's completely in the right. This isn't a police state. You, your department, and the city have been warned. Any more incidents, and I'll call a press conference to let every potential juror know why we're filing the law suit.'

With a final searing gaze, Daly left the room. John followed almost immediately but not before he gave Romero a victimized look that made Romero's face turn warm with anger.

The office became silent.

The city attorney cleared his throat. 'I don't suppose I have to tell you to stay away from him.'

'But I haven't done anything wrong.'

'Did you follow him? Did you go to his home? Did you ask the state police in Taos for backup when you entered the property?'

Romero looked away.

'You were out of your jurisdiction, acting completely on your own.'

'These brothers have something to do with—'

'They were investigated and cleared.'

'I can't explain. It's a feeling that keeps nagging at me.'

'Well, *I* have a feeling,' the attorney said. 'If you don't stop exceeding your authority, you're going to be out of a job, not to mention in court trying to explain to a jury why you harassed a group of brothers who look like advertisements for hard work and family values. Matthew, Mark, Luke, and John, for God's sake. If it wouldn't look like an admission of guilt, I'd recommend your dismissal right now.'

★　★　★

Romero got the worst assignments. If a snowstorm took out power at an intersection and traffic needed to be directed by hand, he was at the top of the list to do it. Anything that involved the outdoors and bad weather, he was the man. Obviously, the police chief was inviting him to quit.

But Romero had a secret defense. The heat that had flooded his face when John gave him that victimized look hadn't gone away. It had stayed and spread, possessing his body. Directing traffic in a foot of snow, with a raging storm, and a wind chill near zero? No problem. Anger made him as warm as could be.

John Parsons had arrogantly assumed he'd won. Romero was going to pay him back. May fifteenth. That was about the time the shoes had appeared two years ago, and the severed feet last year. The chief was planning some surveillance on that section of Old Pecos Trail, but nobody believed that if the killer planned to act again he'd be stupid enough to be that predictable. For certain, Romero wasn't going to be predictable. He wasn't going to play John's game and risk his job by hanging around Old Pecos Trail so John could drive by and claim that the harassment had started again. No, Old Pecos Trail didn't interest him anymore. On 15 May, he was going to be somewhere else.

Outside Dillon. In the Rio Grande gorge.

He planned it for quite a while. First, he had to explain his absence. A vacation. He hadn't taken one last year. San Francisco. He'd never been there. It was supposed to be especially beautiful in the spring. The chief looked pleased, as if he hoped Romero would look for a job there.

Second, his quarry knew the kind of car he drove. He traded his blue Jeep for a green Ford Explorer.

Third, he needed equipment. The night-vision telescope he'd used to watch Old Pecos Trail from the top of the church had made darkness so vivid that he bought a similar model from a military surplus store. He went to a camera store and bought a powerful zoom lens for the 35mm camera he had at home. Food and water for several days. Outdoor clothing. Something to carry everything in. Hiking shoes sturdy enough to support all the weight.

His vacation started on 13 May. When he'd last driven to Dillon, autumn had made the Rio Grande calm, but now the spring snow-melt widened and deepened it, cresting it into a rage. Green trees and shrubs bordered the foaming water as white-water rafters shot through roiling channels and jounced over hidden rocks. As he drove past the entrance to the Parsons farm, he worried that one of the brothers might drive out and notice him, but then he reminded himself that they didn't know this car. He stared to his left at the rich black land, the white buildings in the distance, and the glinting metal roof of the house. At the far edge of the farm, the river raged high enough that it almost snagged the raised footbridge.

He put a couple of miles between him and the farm before he stopped. On his left, a rest area underneath cottonwoods looked to be the perfect place. A few other cars were there, all of them empty. White-water rafters, he assumed. At the end of the day, someone would drive them back to get their vehicles. In all the coming and going, his car would be just one of many that were parked there. To guard against someone wondering why the car was there all night and worrying that he'd drowned, he left a note on his dashboard that read, *Hiking and camping along the river. Back in a couple of days.*

He opened the rear hatch, put on the heavy backpack, secured its straps, locked the car, and walked down a rocky slope, disappearing among bushes. He had spent several evenings at home, practicing with the fully loaded knapsack, but his brick floors hadn't prepared him for the uneven terrain that he now labored over – rocks, holes, and fallen branches, each jarring step seeming to add weight to his backpack. More, he had practiced in the cool of evening, but now in the heat of the day, with the temperature predicted to reach a high of eighty, he sweated profusely, his wet clothes clinging to him.

His pack weighed sixty pounds. Without it, he was sure he could have reached the river in ten minutes. Under the circumstances, he took twenty. Not bad, he thought, hearing the roar of the current. Emerging from the scrub brush, he was startled by how fast and high the water was, how humblingly powerful. It was so swift that it created a breeze, for which he was grateful as he set down his backpack and flexed his stiff shoulders. He drank from his canteen. The water had been cool when he'd left the house but was now tepid, with a vague metallic taste.

Get to work, he told himself.

Without the backpack, the return walk to the car was swift. In a hurry, he unlocked the Explorer, removed another sack, relocked the car, and carried his second burden down the slope into the bushes, reaching the river five minutes sooner than he had earlier. The sack contained a small rubber raft, which after he used a pressurized cannister to inflate it had plenty of room for himself and his backpack. Making sure that the latter was securely attached, he studied the heaving water, took a deep breath, exhaled, and pushed the raft into the river.

Icy water splashed across him. If not for his daily workouts on exercise machines, he never would have had the strength to paddle so hard and fast, constantly switching sides, keeping the raft from spinning. But the river carried him downstream faster than he'd anticipated. He was in the middle, but no matter how hard he fought, he didn't seem to be getting closer to the other side. He didn't know what scared him worse, being overturned or not reaching the opposite bank before the current carried him to the farm. Jesus, if they see me . . . He worked his arms to their maximum. Squinting to see through spray, he saw that the river curved to the left. The current on the far side wasn't as strong. Paddling in a frenzy, he felt the raft shoot close to the bank. Ten feet. Five. He braced himself. The moment the raft jolted against the shore, he scrambled over the front rim, landed on the muddy bank, almost fell into the water, righted himself, and dragged the raft onto the shore.

His backpack sat in water in the raft. Hurriedly, he freed the straps that secured it, then dragged it onto dry land. Water trickled out the bottom. He could only hope that the waterproof bags into which he'd sealed his food, clothes, and equipment had done their job. Had anyone seen him? He scanned the ridge behind him and the shore across from him – they seemed deserted. He overturned the raft, dumped the water out of it, tugged the raft behind bushes, and concealed it. He set several large rocks in it to keep it from blowing away, then returned to the shore and satisfied himself that the raft couldn't be seen. But he couldn't linger. He hoisted his pack onto his shoulders, ignored the strain on his muscles, and started inland.

★ ★ ★

Three hours later, after following a trail that led along the back of the ridge that bordered the river, he finished the long, slow, difficult hike to the top. The scrub brush was sparse, the rocks unsteady under his waffle-soled boots. Fifteen yards from the summit, he lowered his backpack and flexed his arms and shoulders to ease their cramps. Sweat dripped from his face. He drank from his canteen, the water even more tepid, then sank to the rocks and crept upward. Cautiously, he peered over the top. Below were the white barn and outbuildings. Sunlight gleamed off the white house's pitched metal roof. Portions of the land were green from early crops, one of which Romero recognized even from a distance: lettuce. No one was in view. He found a hollow, eased into it, and dragged his backpack after him. Two rocks on the rim concealed the silhouette of his head when he peered down between them. River, field, farmhouse, barn, more fields. A perfect vantage point.

Still, no one was in view. Some of them are probably in Santa Fe, he thought. As long as nothing's happening, this is a good time to get settled. He removed his night-vision telescope, his camera, and his zoom lens from the backpack. The waterproof bags had worked – the equipment was dry. So were his food and sleeping bag. The only items that had gotten wet were a spare shirt and pair of jeans that, ironically, he'd brought with him in case he needed a dry change of clothes. He spread them out in the sun, took another look at the farm – no activity – and ravenously reached for his food. Cheddar cheese, wheat crackers, sliced carrots, and a dessert of dehydrated apricots made his mouth water as he chewed them.

Five o'clock. One of the brothers crossed from the house to the barn. Hard to tell at a distance, but through the camera's zoom lens Romero thought he recognized Mark.

Six thirty. Small down there, the pickup truck arrived. It got bigger as Romero adjusted the zoom lens and recognized John getting out. Mark came out of the barn. Matthew came out of the house. John looked displeased about something. Mark said something. Matthew stayed silent. They entered the house.

Romero's heart beat faster with the satisfaction that he was watching his quarry and they didn't know it. But his exhilaration faded as dusk thickened, lights came on in the house, and nothing else happened. Without the sun, the air cooled rapidly. As frost came out of his mouth, he put on gloves and a jacket.

Maybe I'm wasting my time, he thought.

Like hell. It's not the fifteenth yet.

The temperature continued dropping. His legs cold despite the jeans he wore, he squirmed into the welcome warmth of his sleeping bag and chewed more cheese and crackers as he switched from the zoom lens to the night-vision telescope. The scope brightened the darkness, turning everything green. The lights in the windows were radiant. One of the brothers left the house, but the scope's definition was a little grainy, and Romero couldn't tell who it was. The person went into the barn and returned to the house ten minutes later.

One by one, the lights went off. The house was soon in darkness.

Looks like the show's over for a while, Romero thought. It gave him an opportunity to get out of his sleeping bag, crawl back from the ridge, and relieve himself behind a bush. When he returned, the house seemed as quiet as when he'd gone away.

Again he reminded himself, today's not important. Tomorrow might not be, either. But the *next* day's the fifteenth.

He checked that his handgun and his cellular phone were within easy reach (all the comforts of home), settled deeper into the sleeping bag, and refocused the night-vision scope on the farm below. Nothing.

The cold made his eyes feel heavy.

A door slammed.

Jerking his head up, Romero blinked to adjust his eyes to the bright morning light. He squirmed from his sleeping bag and used the camera's zoom lens to peer down at the farm. John, Mark and Matthew had come out of the house. They marched toward the nearest field, the one that had lettuce in it. The green shoots glistened from the reflection of sunlight off melted frost. John looked as displeased as on the previous evening, speaking irritably to his brothers. Mark said something in return. Matthew said nothing.

Romero frowned. This was too many times that he hadn't seen Luke. What had happened to him? Adjusting the zoom lens, he watched the group go into the barn. Another question nagged at him. The police report had said that the brothers worked for their father, that this was their father's land. But when Romero had come to the farm the previous fall, he hadn't seen the father.

Or yesterday.

Or this morning.

Where the hell was he? Was the father somehow responsible for the shoes and . . .

Were the father and Luke not on the farm because they were somewhere else, doing . . .

The more questions he had, the more his mind spun.

He tensed, seeing a glint of something reflect off melted frost on grass beside the barn door. Frowning harder, he saw the glint dart back and forth, as if alive. Oh, my Jesus, he thought, suddenly realizing what it was, pulling his camera away from the rim. He was on the western ridge, staring east. The sun above the opposite ridge had reflected off his zoom lens. If the light had reflected while the brothers were outside . . .

The cold air felt even colder. Leaving the camera and its zoom lens well below the rim, he warily eased his head up and studied the barn. Five minutes later, the three brothers emerged and began to do chores. Watching, Romero opened a plastic bag of Cheerios, Wheat Chex, raisins, and nuts that he'd combined, munching the trail mix, washing it down with water. From the drop in temperature the previous night, the water in his canteen was again cold. But the canteen was almost empty. He had brought two others, and they would last him for a while. Eventually, though, he was going to have to return to the river and use the filtration pump to refill the canteens. Iodine tablets would kill the bacteria.

By mid-afternoon, the brothers were all in one field, Matthew on a tractor, tilling the soil, while John and Mark picked up large rocks that the winter had forced to the surface, carrying them to the back of the pickup truck.

222

I'm wasting my time, he thought. They're just farmers, for God's sake.

Then why did John try to get me fired?

He clenched his teeth. With the sun behind his back, it was safe to use the camera's zoom lens. He scanned the farm, staring furiously at the brothers. The evening was a replay of the previous one. By ten, the house was in darkness.

Just one more day, Romero thought. Tomorrow's the fifteenth. Tomorrow's what I came for.

Pain jolted him into consciousness. A walloping burst of agony made his mind spin. A third cracking impact sent a flash of red behind his eyes. Stunned, he fought to overcome the shock of the attack and thrashed to get out of his sleeping bag. A blow across his shoulders knocked him sideways. Silhouetted against the starry sky, three figures surrounded him, their heavy breath frosty as they raised their clubs to strike him again. He grabbed his pistol and tried to free it from the sleeping bag, but a blow knocked it out of his numbed hand an instant before a club across his forehead made his ears ring and his eyes roll up.

He awoke slowly, his senses in chaos. Throbbing in his head. Blood on his face. The smell of it. Coppery. The nostril-irritating smell of stale straw under his left cheek. Shadows. Sunlight through cracks in a wall. The barn. Spinning. His stomach heaved.

The sour smell of vomit.

'Matthew, bring John,' Mark said.

Rumbling footsteps ran out of the barn.

Romero passed out.

The next time he awoke, he was slumped in a corner, his back against a wall, his knees up, his head sagging, blood dripping onto his chest.

'We found your car,' John said. 'I see you changed models.'

The echoing voice seemed to come from a distance, but when Romero looked blearily up, John was directly before him.

John read the note Romero had left on the dashboard. ' "*Hiking and camping along the river. Back in a couple of days.*" '

Romero noticed that his pistol was tucked under John's belt.

'What are we going to do?' Mark asked. 'The police will come looking for him.'

'So what?' John said. 'We're in the right. We caught a man with a pistol who trespassed on our property at night. We defended ourselves and subdued him.' John crumpled the note. 'But the police won't come looking for him. They don't know he's here.'

'You can't be sure,' Mark said.

Matthew stood silently by the closed barn door.

'Of course I can be sure,' John said. 'If this was a police operation, he wouldn't have needed this note. He wouldn't have been worried that someone would wonder about the abandoned car. In fact, he wouldn't have needed his car at all. The police would have driven him to the drop-off point. He's on his own.'

Matthew fidgeted, continuing to watch.

'Isn't that right, Officer Romero?' John asked.

Fighting to control the spinning in his mind, Romero managed to get his voice to work. 'How did you know I was up there?'

No one answered.

'It was the reflection from the camera lens, right?' Romero sounded as if his throat had been stuffed with gravel.

'Like the Holy Spirit on Pentecost,' John said.

Romero's tongue was so thick he could barely speak. 'I need water.'

'I don't like this,' Mark said. 'Let him go.'

John turned toward Matthew. 'You heard him. He needs water.'

Matthew hesitated, then opened the barn door and ran toward the house.

John returned his attention to Romero. 'Why wouldn't you stop? Why did you have to be so persistent?'

'Where's Luke?'

'See, that's what I mean. You're so damnably persistent.'

'We don't need to take this any further,' Mark warned. 'Put him in his car. Let him go. No harm's been done.'

'Hasn't there?'

'You just said we were in the right to attack a stranger with a gun. After it was too late, we found out who he is. A judge would throw out an assault charge.'

'He'd come back.'

'Not necessarily.'

'I guarantee it. Wouldn't you, Officer Romero? You'd come back.'

Romero wiped blood from his face and didn't respond.

'Of course you would,' John said. 'It's in your nature. And one day you'd see something you shouldn't. It may be you already have.'

'Don't say anything more,' Mark warned.

'You want to know what this is about?' John asked Romero.

Romero wiped more blood from his face.

'I think you should get what you want,' John said.

'No,' Mark said. 'This can't go on any more. I'm still not convinced he's here by himself. If the police are involved . . . It's too risky. It has to stop.'

Footsteps rushed toward the barn. Only Romero looked as Matthew hurried inside, carrying a jug of water.

'Give it to him,' John said.

Matthew approached warily, like someone apprehensive about a wild animal. He set the jug at Romero's feet and darted back.

'Thank you,' Romero said.

Matthew didn't answer.

'Why don't you ever speak?' Romero asked.

Matthew didn't say anything.

Romero's skin prickled. 'You can't.'

Matthew looked away.

'Of course. Last fall when I was here, John told you to bring him the phone so he could call the state police. At the time, I didn't think anything of it.' Romero waited for the swirling in his mind to stop. 'I figured he was sending the weakest one of the group, so if I made trouble he and Mark could take care of it.' Romero's lungs felt empty. He took several deep breaths. 'But all the time I've been watching the house, you haven't said a word.'

Matthew kept looking away.

'You're mute. That's why John told you to bring the phone. Because you couldn't call the state police yourself.'

'Stop taunting my brother, and drink the water,' John said.

'I'm not taunting him. I just—'

'*Drink it.*'

Romero fumbled for the jug, raised it to his lips, and swallowed, not caring about the sour taste from having been sick, wanting only to clear the mucus from his mouth and the gravel in his throat.

John pulled a clean handkerchief from his windbreaker pocket and threw it to him. 'Pour water on it. Wipe the blood from your face. We're not animals. There's no need to be without dignity.'

Baffled by the courtesy, Romero did what he was told. The more they treated him like a human being, the more chance he had of getting away from them. He tried desperately to think of a way to talk himself out of this. 'You're wrong about the police not being involved.'

'Oh?' John raised his eyebrows, waiting for Romero to continue.

'This isn't official, sure. But I do have backup. I told my sergeant what I planned to do. The deal is, if I don't use my cell phone to call him every six hours, he'll know something's wrong. He and a couple of friends on the force will come here looking for me.'

'My, my. Is that a fact?'

'Yes.'

'Then why don't you call him and tell him you're all right?'

'Because I'm *not* all right. Look, I have no idea what's going on here, and all of a sudden, believe me, it's the last thing I want to find out. I just want to get out of here.'

The barn became terribly silent.

'I made a mistake.' Romero struggled to his feet. 'I won't make it again. I'll leave. This is the last time you'll see me.' Off balance, he stepped out of the corner.

John studied him.

'As far as I'm concerned, this is the end of it.' Romero took another step toward the door.

'I don't believe you.'

Romero stepped past him.

'You're lying about the cell phone and about your sergeant,' John said.

Romero kept walking. 'If I don't call him soon—'

John blocked his way.

'—he'll come looking for me.'

'And here he'll find you.'
'Being held against my will.'
'So we'll be charged with kidnaping?' John spread his hands. 'Fine. We'll tell the jury we were only trying to scare you to keep you from continuing to stalk us. I'm willing to take the chance they won't convict us.'
'*What are you talking about?*' Mark said.
'Let's see if his friends really come to the rescue.'
Oh, shit, Romero thought. He took a further step toward the door.
John pulled out Romero's pistol.
'No!' Mark said.
'Matthew, help Mark with the trapdoor.'
'This has to stop!' Mark said. '*Wasn't what happened to Matthew and Luke enough?*'
Like a tightly wound spring that was suddenly released, John whirled and struck Mark with such force that he knocked him to the floor. 'Since when do you run this family?'
Wiping blood from his mouth, Mark glared up at him. 'I don't. *You* do.'
'That's right. I'm the oldest. That's always been the rule. If you'd have been meant to run this family, you'd have been the first-born.'
Mark kept glaring.
'Do you want to turn against the rule?' John asked.
Mark lowered his eyes. 'No.'
'Then help Matthew with the trapdoor.'
Romero's stomach fluttered. All the while John aimed the pistol at him, he watched Mark and Matthew go to the far left corner, where it took both of them to shift a barrel of grain out of the way. They lifted a trapdoor, and Romero couldn't help bleakly thinking that someone pushing from below wouldn't have a chance of moving it when the barrel was in place.
'Get down there,' John said.
Romero felt dizzier. Fighting to repress the sensation, he knew that he had to do something before he felt any weaker.
If John wanted me dead, he'd have killed me by now.
Romero bolted for the outside door.
'Mark!'

Something whacked against Romero's legs, tripping him, slamming him face hard onto the floor.

Mark had thrown a club.

The three brothers grabbed him. Dazed, the most powerless he'd ever felt, he thrashed, unable to pull away from their hands, as they dragged him across the dusty floor and shoved him down the trapdoor. If he hadn't grasped the ladder, he'd have fallen.

'You don't want to be without water.' John handed the jug down to him.

A chill breeze drifted from below. Terrified, Romero watched the trapdoor being closed over him and heard the scrape of the barrel being shifted back into place.

God help me, he thought.

But he wasn't in darkness. Peering down, he saw a faint light and warily descended the ladder, moving awkwardly because of the jug he held. At the bottom, he found a short tunnel and proceeded along it. An earthy, musty smell made his nostrils contract. The light became brighter as he neared its source in a small plywood-walled room that he saw had a wooden chair and table. The floor was made from plywood also. The light came from a bare bulb attached to one of the sturdy beams in the ceiling. Stepping all the way in, he saw a cot on the left. A clean pillow and blanket were on it. To the right, a toilet seat was attached to a wooden box positioned above a deep hole in the ground. I'm going to lose my mind, he thought.

The breeze, weak now that the trapdoor was closed, came from a vent in an upper part of the farthest wall. Romero guessed that the duct would be long and that there would be baffles at the end so that, if he screamed for help, no one who happened to come onto the property would hear him. The vent provided enough air that Romero wasn't worried about suffocating. There were plenty of other things to worry about, but at least not that.

The plywood of the floor and walls was discolored with age. Nonetheless, the pillow and the blanket had been stocked recently – when Romero raised them to his nose, there was a fresh laundry smell beneath the loamy odor that it had started absorbing.

The brothers couldn't have known I'd be here. They were expecting someone else.

Who?

Romero smelled something else. He told himself that it was only his imagination, but he couldn't help sensing that the walls were redolent with the sweaty stench of fear, as if many others had been imprisoned here.

His own fear made his mouth so dry that he took several deep swallows of water. Setting the jug on the table, he stared apprehensively at a door across from him. It was just a simple old wooden door, vertical planks held in place by horizontal boards nailed to the top, middle, and bottom, but it filled him with apprehension. He knew that he had to open it, that he had to learn if it gave him a way to escape, but he had a terrible premonition that something unspeakable waited on the other side. He told his legs to move. They refused. He told his right arm to reach for the doorknob. It, too, refused.

The spinning sensation in his mind was now aggravated by the short, quick breaths he was taking. I'm hyperventilating, he realized, and struggled to return his breath rate to normal. Despite the coolness of the chamber, his face dripped sweat. In contrast, his mouth was drier than ever. He gulped more water.

Open the door.

His body reluctantly obeyed, his shaky legs taking him across the chamber, his trembling hand reaching for the doorknob. He pulled. Nothing happened, and for a moment he thought that the door was locked, but when he pulled harder, it creaked slowly open, the loamy odor from inside reaching his nostrils before his eyes adjusted to the shadows in there.

For a terrible instant he thought he was staring at bodies. He almost stumbled back, inwardly screaming, until a remnant of his sanity insisted that he stare harder, that what he was looking at were bulging burlap sacks.

And baskets.

And shelves of . . .

Vegetables.

Potatoes, beets, turnips, onions.

Jesus, this was the root cellar under the barn. Repelled by the musty odor, he searched for another door. He tapped the walls, hoping for a hollow sound that would tell him there was an open space, perhaps another room or even the outside, beyond it.

He found nothing to give him hope.

'Officer Romero?' The faint voice came from the direction of the trapdoor.

Romero stepped out of the root cellar and closed the door.

'Officer Romero?' The voice sounded like John's.

Romero left the chamber and stopped halfway along the corridor, not wanting to show himself. A beam of pale light came down through the open trapdoor. 'What?'

'I've brought you something to eat.'

A basket sat at the bottom of the ladder. Presumably John had lowered it by a rope and then pulled the rope back up before calling to Romero.

'I'm not hungry.'

'If I were you, I'd eat. After all, you have no way of telling when I might bring you another meal.'

Romero's empty stomach cramped.

'Also, you'll find a book in the basket, something for you to pass the time. D.H. Lawrence. Seems appropriate since he lived on a ranch a little to the north of us outside Taos. In fact, he's buried there.'

'I don't give a shit. What do you intend to do with me?' Romero was startled by how shaky his voice sounded.

John didn't answer.

'If you let me go right now, I'll forget this happened. None of this has gone so far that it can't be undone.'

The trapdoor was closed. The pale beam of light disappeared.

Above, there were scraping sounds as the barrel was put back into place.

Romero wanted to scream.

He picked up the basket and examined its contents. Bread, cheese, sliced carrots, two apples . . . and a book. It was a tattered blue hardback without a dust cover. The title on its spine read, *D.H. Lawrence: Selected Stories*. There was a bookmark at a story called 'The Woman Who Rode Away'. The pages in that section of the book had been so repeatedly turned that the upper corners were almost worn through.

The blows to Romero's head made him feel as if a spike had been driven into it. Breathing more rapidly, dizzier than ever, he went back to the chamber. He put the basket on the table, then sat on the cot and felt so weak that he wanted to lie down, but he told himself that he had to look at the story. One thing you could say for certain about John, he wasn't whimsical. The story was important.

Romero opened the book. For a harrowing moment, his vision doubled. He strained to focus his eyes, and as quickly as the problem had occurred, it went away, his vision again clear. But he knew what was happening. I've got a concussion.

I need to get to a hospital.

Damn it, concentrate.

'The Woman Who Rode Away'.

The story was set in Mexico. It was about a woman married to a wealthy industrialist who owned bountiful silver mines in the Sierra Madre. She had a healthy son and daughter. Her husband adored her. She had every comfort she could imagine. But she couldn't stop feeling smothered, as if she was another of her husband's possessions, as if he and her children owned her. Each day, she spent more and more time staring longingly at the mountains. What's up there? she wondered. Surely it must be something wonderful. The secret villages. One day, she went out horseback riding and never came back.

Romero stopped reading. The shock of his injuries had drained him. He had trouble holding his throbbing head up. At the same time, his empty stomach cramped again. I have to keep up my strength, he thought. Forcing himself to stand, he went over to the basket of food, chewed on a carrot, and took a bite out of a freshly baked, thickly crusted chunk of bread. He swallowed more water and went back to the cot.

The break hadn't done any good. As exhausted as ever, he reopened the book.

The woman rode into the mountains. She had brought enough food for several days, and as she rode higher, she let her horse choose whatever trails it wanted. Higher and higher. Past pines and aspens and cottonwoods until, as the vegetation thinned and the altitude made her light-headed, Indians greeted her on the trail and asked where she was going. To the secret villages, she told them. To see their houses and to learn about their gods. The Indians escorted her into a lush valley that had trees, a river, and groups of low, flat, gleaming houses. There, the villagers welcomed her and promised to teach her.

Romero saw double again. Frightened, he struggled to control his vision. The concussion's getting worse, he thought. Fear made him weaker. He wanted to lie down, but he knew that, if he fell asleep, he might never wake up. Shout for help, he thought in a panic.

To whom? Nobody can hear me. Not even the brothers.

Rousing himself, he went over to the table, bit off another chunk of bread, ate a piece of apple, and sat down to finish the story. It was supposed to tell him something, he was sure, but so far he hadn't discovered what it was.

The woman had the sense of being in a dream. The villagers treated her well, bringing her flowers and clothes, food and drinks made of honey. She spent her days in a pleasant languor. She had never slept so long and deeply. Each evening, the pounding of drums was hypnotic. The seasons turned. Fall became winter. Snow fell. The sun was angry, the villagers said on the shortest day of the year. The moon must be given to the sun. They carried the woman to an altar, took off her clothes, and plunged a knife into her chest.

The shocking last page made Romero jerk his head up. The woman's death was all the more unnerving because she knew it was coming and she surrendered to it, didn't try to fight it, almost welcomed it. She seemed apart from herself, in a daze.

Romero shivered. As his eyelids drooped again, he thought about the honey drinks that the villagers had kept bringing her.

They must have been drugged.

Oh, shit, he thought. It took all of his will power to raise his sagging head and peer toward the basket and the jug on the table.

The food and water are drugged.

A tingle of fear swept through him, the only sensation he could still feel. His head was so numb that it had stopped aching. His hands and feet didn't seem to be a part of him. I'm going to pass out, he thought sickly.

He started to lie back.

No.

Can't.

Don't.

Get your lazy ass off this cot. If you fall asleep, you'll die.

Mind spinning, he wavered to his feet. Stumbled toward the table. Banged against it. Almost knocked it over. Straightened. Lurched toward the toilet seat. Bent over it. Stuck his finger down his throat. Vomited the food and water he'd consumed.

He wavered into the corridor, staggered to the ladder, gripped it, turned, staggered back, reached the door to the root cellar, turned, and stumbled back to the ladder.

He did it again.

You have to keep walking.

And again.

You've got to stay on your feet.

His knees buckled. He forced them to straighten.

His vision turned gray. He stumbled onward, using his arms to guide him.

It was the hardest thing he had ever done. It took more discipline and determination than he knew he possessed. I won't give up, he kept saying. It became a mantra. I won't give up.

Time became a blur, delirium a constant. Somewhere in his long ordeal, his vision cleared, his legs became stronger. When his headache returned, he allowed himself to hope the drug was wearing off. Instead of wavering, he walked.

And kept walking, pumping himself up. I have to be ready, he thought. As his mind became more alert, it was seized by confusion. Why had John wanted him to read the story? Wasn't it the same as a warning not to eat the food and drink the water?

Or maybe it was an explanation of what was happening. A choice that was offered. Spare yourself the agony of panic. Eat from the bounty of the earth and surrender as the woman had done.

Like hell.

Romero dumped most of the water into the latrine. It helped to dissipate his vomit down there, concealing what he had done. He left a small piece of bread and a few carrot sticks. He bit into the apples

233

and spit out the pieces, leaving the cores. He took everything else into the root cellar and hid it in the darkest corner behind baskets of potatoes.

He checked his watch. It had been eleven in the morning when they'd forced him down here. It was now almost midnight. Hearing the faint scrape of the barrel being moved, he lay down on the cot, closed his eyes, dangled an arm onto the floor, and tried to control his frantic breathing enough to look unconscious.

'Be careful. He might be bluffing.'

'Most of the food's gone.'

'Stay out of my line of fire.'

Hands grabbed him, lifting. A dead weight, he felt himself being carried along the corridor. He murmured as if he didn't want to be wakened. After securing a harness around him, one brother went up the ladder and pulled on a rope while the other brothers lifted him. In the barn, as they took off the harness, he moved his head and murmured again.

'Let's see if he can stand,' John said.

Romero allowed his eyelids to flicker.

'He's coming around,' Mark said.

'Then he can help us.'

They carried him into the open. He moved his head from side to side, as if aroused by the cold night air. They put him in the back of the pickup truck. Two brothers stayed with him while the other drove. The night was so cold that he allowed himself to shiver.

'Yeah, definitely coming around,' John said.

The truck stopped. He was lifted out and carried into a field. Allowing his eyelids to open a little farther, Romero was amazed at how bright the moon was. He saw that the field was the same one that he had seen the brothers tilling and removing the stones from the day before.

They set him on his feet.

He pretended to waver.

Heart pounding, he knew that he had to do something soon. Until now, he had felt helpless against the three of them. The barn had been too constricting a place in which to try to fight. He needed somewhere in the open, somewhere that allowed him to run. This field was going to have to be it. Because he knew without a doubt that this was where they intended to kill him.

'Put him on his knees,' John said.

'It's still not too late to stop this,' Mark said.

'Have you lost your faith?'

'I . . .'

'Answer me. Have you lost your faith?'

'. . . No.'

'Then put him on his knees.'

Romero allowed himself to be lowered. His heart was beating so frantically that he feared it would burst against his ribs. A sharp stone hurt his knees. He couldn't allow himself to react.

They leaned him forward on his hands. Like an animal. His neck was exposed.

'Prove your faith, Mark.'

Something scraped, a knife being pulled from a scabbard.

It glinted in the moonlight.

'Take it,' John said.

'But—'

'Prove your faith.'

A long tense pause.

'Yes,' John said. 'Lord, accept this sacrifice in thanks for the glory of your earth and the bounty that comes from it. The blood of—'

Feeling another sharp rock, this one beneath his palm, Romero gripped it, spun, and hurled it as strongly as he could at the head of the figure nearest him. The rock made a crunching noise, the figure groaning and dropping, as Romero charged to his feet and yanked the knife from Mark's hands. He drove it into Mark's stomach and stormed toward the remaining brother, whom he recognized as John because of the pistol in his hand. But before Romero could strike him with the knife, John stumbled back, aiming, and Romero had no choice except to hurl the knife. It hit John, but whether it injured him, Romero couldn't tell. At least it made John stumble back farther, his aim wide, the shot ploughing into the earth, and by then Romero was racing past the pickup truck, into the lane, toward the house. John fired again. The bullet struck the pickup truck.

Running faster, propelled by fear, Romero saw the lights of the house ahead and veered to the left so he wouldn't be a silhouette. A third shot, a bullet buzzing past him, shattered a window in the house. He stretched his legs to the maximum. His chest heaved. As the house got larger before him, he heard the roar of the pickup truck behind him. I have to get off the lane, he thought. He veered farther to the left, scrambled over a rail fence, and raced across a field of chard, his panicked footsteps mashing the tender shoots.

Headlights gleamed behind him. The truck stopped. A fourth shot broke the silence. John obviously assumed that in this isolated area there was a good chance a neighbor wouldn't hear. Or care. Trouble with coyotes.

A fifth shot stung Romero's left shoulder. Breathing rapidly and hoarsely, he zig-zagged. At the same time he bent forward, running as fast as he could while staying low. He came to another fence, squirmed between its rails, and rushed into a further field, crushing more crops, radishes he dimly thought.

The truck roared closer along the lane.

Another roar matched it, the roiling power of the Rio Grande as Romero raced nearer. The lights of the house were to his right now. He passed them, reaching the darkness at the back of the farm. The river thundered louder.

Almost there. If I can—

Headlights glaring, the truck raced to intercept him.

Another fence. Romero lunged between its rails so forcefully that he banged his injured shoulder, but he didn't care – moonlight showed him the path to the raised footbridge. He rushed along it, hearing the truck behind him. The churning river reflected the headlights, its fierce white caps beckoning. With a shout of triumph, he reached the footbridge. His frantic footsteps rumbled across it. Spray from the river slicked the boards. His feet slipped. The bridge swayed. Water splashed over it. He lost his balance, nearly tumbled into the river, but righted himself. A gunshot whistled past. Abruptly, he was off the bridge, diving behind bushes, scurrying through the darkness on his right. John fired twice toward where Romero had entered the bushes as Romero dove to the ground farther to the right. Desperate not to make noise, he fought to slow his frenzied breathing.

His throat was raw. His chest ached. He touched his left shoulder and felt cold liquid mixed with warm: water and blood. He shivered. Couldn't stop shivering. The headlights of the truck showed John walking onto the footbridge. The pistol was in his right hand. Something else was in his left. It suddenly blazed. A powerful flashlight. It scanned the bushes. Romero pressed himself lower on the ground.

John proceeded across the bridge. 'I've been counting the same as you have!' He shouted to be heard above the force of the current. 'Eight shots! I checked the magazine before I got out of the truck. Seven more rounds, plus one in the firing chamber!'

Any moment the flashlight's glare would reach where Romero was hiding. He grabbed a rock, thanked God that it was his left shoulder that had been injured, and used his right arm to hurl the rock. It bounced off the bridge. As Romero scurried farther upriver, John swung the flashlight toward where he'd been hiding and fired.

This time, Romero didn't stop. Rocks against a pistol weren't going to work. He might get lucky, but he doubted it. John knew which direction he was taking, and whenever Romero risked showing himself to throw another rock, John had a good chance of capturing him in a blaze of the flashlight and shooting him.

Keep going upriver, he told himself. Keep making John follow. Without aiming, he threw a rock in a high arc toward John but didn't trick him into firing without a target. Fine, Romero thought, scrambling through the murky bushes. Just as long as he keeps following.

The raft, he kept thinking. They found my campsite. They found my car.

But did they find the raft?

In the darkness, it was hard to get his bearings. There had been a curve in the river, he remembered. Yes. And the ridge on this side angled down toward the water. He scurried fiercely, deliberately making so much noise that John was bound to hear and follow. He'll think I'm panicking, Romero thought. To add to the illusion, he threw another high arcing rock toward where John was stalking him.

A branch lanced his face. He didn't pay attention. He just

237

rushed onward, realized that the bank was curving, saw the shadow of the ridge angling down to the shore, and searched furiously through the bushes, tripping over the raft, nearly banging his head on one of the rocks that he'd put in it to prevent a wind from blowing it away.

John's flashlight glinted behind him, probing the bushes.

Hurry!

Breathless, Romero took off his jacket, stuffed it with large rocks, set it on the rocks that were already in the raft, and dragged the raft toward the river. Downstream, John heard him and redirected the flashlight, but not before Romero ducked back into the bushes, watching the current suck the raft downstream. In the moonlight and the glint of the flashlight, the bulging jacket looked as if Romero were hunkered down in the raft, hoping not to be shot as the raft sped past.

John swung toward the river and fired. He fired again, the muzzle flash bright, the shots barely audible in the roar of the current, which also muted the noises that Romero made as he charged from the bushes and slammed against John, throwing his injured arm around John's throat while he used his other hand to grab John's gun arm.

The force of hitting John propelled them into the water. Instantly, the current gripped them, its violence as shocking as the cold. John's face was sucked under. Clinging to him, straining to keep him under, Romero also struggled with the river, its power thrusting him through the darkness. The current heaved him up, then dropped him. The cold was so fierce that already his body was becoming numb. Even so, he kept squeezing John's throat and struggling to get the pistol away from him. A huge tree limb scraped past. The current upended him. John broke the surface. Romero went under. John's hands pressed him down. Frenzied, Romero kicked. He thought he heard a scream as John let go of him and he broke to the surface. Five feet away, John fought to stay above the water and aim the pistol. Romero dove under. Hearing the shot, he used the force of the current to add to his effort as he thrust himself farther under water and erupted from the surface to John's right, grabbing John's gun arm, twisting it.

You son of a bitch, Romero thought. If I'm going to die, you're going with me. He dragged him under. They slammed against a boulder, the pain making Romero cry out underwater. Gasping, he broke to the surface. Saw John ahead of him, aiming. Saw the headlights of the truck illuminating the footbridge. Saw the huge tree limb caught in the narrow space between the river and the bridge. Before John could fire, he slammed into the branch. Romero collided with it a moment later. Trapped in its arms, squeezed by the current, Romero reached for the pistol as John aimed it point-blank. Then John's face twisted into surprised agony as a boulder crashed down on him from the bridge and split his skull open.

Romero was barely aware of Matthew above him on the footbridge. He was too paralyzed with horror, watching blood stream down John's face. An instant later, a log hurtled along the river, struck John, and drove him harder against the tree branch. In the glare of the headlights, Romero thought he saw wood protruding from John's chest as he, the branch, and the log broke free of the bridge and swirled away in the current. Thrust along with him, Romero stretched his arms up, trying to claw at the bridge. He failed. Speeding under it, reaching the other side, he tensed in apprehension of hitting a boulder and being knocked unconscious, when something snagged him. Hands. Matthew was on his stomach on the bridge, stretching as far down as he could, clutching Romero's shirt. Romero struggled to help him, trying not to look at Matthew's crushed forehead and right eye from where Romeo had hit him with a rock. Gripping Matthew's arms, pulling himself up, Romero felt debris crash past his legs, and then he and Matthew were flat on the footbridge, breathing hoarsely, trying to stop trembling.

'I hate him,' Matthew said.

For a moment, Romero was certain that his ears were playing tricks on him, that the shots and the roar of the water were making him hear sounds that weren't there.

'I hate him,' Matthew repeated.

'My God, you can talk.'

For the first time in twelve years, he later found out.

'I hate him,' Matthew said. 'Hatehimhatehimhatehimhatehim.'

★　★　★

Relieving the pressure of silence that had built up for almost two thirds of his life, Matthew gibbered while they went to check Mark and found him dead, while they went to the house and Romero phoned the state police, while they put on warm clothes and Romero did what he could for Matthew's injury and they waited for the police to arrive, while the sun rose and the investigators swarmed throughout the farm. Matthew's hysterical litany became ever more speedy and shrill until a physician finally had to sedate him and he was taken away in an ambulance.

The state trooper whom Romero had asked for backup was part of the team. When Romero's police chief and sergeant heard what had happened, they drove up from Santa Fe. By then the excavations had started, and the bodies were showing up. What was left of them, anyway, after their blood had been drained into the fields and they'd been cut into pieces.

'Good God, how many?' the state trooper exclaimed as more and more body parts, most in extreme stages of decay, were found under the fields.

'As long as Matthew can remember, it's been happening,' Romero said. 'His mother died giving birth to him. She's under one of the fields. The father died from a heart attack three years ago. They never told anybody. They just buried him out there someplace. Every year on what's usually the last frost date, May fifteenth, they've sacrificed someone. Most of the time it was a homeless person, no one to be missed. But last year it was Susan Crowell and her fiancé. They had the bad luck of getting a flat tire right outside the farm. They walked down here and asked to use a phone. When John realized they were from out of state . . .'

'But why?' the police chief asked in dismay as more body parts were discovered.

'To give life to the earth. That's what the D.H. Lawrence story was about. The fertility of the earth and the passage of the seasons. I guess that's as close as John was able to come to explaining to his victims why they had to die.'

'What about the shoes?' the police chief asked. 'I don't understand about the shoes.'

'Luke dropped them.'

'The fourth brother?'

'That's right. He's out there somewhere. He committed suicide.'

The police chief looked sick.

'Throughout the spring, until the vegetables were ready for sale, Luke drove back and forth from the farm to Santa Fe to sell moss rocks. Each day, he drove along Old Pecos Trail. Twice a day, he passed the Baptist church. He was as psychologically tortured as Matthew, but John never suspected how close he was to cracking. That church became Luke's attempt for absolution. One day, he saw old shoes on the road next to the church.'

'You mean he didn't drop the first ones?'

'No, they were somebody's idea of a prank. But they gave him an idea. He saw them as a sign from God. Two years ago, he started dropping the shoes of the victims. They'd always been a problem. Clothes will decay readily enough. But shoes take a lot longer. John told him to throw them in the trash somewhere in Santa Fe. Luke couldn't bring himself to do that any more than he could bring himself to go into the church and pray for his soul. But he could drop the shoes outside the church in the hope that he'd be forgiven and that the family's victims would be granted salvation.'

'And the next year, he dropped shoes with feet in them,' the sergeant said.

'John had no idea that he'd taken them. When he heard what had happened, he kept Luke a prisoner here. One morning, Luke broke out, went into one of the fields, knelt down, and slit his throat from ear to ear.'

The group became silent. In the background, amid a pile of upturned rich black soil, someone shouted that they'd found more body parts.

Romero was given paid sick leave. He saw a psychiatrist once a week for four years. On those occasions when people announced that they were vegetarians, he answered, 'Yeah, I used to be one, but now I'm a carnivore.' Of course, he couldn't subsist on meat alone. The human body required the vitamins and minerals that vegetables provided, and although Romero tried vitamin pills as a substitution, he found that he couldn't do without the bulk that vegetables provided. So he grudgingly ate them, but never without thinking of those delicious, incredibly large, shiny, healthy-looking tomatoes, cucumbers, peppers, squash, cabbage, beans, peas, carrots, and chard that the Parsons brothers had sold. Remembering what had fertilized them, Romero chewed and chewed, but the vegetables always stuck in his throat.